VERDICT JUSTICE

Brian R. Toung, MS, JD, BCS, PhD

LifeRich
PUBLISHING

LifeRich Publishing is a registered trademark of The Reader's Digest Association, Inc.

LifeRich Publishing books may be ordered through booksellers or by contacting:

LifeRich Publishing
1663 Liberty Drive
Bloomington, IN 47403
www.liferichpublishing.com
1 (888) 238-8637

Because of the dynamic nature of the Internet, any web addresses or links contained in this book may have changed since publication and may no longer be valid. The views expressed in this work are solely those of the author and do not necessarily reflect the views of the publisher, and the publisher hereby disclaims any responsibility for them.

Any people depicted in stock imagery provided by Getty Images are models, and such images are being used for illustrative purposes only.
Certain stock imagery © Getty Images.

Cover Design by Greg Dean of New Smyrna Beach, Florida

ISBN: 978-1-4897-2494-6 (sc)
ISBN: 978-1-4897-2493-9 (hc)
ISBN: 978-1-4897-2495-3 (e)

Library of Congress Control Number: 2019913943

Print information available on the last page.

LifeRich Publishing rev. date: 07/23/2020

PART I

THE EVENT

CHAPTER 1

OMAR

The Alabama sun was beating down relentlessly, and if there was any breeze at all, the pitcher couldn't feel it as he stared at the crotch of the catcher whose fingers flashed signals from sixty feet away. It was so hot the air appeared to be thickening, and he was sweating like a thief in the confessional. The count was full on the big outfielder from Tuskegee who waggled his bat in challenge as Omar nodded his head and stood upright. He glanced at the runners at first and second as he took a deep breath and relaxed for the delivery.

This was it, the last game of his senior season, and he was on the bump to close out a win and a division championship against a longtime rival. The score was Florida A&M 4, and Tuskegee 2, with two outs in the bottom of the ninth. Both outs could be credited to Omar's arm as he came in and struck out batters three and four after the first two reached base on walks issued by the previous pitcher who failed to close the deal. His coach had let the starting pitcher try to go the distance, and he began the ninth inning on the mound, but after he demonstrated a clear lack of stamina to finish, Omar was sent in to close. He had to be very careful, however, as Marteen Wilson, the batter, was capable of slamming one out of the park for a Tuskegee win. It didn't help that at this very moment, at the apex of his college baseball career, Omar had to piss like a racehorse.

Satisfied with the pitch called and the placement of the runners, he nodded to the catcher and went into his tight windup. He concealed the ball in his glove, reared back, and then with an audible grunt, heaved the

1

little pill homeward as his left leg fell forward on the mound. Just after his foot hit the ground, the batter strode toward the mound, uncoiled his shoulders, and swung the aluminum bat in a vicious arc along the general path of the ball. Had the ninety-seven-mile-per-hour fastball not slammed into the catcher's mitt before the bat reached the intended point of impact, the collision would have been prodigious, and the result a likely home run. As it was, strike three was called.

The A&M bench players erupted with joy and charged the mound. Omar was as delighted with the victory as he was with the fact that he would soon be able to relieve the acute distress in his bladder. He had to face numerous high fives from teammates, and he prayed they wouldn't jump on his back and form a pig pile over his prostrate body with its very swollen bladder slowly leaking its contents.

As Omar ran toward his dugout against the flow of approaching teammates who were screaming like banshees, a thought occurred to him: *What the hell is a banshee anyway?* He grimaced from the combination of happiness and bladder pain. Fortunately, everyone remained vertical during the celebration, and he was able to prevent the venting of his bodily fluids until he was in the dugout and nearly to the urinal. After standing at the urinal amid the shouts of happy teammates for what seemed like an eternity, the process feeling nearly as good as sex, he finally was able to join the party.

The coach called him over, gave him a hug, and whispered into his ear, which was beginning to fill up with champagne, "You need to step outside, Lou Pinella, the talent scout from the Cubs, is here to talk to you."

Omar said, "No shit?" Upon seeing the affirming nod of his coach, Omar said, "Thanks, Coach!" He bolted for the locker room door.

Lou was lounging by the third base fence talking to some eager youngsters when Omar approached in his wet T-shirt, unmarked baseball pants, and socks. He was beaming as he extended his meaty fist to Lou who accepted it with a smile as he spit a stream of tobacco juice into the grass. Lou was an ageless talent scout who had been in the business since Moby Dick was a minnow. He was a man of average height, five eleven, with a bald dome perpetually covered by a ratty old ball cap, gray beard, and a pronounced beer belly. He always wore jeans that looked like he shopped mostly at the Salvation Army, held up by suspenders and an untucked T-shirt. His influence in the game of baseball was far more significant than his appearance, and he was sharp as a tack, and not to be underestimated. "That was some toss to end the game, stud. I reckon ninety-five plus."

Omar struggled to appear respectful and humble. "Yeah, I got all a that un."

"Hey, Lou, have you heard the latest on the draft?"

"Yep," Lou drawled, spitting again into a spot on the grass that was becoming decidedly brown. "Word is you're going in the first round with our pick in the seven spot unless those bastards from Atlanta trade up. The other six teams are recruiting bats, and we've got you pegged as the top closer on the block, which happens to be just what we need."

"That's great, man," Omar said, even though as a Florida boy, he was dubious about moving to the Windy City to live and work. The huge signing bonus that a first-round pick would garner would make Chicago much easier to tolerate. Besides, he knew they had great pizza there, and a buddy of his from high school was also on the team.

Lou said, "Listen, Omar, I've gotta jet, but I wanted to see you work and tell you to be careful and keep your nose clean for three more weeks. Do that, and you'll be headed for the show."

"You got it, Lou," said Omar as they shook hands again.

Lou winked as he wiped a brown stain from his chin, applied it to his jeans, and hitched up his large-girth britches before heading for the parking lot. Lou obviously hadn't missed a meal in recent history. His industrial-strength suspenders were working overtime.

Omar Steele, on the other hand, was a lean and muscular young man with light brown skin, six pack abs, almond eyes, and a well-groomed appearance. At six feet two inches tall and 190 pounds, he was a dashing man with a nice smile framed by perfect white teeth. His look said class act. As an athlete, Omar was in the top 1 percent in the nation. His talent was mostly natural, with 4.3 speed in the forty-yard dash and great balance, agility, and hand-eye coordination. He didn't need to practice like most people to be good—only to be great. He had lettered in four sports every year in high school and owned several local sports records. He had been highly recruited coming out of high school and could have gone most anywhere he wanted. He chose Florida A&M because his father had attended there, and he had been a fan for as long as he could remember. He dad was gone now, but his mother was a graduate, and so she approved of his choice—plus it was just far enough away from home to feel like being away, yet close enough to easily come home for a weekend.

Needless to say, Omar did extremely well with the ladies. At the moment, his main squeeze, Diandra, was a graduating senior at Martin Luther College in Daytona Beach. They had talked about getting married after graduation, but he was leaning more toward his current Tallahassee girl as the one with the most long-term potential. However, with the Major Leagues beckoning, he was in no hurry to be tied to just one woman. Of course, there were plenty of part-timers back home in South Florida, along with some yummy acquaintances in cities where his ball club visited frequently. Life was good, and in his mind, there was no such thing as too much talent. All he needed now was the cash to back up his looks, and he knew that the lifestyle that his friends who had already made it to the big show always bragged about would come soon after the draft.

Two of his best mates from high school were already in their third year in the majors, having been taken in the draft right out of high school. He wasn't sorry that he chose to go to college and to graduate, however, as he knew that his time would come, and not everyone makes it in the pros, so a degree would be good to fall back on, if needed. The extra seasoning and development afforded by college was extremely beneficial to pitchers. Everyone knew this, right?

Just then, a tall, well-built lady named Wanda strode up, as stealthy as a cheetah, grabbed him from behind, and stuck her wet tongue in his ear.

"Well, if it isn't my Tallahassee lassie!" He reached behind them both and grabbed a firm bubble butt in both hands.

She laughed and squeaked, "Wouldn't you like to know, big guy."

He turned, grabbed her head, and placed his mouth over hers. They kissed long and deep, and then he grabbed her hand and dragged her in the direction of the parking lot and his car.

"Where do you think you're taking me?" she protested ineffectually.

He pulled her up and whispered in her ear of his unspeakably pleasurable intentions with his tongue when they got back to his apartment.

"Promises, promises." She laughed, and Omar could see her struggling in vain to resist. In the end, he knew her inability to suppress her anticipation would win out, and off they went for some afternoon delight.

Their relationship was only six months old, but it was moving along pretty well so far. Wanda was a senior at the same college. She had a white dad and black mom. She had a Halle Berry look with green eyes and a body that stopped traffic.

He knew that Wanda wasn't thrilled about her suspicions that he was still seeing other girls, but she figured on changing that behavior very soon. This wasn't her first rodeo, and she knew how to make a man toe the line.

Omar returned to his dorm room dripping with sweat and excitement at the prospects of being drafted into the pros. He settled on his tattered couch with a gallon of cold Gatorade and grasped the remote control, which harnessed all the power of his nineteen-inch low-definition color TV. As he clicked it on, he muttered, "You're gonna be the first thing replaced when that contract comes in, bubba." The television responded by slowly bringing in ESPN with a light fuzz over the screen. It was not a 4K HD version.

The phone rang and Omar grabbed it. "Yo, this is me. Is that you?"

"Hey, pro, wassup?"

"Yo, Short man, what's turnin', brother?"

Ronnie Short said, "I was checkin' ta see if we was still on for the weekend at the beach."

Omar responded, "You betcha, buddy. We're gonna have too much fun. Who's all gonna be there?" Omar asked.

Short replied, "Me and Dump Truck are coming over early on Friday. We're all crashing at Speed's crib."

"Tha's cool," said Omar. "I'll be there by six and meet y'all at Speed's."

The conversation drifted from weekend plans to other more mundane matters.

Omar clicked off with a grunt and headed for the shower. It was Wednesday. Wanda tonight if all went as planned. He had to laugh thinking about Ronnie and his little brother, Dump Truck, driving from Tampa to Daytona in Ronnie's rattletrap of a car.

Ronnie was his best friend from high school and was a pretty fair athlete in his own right. At six two and lean with pretty fair looks, he also did all right with the ladies, but he lacked the speed needed to make it to the ranks of a scholarship athlete. As a result, he was working as a stockman at the local Food Lion, and his wheels were a rusted-out Toyota from the early seventies, which lacked air conditioning. What it lacked in appearance, it made up for in a master-blaster sound system that was no doubt worth more than the car itself.

Dump Truck was also a member of his high school crew, and he had earned his nickname through his girth, which he had developed through years of fast-food consumption. He was Omar's younger brother, properly named Orson, but he had always hated his given name. Truth be known, he resembled a black Orson Welles, minus the beard. Omar was realistically afraid that Ronnie's car could succumb to Dump Truck's weight of more than three hundred pounds during the trip if the stereo system's bass didn't blast it apart first. He also knew that the boys liked to party on road trips, and they always seemed to reach their objective in various states of fucked up. This weekend was definitely going to be a party to remember.

Speed was another Tampa-grown athlete who had the significant athletic talent, size, and speed to be a terror to quarterbacks and running backs, and up until recently, he had been a star defensive player at Martin Luther College. It seems that he had run afoul with the powers that be for carrying a loaded assault rifle in his car on campus, and, as a result, he had been tossed from the team after an outstanding junior season. With only one year of eligibility left, Omar knew his college football playing days were over, but he was apparently staying in shape. He claimed to have hopes of making it to the NFL combine and getting picked up by a team in search of someone with his talent and penchant for violence on their defense. Omar thought Speed would be a natural for the Oakland Raiders, and Speed had already enlisted a local tattoo artist to render the Raider logo on one of his ham-sized biceps.

Speed lived off campus in a shady part of town with an iron-pumping monster named Cooter who tried to keep Speed in the weight room and off the streets as much as possible. Speed had so far managed to avoid gainful employment, so the chore was not an easy one. Keeping Speed out of trouble was a task Omar fondly referred to as "Speed duty." Omar knew that Speed would be looking forward to the weekend reunion with his friends from home and had already lined up a party for them to crash. It was graduation weekend at Martin Luther, and the town would be revved up to jam.

CHAPTER 2

BRANDON

Brandon Michaels was stretched across the bow of his eighteen-foot Hewes flats boat, drifting in the Mosquito Lagoon, and with one eye, he was watching his bobber skitter about on the surface. The early morning dew was rising with the sun, but the temperature was still rather brisk. His fishing buddy, Steve, a female Australian shepherd, was curled up on a fleece blanket in the stern, oblivious to the proceedings and trying to stay warm. Beneath the bobber was a nervous pigfish, a small baitfish considered by redfish or red drum fisherman to be the "pizza" of baits. Pigfish were seemingly irresistible to redfish, whether they were hungry or not, presumably because of the grunting noises they made when hooked or nervous. It was the first Saturday of April, and Brandon was engaged in the first half of his usual weekend ritual: fishing on Saturday and golf on Sunday. It was a typical existence for a single lawyer residing on the upper east coast of Florida, and in his view, it didn't suck. His system was working to perfection thus far. All he needed now was the cooperation of the fish.

Brandon was single, Caucasian, six feet tall, and 230 pounds. He was broad at the shoulders from years of football, rugby, and weight training, and he had thinning brown hair and green eyes. He sported a redneck tan from his weekend activities: olive/tan arms and lower legs from where shirtsleeves and shorts stopped and socks started. He had calves like hams to go with a muscular physique. He owned a modest but well-placed Florida-style house on the east side of the Intracoastal Waterway, and he kept his boat in a rickety pre-WWII boathouse built on the end of his dock. He and Steve would often go fishing on a moment's notice, depending on work, his mood, and, of course, the weather.

His golfing habit got a bit more complicated by his other hobby: flying. He spent half of most weekends these days with three other characters, all of whom liked to fly and play golf. As a result, Brandon and his buds would fly off at the crack of dawn nearly every Sunday morning with the sun rising in the east, and land somewhere within two hours away at a private FBO that was within reasonable cab or courtesy car distance from a golf course on their wish list. When he bought his Beach Bonanza, one of his goals was to play each of the top hundred golf courses in the state of Florida using the aircraft as transportation. Afterward, he sold quarter interests to three of his flying friends. With four of them splitting the flying and the bills, it wasn't unreasonably expensive, and they all enjoyed their weekly adventures immensely. Each week, a different partner was responsible for picking the course, securing a tee time, and acting as pilot in command. He also had to pick up the tab and take enormous amounts of verbal abuse should any part of the plan go awry.

This morning, Steve was leashed to her usual spot on the center console of the boat due her propensity to jump out and literally chase fish on the hook and try to bite/eat them. While the Australian shepherd is a herding dog by nature, it seemed that Steve had evidently received a bizarre twist in her genetic recipe book; she found a hooked fish to be a most desirable creature to chase. Brandon had lost one prize redfish and a two hundred-plus-pound tarpon learning this lesson the hard way. It had turned out to be worth the sacrifice, however, considering the huge laughs he got every time he recounted the incidents. Unlike most yuppie business types, Brandon refused to turn on his cell phone unless he needed to make a call, so when he was fishing or playing golf, he was truly unreachable by the outside world. He simply forwarded his calls to his reluctant secretary, Patty, and often left the iPhone in the truck unless a call was expected. On this day, he was concentrating on his increasingly active bobber when it submerged suddenly with a loud plop.

One thing about large redfish is they don't sneak up quietly on a bait; rather, they hit it like a ton of bricks and take off immediately upon being hooked, peeling off large chunks of twelve-pound test line. Since the banning of the gill nets in the early nineties, the Mosquito Lagoon's redfish population had become both larger and more plentiful—in spite of the craze for blackened redfish in New Orleans restaurants. With a two fish per person keep limit, and a length limit of between eighteen and twenty-seven inches, sport fishing alone was putting very little pressure on the redfish stock.

What that meant in essence was that once a redfish exceeded twenty-seven inches in length, she could not be legally killed by a fisherman and was home free for life. As a result, fish in excess of twenty pounds and thirty inches were becoming commonplace in these waters and had only to worry about underwater predators.

Brandon figured that whatever was currently dumping the line from his Daiwa spin-casting reel was a monster. Steve whined and strained at her leash, sensing the presence of her antagonist of choice, while Brandon held on and watched the spinning spool. The fish took a good seventy-five yards of line before he was able to turn it and begin to work it back toward the boat. It took nearly twenty minutes of steady pressure to get the fish into view, and as soon as it saw the boat, it bolted again, causing the whole process to repeat itself.

After nearly thirty minutes the great fish was tiring—as was Steve, whose attention had diminished to a plaintive whine and a light drool. Brandon grabbed the "N-E-T" (he told the dog never to let him say that word out loud while fighting a fish or it will surely get off) and hauled in the catch of the day for a brief period of measurement, admiration, revival, and release. The redfish measured thirty-four inches, and he conservatively estimated its weight to be well over twenty-five pounds. What a specimen! Now all he needed was a smaller one for lunch—or perhaps a trout or snapper.

Had he allowed himself a camera in the boat (also bad luck), this one would have made a worthy photo opportunity. The whole ordeal, including fighting, admiration, and release, took more than forty-five minutes and satisfied Brandon's "catch a large fish" craving. In Florida, it is illegal to keep a redfish that is more than twenty-seven inches in length.

"Time for breakfast, Steve, old girl," he said as he poured half of an Icehouse beer (she wouldn't drink Budweiser or its ilk) into a bowl for her and tossed her half of a pastrami sandwich, which she caught in midair and swallowed after very little chewing. "Breakfast of champions," he said between swallows of beer as he cranked up the two hundred-horse Yamaha engine and engaged the throttle.

The nimble little Hewes jumped up on plane and sped along at a brisk clip, Brandon keeping it generally in the edges of the channel, dodging crab trap floats. He steered the boat for sea trout country, hoping to catch a fish or two suitable for lunch. Luckily for them, the blackened redfish craze had passed by the time the fish was de-commercialized, but the truth be known, sea trout was a sweeter meat, and it was easier to find in legal sizes. Also, there was no maximum limit on one fish, so big ones called "gator trout" were keepers as well. Brandon had caught several that were more than ten pounds over the years.

Thirty minutes later, with six speckled trout in the three-to-five-pound class in his live well, Brandon and Steve headed toward the old fish camp in Oak Hill. By eleven, the W-I-N-D (another verbal no-no) was coming up from the east along with the wakes of yachts owned by northerners returning from their winter homes in South Florida. Brandon reflected on how nice it would be to have enough money to buy and operate an eighty-foot sport fisherman between a winter home on the Intracoastal Waterway in the colder months and a lavish mansion in the North in the warmer months. Brandon could think of two principle ways to become rich: to be born that way or to marry into it. He was so far oh for two in that regard. He loved the ladies, but he felt that thirty-two years old was far too young to settle down. So many women, such little time, as they say. Besides, he had yet to meet a wealthy man's gorgeous daughter who was both a practicing nymphomaniac and a liquor store owner.

Brandon had been practicing law in northeast Florida for more than eight years since graduation from Florida State University Law School. Personal injury law was his forte, and after seven years of being tutored by the insurance companies as a defense lawyer, he had recently struck out on his own, "hung the shingle" so to speak, and was turning his sword on the insurance companies. Being the eternal optimist, he hoped that he would someday soon stumble into the third way to get rich, which was to handle a few multimillion-dollar personal injury cases with attorney's fees being 30–40 percent of the total recovery.

Unfortunately, young lawyers quickly learn upon striking out on their own that those cases don't grow on trees, and if one wants to pay the rent, the secretary, the costs, and the rest of the overhead, at least in the beginning, one needs to take most everything that pokes its head in the office door with fee potential. That, in practice, meant that Brandon was representing drunk drivers and other petty criminals, suing deadbeat debtors and contract breakers for his buddies who owned businesses, handling divorces when unavoidable, and presiding over real estate closings. An incredible amount of Florida residents own Real Estate salesperson's licenses, and Brandon, having been born and raised in Florida, had gotten a salesman's license and then a broker's license just to bone up on the subject for his practice. He was always very thorough when he set his mind to a task, and the current task upon returning to the dock was to filet his catch and then load up the boat. He had trailered his boat the thirty or so miles south to the fishing grounds today in order to avoid the long, wet boat ride home.

Upon arrival back at the city dock at Oak Hill, Steve bounded from the boat on contact with the dock and darted off to partake of one of her favorite pastimes: "chasing stuff." Birds, squirrels, lizards, it didn't matter what species of critter, so long as it was game enough to flee. Steve was the fastest Aussie Brandon had ever known. At twenty-nine pounds and two and a half feet tall, she was a bit larger than a Shetland Sheepdog, with a similarly shaped body, face, and coat. Her coloring was jet-black with the exception of a white collar, which ran from her shoulders to her head, covered half her muzzle and split her eyes to the top of her head, kind of like a black and white Lassie. Her piercing brown eyes spoke of an intelligence that belied the silly behavior she was presently exhibiting. She quickly had a squirrel treed in a palm tree with no nearby wires or limbs to leap upon to freedom, so the squirrel was reduced to jabbering at her from safety and spitting in Steve's direction as she barked her brains out. She bounded like a deer when approaching her prey, and Brandon often wondered what would happen if she ever caught a squirrel, nothing good for either was his guess, but he enjoyed watching her work, so long as the barking didn't bother the neighbors.

CHAPTER 3

GUS

Oak Hill dock was an old fisherman's dock that had remained unchanged for many years. It sported several mobile homes on wheels that harbored gnarled old fisherman who chose to live within yards of access to their boats. It had an old bait and tackle store that supplied bait, beer, and ice along with a poor selection of fishing gear manned by Gus, the ornery old fisherman who managed it. He was a throwback to the days of Hemingway and looked a lot like him. He was probably over six foot two in his youth, but sixty plus years of backbreaking work had left him stoop shouldered and bowlegged to the point where he was now barely five ten. His shop was just as old and smelled like dead things as one would imagine.

Hearing the familiar barking, Gus came out of the bait shack and called to Steve. She knew that he always kept a morsel of something generally edible for her, so she abandoned the squirrel and trotted over to scope him out. Her stump of a tail wagged as she sat at his feet and looked up in anticipation. As much as Brandon enjoyed watching, Steve's antics, he momentarily ignored her while proceeding with the odiferous chore of cleaning the trout and tossing the heads, skins, and guts into the river, whereupon a veritable rugby match ensued between a dozen brown pelicans doing battle with several plump catfish for the scraps. It always amazed Brandon how much stuff a pelican could get into its mouth and down that narrow neck. They were bottomless pits when it came to fish remains. Brandon drained off his beer, tossed the trout filets into a

14

ziplock bag and then into the cooler, and strolled down the dirt road to retrieve his truck and trailer.

His truck was a white Chevy Silverado Cowboy king cab with all the bells and whistles. It came with a mortgage-sized payment, but it was very comfortable and useful, and the girls at the country bars loved it. It could also pull the Hewes out of the water off any boat ramp, no matter how bad, and in this part of Florida, most ramps were in various stages of ruin.

Brandon handled the loading of the boat himself in five minutes. He was fairly expert at backing a truck and trailer, which was an uncommon attribute. Anyone needing a good laugh need only park next to a boat launch on a Saturday anywhere in Florida and watch the amateurs attempt to load and unload their boats. Not a day went by without someone taking forty tries before getting it right, or, better yet, sinking a boat, truck, or both after forgetting to install the plug or backing in too far.

Brandon hauled out the Hewes, pulled the plug to let it drain, tied it securely, and secured the rods and reels. Then he popped a new beer and went into the bait shack to shoot the shit with Gus and retrieve his roommate. The store wasn't much larger than a normal bedroom, with a live well for shrimp, an icebox, a cooler for drinks, some snacks, and a few items of tackle. Gus charged a modest fee of five bucks per boat to launch and probably made barely enough to survive, but he wasn't complaining since he got to fish every day.

In the bait shop, which was a small, stark concrete structure offering all manner of snacks, drinks, and fishing gear for sale, Gus was talking to Steve, who was acting like she understood every word and wagging her stubby tail to show the proper amusement to Gus's story. She was really hoping to boost another snack, but Gus wasn't fooled. "All right, ya shit-bird," he hollered as he tossed her another snack, which she caught in midair. The snack's origin was not readily apparent to Brandon, but she caught it as usual and swallowed it whole. Most likely, it was a hunk of smoked mullet, a delicacy in these parts.

"How's it hanging, Gus," Brandon said as he entered the shack. The smell of the bait shack took some getting used to every time he entered, and today was no different. "Yep, still smells like a French whore died in here."

"I'll have to rely on your olfactory experience in that regard." Gus reached out his liver-spotted, leather-skinned hand to shake Brandon's. Gus was wearing a pair of ancient overalls that looked like hand-me-downs from Jed from the *Beverly Hillbillies*. With an unfiltered Camel hanging from a craggy, lined mouth missing several front teeth, he asked with a lisp, "So, you keeping the streets clean of criminals and other such vermin, Counselor?"

"I do my best, Gus. You know the saying: Blessed is he who busts my client …"

"Or runs his ass over," Gus completed the thought that accompanied the typically slanderous ambulance-chaser accusation.

Personal injury lawyers had developed a bad rap of late with the public, and it was showing in the pathetically small verdicts being handed down.

Gus said, "You can't turn on the TV these days without some greedy lawyer looking out at ya and wanting ya to sue somebody."

"Don't start with me, Gus. I don't like the TV lawyers any more than you, and the goddamned insurance companies have everyone convinced that there is a flood of litigation driving out insurance carriers and driving up rates. It's bullshit, and you know it. They lost their asses in the real estate market in the late eighties by investing mountains of premiums on projects destined for failure, and again in 2008 when the real estate market went to shit—and now they're blaming their poor planning on the trial lawyers." Of course, hurricanes like Andrew, Charlie, Francis, Matthew, Ivan, Michael, and Jeanne hadn't cheered them up much either.

It was a trend that Brandon knew well. His past ten jury trials as a defense lawyer had resulted in the plaintiff receiving the proverbial goose egg in nine of them and barely netting the plaintiff lunch money in the tenth. He was hoping to get a chance to help turn that trend around from the other side, and he took every opportunity to dispel the rumors by educating laymen like Gus whenever the opportunity arose. The problem was that Brandon knew that Gus didn't really give a shit. He was just busting his balls.

"Did I get any calls?" Brandon inquired to change the subject. His secretary knew his general pattern, and if necessary, where or when he could be reached if anything needed his immediate attention, preferably new clients.

"Oh yeah," Gus said. "Some guy who got run over and turned into paraplegic cauliflower by the Coca-Cola truck called looking for ya. I told him to buzz off," he said with a grin.

Brandon threw a smelly rag at him as he ducked behind the counter and giggled. "I don't know why I bother making civilized conversation with you, you smelly old river rat. "Come on, Steve. Let's blow this pop stand."

Brandon and Steve departed, and Gus waved as he clutched his ample belly with gnarled hands, amusing himself greatly with his wit. Heading the truck back toward home, Steve rode in the front with her head out the window. It always reminded Brandon of the cartoon that showed why dogs could never go into space: their heads would burn up on reentry.

CHAPTER 4

THE PRACTICE

Up to speed and driving north on US-1, the wind was doing ridiculous things to Steve's muzzle, and Brandon nearly rear-ended a cop while watching her in the side-view mirror. Not a good thing with an open beer between his legs. He slowed down the Cowboy Cadillac as he called his truck, tossed the empty beer can out the window, rationalizing this littering as his contribution to someone's aluminum collection, and dialed the office on his cell phone.

Patty worked Saturday mornings as a favor while they tried to get the practice going. She had migrated from the insurance defense firm with him, along with a total of seven clients. Six months later, the client list had nearly tripled.

"Law offices."

"Anything doing?" he asked.

"Hey, boss, did ya catch lunch for Monday?"

"Sure did, sugar. Bring in some of that special beer batter, and we'll pig out on trout and hush puppies."

Her reply sounded like a sarcastic "Yum," primarily since he had been catching lunch for Mondays and sometimes Tuesdays and Wednesdays almost every weekend for six months in order to go easy on the cash flow. He correctly suspected that she was thoroughly sick of eating fish.

"Give me some good news," Brandon said, getting to the point. He despised talking on the cell phone while driving. He had used it as a defense in several cases as an excuse to blame the plaintiff for his or her own car crashes, and he never wanted that to happen to him should he get in a crash. Texting was even worse.

Patty said, "You got a collect call from the jail. A guy named Carl Rust got you appointed to represent him on armed robbery charges. The public defender got the codefendant."

"Great," Brandon lamented. "A major felony with a lovely $1,500 fee at the end. With my luck, it will probably result in a six-week trial."

The public defender's office represented persons who couldn't afford a private lawyer, which meant those earning less than one hundred and fifty bucks per week, which was basically limited to those criminals who were homeless and jobless. The problem arose when two or more broke people were involved in committing the same crime. The public defender couldn't represent them both. When the two characters did not always share the same interests, what is referred to in the business as a "conflict" develops, usually because one wise guy might squeal on the other to get himself a better deal. In that case, special public defenders were appointed from a list of lucky volunteers, and Brandon had put himself on that list in his quest for new clients.

"Okay, I'll stop by the branch jail after my nap. You can take the rest of the day off." Brandon clicked off without saying goodbye. It would probably be Monday or Tuesday before he actually visited his latest jewel, but there were no worries since the guy wasn't going anywhere.

That following Wednesday, Brandon was finally getting around to meeting his new client. Carl Rust was not so comfortably ensconced in the local branch jail. Brandon parked the white Chevy in the parking lot at around ten. It was hot, as usual, and he was sporting his usual out-of-court look: Dockers, no socks, shorts, and a golf shirt. One never knew when a golf match would beckon, and he kept an assortment of suits, clean shirts, and ties in the office closet in case a court appearance necessitated a change. He had initially worn a suit and tie to work every day after opening his new practice, but he soon learned that clients understood the practicality of casual attire in Florida's heat, and most seemed to be more at ease when he was at ease.

This practice had begun when an unscheduled client called on a day when his suits were at the cleaners. He had thrown on a white shirt and tie over his Docker shorts and Timberline walking shoes, figuring he could stay seated behind the desk and the client would be none the wiser. Unfortunately, the client insisted upon showing him the damage that his car had sustained in the crash, and Brandon had to reveal his lower half in order to follow the client to the parking lot. As it turned out, the client had said, "Hell, I don't blame ya, boy. It's too damn hot for long trousers in this state." After that, he gave up on the pretense, and nobody complained. So much for dress for success.

Fortunately, the only attire the jail required of visiting attorneys was long pants, a picture ID, preferably a driver's license, and a Florida Bar card, which Brandon had taped together for convenience's sake. It also came in handy sometimes when he got pulled over. Cops weren't overly fond of defense attorneys, but they realized it sometimes paid off to have them on their side since none of them relished being cross-examined by a lawyer with a grudge against cops. Brandon deposited his credentials and scrawled his name on the sign-in book along with that of Mr. Rust and awaited the familiar click of the outer door to the jail's visiting area. Once through the outer door, one had to wait in a small cell for the outer door to slam shut before the inner door would open. When the inner door locked shut, and he was securely inside the jail's confines, he always shuddered at the prospect that but for the grace of God go I …

Brandon walked into one of the four interview rooms, flicked on the light, sat in a hard chair, and reviewed the flimsy file while awaiting the appearance of his newest charge. Next to him on the wall was a red button he could push to alert the guards in the unlikely case that the client attacked him. Brandon was dying to push it just to see what would happen. The place had a unique smell of something stale or recently dead, and there were always echoes of shouts and voices bouncing about. His file contained little more that the court's order appointing him and a copy of the information. This was the charging document that laid out the bare essentials of Mr. Rust's alleged deed against the people of the State of Florida. He kept all of his criminal files in red folder jackets to signify trouble. Personal injury files were kept in green folders for the obvious reason, greenbacks, and all others in manila because their contents were usually rather bland compared to the juicier criminal and personal injury cases.

Rust had been charged with eighteen counts of armed robbery involving various small branches of local banks. That was extremely good news because it meant that his fee would be at least fifteen hundred bucks for each offense. Thus, his fee would be twenty-seven grand, more akin to, but still much less than, the actual fee he would levy for a paying client facing the same charges. He would have to remember to send flowers to the judicial assistant who had appointed him on this jewel.

Rust shuffled to the open door of Brandon's cubicle in the standard prison attire: sandals, handcuffs, an ill-fitting, well-used orange onesie, and slip-on shoes. Being a Florida State Seminole, Brandon loved the irony of the color that represented half of the famous orange and blue of the University of Florida Gators. He loved to sit in court among a group of attorneys when the prisoners were led in together for arraignment or pretrial. He would hold his hand over his mouth and say in a low but deep announcement, "Here come the Gators!" He would hope neither the judge nor his armed bailiff heard him. The Gator alumni among the attorneys always grimaced at this and sometimes threw things at him.

"Have a seat, Mr. Rust," Brandon cheerfully said, indicating the only other piece of furniture in the room besides the desk that was secured to the wall. Rust took his seat and said, "Howdy."

"So, you've gotten yourself in a bit of trouble, I see," said Brandon.

"Yeah," said Rust. "It's all a cuz a the crack." He had the look of a man who had been ridden hard and put away wet, common among frequent drug abusers. He was a white dude in his sixties, about five foot five with white hair that hadn't seen a barber's blade since Nixon was president, the beginning of a beard, stooped shoulders, and bad posture.

"Well, why don't you just tell me about it?" said Brandon. "And don't leave anything out if you want me to represent you effectively."

"Okay," said Rust, and he began.

Brandon came from the school of thought that basically held that most criminal defendants were guilty of something, and it was better to know the whole truth in cases not subject to capital punishment. In the movies, lawyers sometimes didn't ask their clients if they were guilty

21

or not to avoid becoming party to a lie. Once an attorney knows that a client plans to lie in court, he must either keep him off the stand, or, if he insists upon testifying, the lawyer must allow him to do so in narrative form without questioning him.

Brandon felt like it was easier to avoid the lies if he knew where they were, and the truly guilty defendants were usually best served by not testifying. Besides, cops often bent the truth nearly as much as the defendants, so it all evened out. When asked by friends how he could defend someone who was guilty, he would reply that the guilty deserved the same representation as the innocent, and if we let the cops make that determination instead of judges and juries, we'd live in a police state. Even when guilt was obvious, the system still required the government to carry the burden of proof beyond and to the exclusion of all reasonable doubt. His job was to make them work for it and then to secure for his client the best possible plea deal when it became apparent that they would be able to do so. The trick was not to make the state work too hard at it—or they would then feel like they had nothing to lose by seeking the maximum sentence. Brandon saw his job as being a facilitator who got the client through the system efficiently and minimized his penalty. In the rare case of the innocent client, he would push like hell for them to drop the charges to a slap on the wrist or dismissal, and, failing that, take it to trial. He had an excellent track record in trials since he only tried the winnable ones, and the prosecutors knew it.

It seemed that Carl Rust had devised a relatively harmless plan to support his crack cocaine habit. When in need of a fix and low on funds, he would take a cab to a small local bank branch in a busy shopping plaza. He would direct the cabbie to park where he couldn't see Carl's destination and tell him to wait. Then he would take a circuitous route to the bank, enter, and wait in line for a teller like everyone else. When it came his turn, he would approach the teller and calmly hand her a note with his left hand while in his right he held a piece of pipe the size of a small gun barrel pointed toward her in his jacket pocket in such a way as to make it obvious to her as soon as she read the note.

The note was always the same. It said simply: "I don't want to hurt you, simply place a handful of twenties and tens in this bag with no dye pack, and I will leave quietly, and don't even think about raising an alarm until I have been gone for five minutes." He would then hand over a brown sack, and the teller would invariably stuff a generous amount of cash into it. They always felt the need to appear generous in their stuffing so as not to anger him.

Carl related that he always wore a hat pulled low over his brow, and his nondescript size and appearance always seemed to frustrate the bank's security cameras. As a result, he claimed to have been successful at least seventeen times, averaging nearly twenty-five hundred dollars per visit, with two visits netting him nearly ten grand on days when his bag happened to be larger. He would then stroll from the bank, return quickly to the cab, and direct the driver to the vicinity of his current crash pad.

According to Carl, after his first few successes, he decided to treat himself to some luxury. Adorned in some recently purchased clothes, he checked into the penthouse suite in the Oceanfront Marriott hotel. The room boasted a great view of the ocean and a hot tub for only four hundred dollars a night, which he paid for in small used bills on a weekly basis after each heist. According to Carl, the management never suspected a thing, in spite of the regular visits from Happy, Carl's crack dealer, who was usually accompanied by a bottle of spirits of one type or another and a local hooker or three.

Carl said that his little joyride had been going along nicely for more than three months until one night in a crack-induced haze, his friendly neighborhood dealer had pried out of Carl the source of his seemingly endless stash of cash. He told Brandon that his codefendant, Happy, had threatened to narc on Carl if he didn't let him in on the action, so Carl said he allowed him to drive the getaway car on what was to be his final heist in this area. Carl sensed the cops were getting sick of his success, and he didn't want to push his luck.

Brandon took notes: "For the latest victim, the two rocket scientists had selected a small Pioneer Bank in the plaza at the corners of Nova and Beville Roads, and Carl directed Happy to wait around back while he did his thing."

Carl claimed that everything went like clockwork until he came out of the bank and headed to the car only to find it missing. Apparently, Happy couldn't resist the temptation to watch the action, and he had driven around to the front of the bank. So, when Carl spotted his car, he panicked and ran to it. At that moment, apparently, a teller was able to spot the car and record the plate number. She then called it in to Daytona's finest via 911. What resulted was a brief chase, which ended five miles up I-95 when Happy's car blew a tire and careened off the interstate and into the trees on the side of the road.

As expected, Happy was caught quickly, and while he protested his innocence to the deputies on the scene, Carl bolted into the woods. According to the police report, Carl had gone nearly a mile into the thick pine forest before digging in. He said he started hearing a helicopter and the unmistakable sound of dogs in pursuit. He decided that a hiding place was called for, so he quickly dug himself a three-foot hole in the soft ground with his hands and the help of a sharp stick. Then he covered himself up with palm fronds from within.

He might have gotten away with it had he been able to resist the strident call of the crack pipe nestled in his jacket pocket. He told Brandon, "The stuff pulls on you harder than a three hundred-pound whore." Shortly after he took a few tokes from his trusty pipe, he found himself sharing his hideout with a very aggressive German shepherd police dog. After several bites, the hound was pulled from Carl's hide none too quickly by his snickering handler. Carl was led to custody dripping pine straw and blood from the dog bites while enjoying his last cocaine high for a long time to come.

His wounds had mostly healed by the time Brandon interviewed him, and he finished his story with an exclamation: "What a ride it was while it lasted!"

Brandon explained that not using a real gun and never hurting anyone would favor his chances for a relatively lenient plea bargain. The truth of the matter was that the state simply could not afford to take to trial every case that came to the courts, and as a result, plea bargains offering defendants a significant break from what one could expect from a guilty verdict were the norm. The unfortunate side effect was that defendants who maintained their innocence and demanded to exercise their Constitutional right to a trial by their peers often were punished for exercising that right by receiving a more severe sentence from the judge when they were found guilty at trial.

Brandon concluded the interview by explaining to Carl the various expected outcomes and promised to see him in court at his first pretrial conference.

As Carl trudged solemnly back to his cell, Brandon reversed the process and exited the jail. It was always a breath of fresh air to step outside again—even if it was hot as hell. Brandon wondered what delicacy Carl would be enjoying for dinner that evening as he steered the truck down US-92 and headed for a cool mug of Foster's lager and a medium-rare steak with all the trimmings at the Outback. Brandon had been with clients in jail on a few occasions when their noon meal was served, and it wasn't a pretty sight. He had to laugh at the stupidity of his newest client's capture and marveled at the strength of the urge that crack cocaine evidently held over its addicts. Apparently, crack cocaine became addictive after only one use, and he couldn't fathom why anyone who knew that would be stupid enough to partake in its use even once. But humans were known to go to great lengths to get high without any regard for the consequences. Unfortunately, this country is full of idiots, but without them, lawyers like Brandon would have very little to do. Thank God you can't coach stupid.

CHAPTER 5

WANDA

Omar bounded into his apartment after finishing his last final exam. Words could not describe the feeling of elation he felt after completing four years of college. He grabbed a beer from the fridge and hopped into the shower to begin the preparation for his date with Wanda. She was due to arrive any minute, and he was tingling with anticipation. Wanda hailed from Mississippi and was the voluptuous daughter of a Baptist minister. What they say about preacher's daughters being on the wild side was certainly the case with Wanda. They had been dating for six months, and the sex was frequently wild and wooly. While she was by no means the only woman he had at his beck and call, she was his favorite. The others he kept in "touch" with lived in various other towns besides Tallahassee as he had learned that this town wasn't big enough for two girlfriends. He had once tried running four locals at one time, and it blew up in his face in a big way.

Five minutes into his shower with his eyes shut and his face covered with suds, Omar sensed the presence of another person in the stall. Wanda pressed her ample breasts against his back, took the bar of soap, and began to lather his front side from behind. "Holy shit, there's a naked woman in my shower!" Omar exclaimed.

"It's your lucky day, stud," Wanda whispered into his wet ear.

Her lathered hand headed south to his stiffening erection.

"I've already washed my johnson, baby," Omar whined.

"Well we're just gonna make sure he's extra clean then," she said as she stroked him.

Omar groaned with pleasure as he rinsed the shampoo from his head so he could open his eyes. He turned to face her, took the soap from her hand, and began to massage her breasts with it while she continued her ministrations with his manhood.

Her nipples hardened under his gentle caress, and she began to moan softly.

"Honey, if you keep that up, this little session is going to be over in a hurry," Omar warned.

She released him and stretched her arms languorously behind her head, allowing him unfettered access to her 36Cs.

"You just cannot get these babies too clean," said Omar, and he dropped his right hand between her legs and began massaging her. She kept her pussy shaved from the clitoris on down—just the way he liked it. Rolling the lips of her vagina around in his slippery fingers was driving them both crazy.

"Oh, baby, I need you now," she said.

He obliged by lifting her buttocks as she encircled him with her legs. He entered her easily and began to lift her up and down while kissing her deeply. It wasn't long before she arched her back and a deep growl began in her throat. He could feel her nails digging into his back as he quickened his pace until matching her orgasm with his own. He continued to hold her as the water cascaded off his back for several moments. Then he gently put her down and said, "Baby, you keep this stuff up, and I may have to make an honest woman of you."

"You keep this up, and I may just let you," she said as she exited the shower, winking seductively at him as she went.

Wanda walked into the living room as she dried her hair with a towel. She was wearing Omar's terry cloth robe and nothing else but a smile.

The phone rang, and she answered, "Hello?"

The gruff voice of an impatient white man said, "Omar!"

"Yeazza, let me go fetch him for ya," she said in her Aunt Jemima voice. "Omar, phone!" She continued drying her hair, grabbed the brain, and flipped on the TV.

Omar came out in his gym shorts and said, "Who is it, baby?"

"Some white man in a hurry," she said.

"Shoot," said Omar as he picked up the phone.

"It's Lou. Who the fuck you got answering your phone?"

"Oh, that would be my main squeeze, Wanda," he said.

"She's a smart-ass. I like her," said Lou.

Wanda whispered, "I'd better be your *only* squeeze if you want to live to see your baseball career. Otherwise, I'll show you squeeze, you bastard."

Omar kept one eye on her and said, "What's up, Lou?"

Lou said, "I just wanted to give you the skinny. I talked to the folks upstairs, and your selection is locked."

Wanda opened the front of the bathrobe and had one breast in each hand. She was squeezing them while slowly licking her lips.

Omar began to sweat, "You mean first round, for sure?" He was trying to concentrate on two things at once.

"You got it, bubba. Now keep your ass in shape and out of trouble for the next twenty days, you got it?"

"No sweat, Lou," Omar said as he felt himself hardening again. "Listen, I'm going down to Daytona for the weekend, so I've really gotta get going, but I'll call you when I get back, and we can schedule some workouts, okay?"

Wanda had squeezed her nipples to full erection, and her left hand held up her right breast so she could suck on it while her right was working an area below the waist which still remained covered by robe.

"Roger that. I'll talk to you soon," said Lou as he clicked off.

Omar hurriedly put the phone in its cradle and began moving toward Wanda as she moaned sleepily. "You've gone and done it now, woman. You've awakened the giant again."

Round 2 was on. Their last date before the break was spent mostly horizontal, and Omar suspected Wanda wasn't taking any chances on his going to Daytona Beach all horny without her.

Wanda had friends in Daytona who would waste no time trying to set Omar up with a budding coed from Martin Luther. Truth be known, one of the reasons he was going to Daytona in the first place was to touch base with his second favorite girl: Diandra. He figured that what Wanda didn't know wouldn't hurt him. He hoped he didn't run into any of her crew while hanging out with Diandra.

After having been shanghaied for one more night in Tallahassee, Omar spent that Saturday morning driving to Daytona. It was a four-hour drive, all interstate highway, but he left at seven thirty and was probably going to just make the graduation ceremony at noon. He had called Diandra that morning after escaping the clutches of wicked Wanda, and she made it clear that if he didn't, the after-graduation celebration would not be nearly as much fun as he expected.

He had also called Speed's place and woken up Cooter. Ronnie and Dump Truck had arrived safely and were currently sleeping off last night's buzz as was Speed.

"Don't you worry though," Speed said. "We're gonna party hard again tonight!"

Omar could hardly wait. The change of scenery would do him good, and besides, he hadn't been with Diandra in two months—and the real world would soon be beckoning. *Nothing like a little strange*, he thought as he sped down the highway while rocking to loud rap and R&B music. *It's good to be king.*

The drive was a straight shot east down I-10, the world's most boring highway, followed by I-295 beltway south around Jacksonville, then eighty miles south on I-95. He was there in well under four hours.

CHAPTER 6

THE PARTY

Brandon awoke with his teeth seemingly stuck together and a pounding headache. In spite of his aroma, Steve was licking his face, her nub of a tail wagging urgently, and her paws planted firmly on his naked chest. The sun was shining into the bedroom, and Brandon felt like a monkey had taken a dump in his mouth during the night. He asked Steve about it, but he got only the usual response.

The dog ran to the sliding glass door that overlooked the backyard and the river and barked to go out.

Brandon struggled up, holding his head in his hands. "God damn, Steve, did you get the license plate on the Mack truck that hit me?"

Steve only looked at him expectantly, cocking her head slightly as smart dogs do, so he climbed out of bed in his underwear, and opened the door, letting out the dog. "And no chasing fish!"

When she was not hunting for fish to chase, Steve delighted in trying to open those nasty oyster shells that existed at water's edge, often cutting her paws on the sharp edges. *You'd think she would have learned by now.* Brandon was sure he would puke if Steve returned with any foul smells. He reminded himself again of the need for a fence at the water's edge to thwart her shenanigans.

As he headed for the kitchen, he began to discover telltale signs of the nature of the end of the evening. He found his pants at the bedroom door with the socks trailing out of the ends of the legs and amazingly into his shoes as if he had been right sucked out of them. A little farther along, he found his shirt in the hallway, and in the kitchen was the clincher, eight empty white boxes with orange stripes scattered atop the counter. These formerly contained those greasy little Krystal cheeseburgers. *You know you've tied one on when you resort to those as a late-night snack.* They were still sitting like a bowling ball in his stomach, so he decided to forego breakfast and popped open a diet Coke in the hope that the carbonation would wash down the sludge in his mouth.

The morning paper reminded him that it was the first Saturday in April as he tried to reconstruct what had happened last night. First things first, after recovering the paper from the front porch, he checked the driveway to make sure the truck was there and undamaged. Good news and bad news: it was there and unhurt, which meant that he must have driven home with one eye open. He hated doing that, but sometimes the irrational side of the brain wins those arguments. "We can do it—we are invisible!" said the little devil sitting on his shoulder.

Friday evening had started normally with happy hour at the local meat market with some colleagues from the courthouse. The usual scene was the usual scene: everyone bragging about the week's legal triumphs and ogling the same women.

Brandon knew almost everyone there, and nothing exciting happened. Around seven, after one or three harmless Heinekens, he had migrated to the Oyster Pub in search of some female companionship as single guys in Daytona are wont to do when happy hour prices end at the latest meat market. Once there, he encountered a group of skydivers who had just made a beach jump and were celebrating having cheated death once again. They never needed much of an excuse to celebrate.

They were doing shots of Patron tequila with beer chasers, and Brandon bought them a round from a nearby bar stool. They were doing it a bit different than the normal salt and lemon, and he was curious. They seemed to be licking cinnamon and sucking on oranges before downing the tequila. Brandon had been on the skydiving team briefly in college so he could relate, and when they found this out, they had insisted that he join them. Since a couple of them were nice-looking and of the female variety, he humbly obliged.

He would not, however, do shots of tequila, as he had once had a bad date with a bottle of Jose Cuervo after a high school football game with two of his teammates (the only one they won his senior year), and he had gotten so sick that he hadn't been able to so much as smell tequila since then without gagging. The skydivers insisted that he participate by doing a shot of something, so he had relented and began doing kamikaze shots while everyone else shot tequila. In Brandon's world, a kamikaze shot consisted of a shot of vodka, a shot of triple sec (a citrus liqueur), and a splash of Rose's lime juice, all strained through ice, so it tended to be twice the size of a shot of tequila and just as potent. In between these, they were drinking Bull Juice, a mix of Red Bull and vodka that kept you up until it knocked you out.

Once into the kamikaze shots, he liked to entertain his fans with the bit from Cheech and Chong or Carlin or some other comedian where he would first make okay signs with each hand joining his thumb and forefinger into a circle, then reverse them with three fingers over the top toward his ears, so that his palms were facing his face and the three fingers were pointing down his cheeks with the circled fingers over his eyes like glasses. The fun of it was that some people, drunk or not, physically could not do this, but they always tried to imitate. Then he would say in his best Japanese accent, "Kamikaze pilots, fly down low, crashing on the deck, killing yourself and all aboard. Are there any questions?" Then turn around and reply, "Honorable Captain, sir, you outta you fucking mind!" By that time, everyone was usually in the frame of mind that most anything was funny, so the Kamikaze pilot usually killed. Last night was no exception.

The events of the evening got pretty vague about an hour or so into the shots program, and the visit to Krystal was a complete blur, let alone the Houdini act with his clothes. After showering and brushing his teeth hard enough to lose a year's worth of enamel, he threw on a pair of Dockers and a golf shirt and sat on the deck with the paper and a new Diet Coke. The paper was full of all the usual crime, drama, and tribulation in the front section, which he usually gave only a cursory glance before turning to the sports. Being April, with no football or much baseball to read about, the only thing of interest to him was golf since

Brandon wasn't much of a basketball fan. Just then, the phone rang. He wasn't going to answer it, but the noise was unbearable, so he did only to stop the ringing. *Why do I still have a landline?*

"This better be good," he said cradling the plastic troublemaker. "Hey, you party animal; it's Genie, from last night." The name sounded vaguely familiar, but he hesitated to speak. She continued, "Remember … your kamikaze copilot from the Oyster Pub?"

"It's all coming back to me now. Did you slip me a mickey?"

"I didn't have to," she said. "You mickeyed your own self. Was that a blast or what?"

"Did I do the kamikaze bit?" he asked.

"Several times, boyfriend. You were a riot."

"Did we get tossed out for dancing naked or causing a riot?" he asked.

"Unfortunately, no," she replied.

"Tell me you drove me home," he said.

"As a matter of fact, I was blitzed too, but Spiderman drove us both in your bad-ass truck, and Jonsey picked us up after a whirlwind tour through the Krystal drive-through. Then you mumbled something about letting the dog out and stumbled into your house without even offering us a tour or a kiss goodbye."

"Bless you, my child. We have now completed the puzzle, unless you are going to tell me that we then made mad passionate love—and I missed it."

"No such luck, big guy, maybe next time," she teased. "So, are you coming to Deland to watch us jump today?"

"Are you kidding? I had trouble jumping into the shower this morning, but I'll take a rain check."

"Wimp! Okay then, I'll catch you later. Give me a call. I wrote my number on the back of your shirt. Bye!"

He signed off, went into his bedroom, and retrieved his shirt from the hamper. Sure enough, across the back and shoulders of his monogrammed tailor-made cotton work shirt imported from England was a seven-digit number scrawled in black magic marker. "Well, at least the night wasn't a total loss," he said to himself as he transferred Genie's name and number to the contacts in his phone for future reference.

Steve was clambering to get in about the time he was soaking the shirt in cold water in a feeble attempt to salvage it. He opened the sliding door, and since it was already too late to go fishing, he asked, "What say we go for a run and sweat out some of this vodka?"

Steve knew the word run and immediately began to whine and twirl around in small circles.

Brandon turned on the answering machine, turned down the air conditioner to seventy-two degrees, and grabbed Steve's retractable leash.

They headed out to Peninsula Drive for a leisurely five-mile jog. The first half always began with Steve out front straining on the leash, pulling Brandon along, followed by the return trip when it gradually became the other way around. Steve wasn't in near the shape she used to be.

Besides keeping one reasonably fit, running for Brandon was a way for him to engage the little tickler system in his mind and go over the cases at the office that needed his attention. Lifting weights, his other fitness-related hobby was different because there were too many spandex-clad women in the gym for him to concentrate on work. Frequently, his runs ended with him scribbling sweaty notes to Patty for the next workday's chores, something she dearly loved. *Not.* She was a great secretary, but she never failed to complain that she had too much work to do. One day, he would probably have to hire her some help, but not just yet.

The practice was picking up since he went out on his own, but he was still handling a lot of junk mixed in with the good cases. He hoped the day would come when he could be more selective with which cases he accepted. He would definitely like to quit doing divorce work because it seemed like after fighting over the pets and the toaster, everyone hated everyone else, including the lawyers. He wanted to focus on personal injury and business litigation where folks didn't usually threaten to kill one another during depositions.

After returning from the run and falling in the pool, Brandon spent the rest of his Saturday in the air-conditioning reading an espionage thriller while watching golf and saying over and over, "I'll never drink again."

While single life seemed to leave him with more hangovers than his married friends, they had their own problems of a different sort, which he wasn't interested in adding to his life at the moment. He didn't necessarily agree with the proposition that among married folks, women controlled all the sex and half of the money. Truth be known, women controlled more than half of the money because the reality was that divorce was a financial sacrifice that most people were better off not undertaking. In his experience, most couples seeking divorce learned early on that they could not afford two households. So, as he often counselled clients, maybe it was worth trying a bit harder to make it work. Get some counselling. He wasn't sure the whole "till death do us part" thing was workable these days.

If women were from Venus and men were from Mars, Brandon was content to stay on Mars—and he was not willing to go over to the dark side just yet. He knew there were tons of happy marriages out there but doing divorce work just highlighted the bad ones and tended to jade his viewpoint. He also came from a broken family; his parents divorced when he was young, which that did not help his viewpoint. This was why he mostly avoided taking on family law matters in his practice.

CHAPTER 7

PHILOSOPHY

Brandon sat on his dock flicking a lure, which was an incredible imitation of a shrimp out from his dock into the river. He mindlessly twitched the rod tip as he slowly wound in the twelve-pound test Stren "Spiderwire". Fishing was what he liked to do when he felt contemplative. It was just after sunrise, around seven on a brisk April morning. There wasn't a puff of breeze, which was usually good for fishing. Gentle waves lapped the shore driven by the seemingly endless stream of yachts headed north in the Intracoastal Waterway as the rich returned from their Gold Coast wintering nests to their summer havens in the Northeast. Brandon could swear he could smell the money as they sailed on by.

He had already fielded two phone calls that morning, and they had sent him to his dock to fish and contemplate instead of taking his usual morning run. Steve was by his side with one ear cocked and one eye open, awaiting that moment of pandemonium when a redfish or trout would explode from the calm water and gobble up the lure. Brandon had Steve securely tied to the bench on the dock to prevent her normal reaction to that moment, which would be to dive from the dock, bark hysterically, and literally chase down the hooked fish like an Olympian after a gold medal. His more serious thoughts were interrupted by the notions of winning some serious bucks on *America's Funniest Video* if he were to film one of her performances. He made a mental note to bring the video camera next time and do just that. He had made this empty promise to himself before and having his cell phone on the dock was a good way to lose it in the river.

Brandon's philosophy was basically that of a realist with a bent toward optimism. This was largely due to the fact that he felt that if one contemplated reality too much, one tended to become pessimistic. As a reasonably intelligent person with a rudimentary knowledge of world affairs, he had several theories on the world's problems. It was logical to believe that the Creator made the act of sex a pleasurable thing to encourage mammals of all kinds to procreate and flourish. Survival of the fittest, and all that rot.

Well, it seemed to him that the Creator failed to build flexibility into the system, because after World War II, most of the civilized world had replaced survival with pleasure and entertainment as the primary goals in life. One natural result was a population explosion around the globe that threatened to destroy us one and all as a result of the inevitable exhaustion of resources such as food and water due to overcrowding, extinction, and pollution. If Brandon were a Miss America contestant, his answer to how would you better the world would not be the standard "world peace," but, rather, change the human makeup such that each woman could only bear one child. His theory was that then, each two people could only bring one more into the world, and the population would gradually decline to a manageable, static number.

He often wondered how that reality would change the way woman were viewed in the world. He had read that in China families, who were limited by law to one child, would often discard female children, preferring to have a boy for financial reasons. He felt girls should be equally treasured. He postulated a female-oriented solution could be to somehow make the male erection and orgasm as painful as childbirth. Or, better yet, he thought, what if men weren't issued a penis until and unless they qualified financially and emotionally as fathers—and promptly returned it to sender when finished. A workable but unrealistic impossible solution.

He then mused that this policy would also cut out huge amounts of crime in the world, presumably eliminating the sex, porn, and the human trafficking trades and ensure that only those men who truly wanted children could have sex. Being a fan of pleasure himself, he opted for the first option. The other banes of the world as he saw it were the destruction of the rain forests and the ozone layer and abuse and neglect of animals and old people. He felt that there was nothing sadder to him than seeing an old person eating a meal alone. He personally hoped he had the funds when he reached the age of geriatrics to start an old farts' frat house for himself and all of his surviving cronies.

Brandon suspected that he may have become a lawyer in part because of his admiration of the Constitution. It was created as a living thing that changed with the times to suit our changing needs. *That's where the "Creator" may have erred. He or she made us the way we are, and now we've become too smart for our own britches. We've developed several methods to eradicate ourselves, and we do not seem to get the idea that if we are to survive as a race, we need to agree on a few things.* He also blamed the religions of the world for being part of the problem in that regard.

As a realist and logical thinker and given the fact that in the past three or four thousand years, so many civilizations had so many completely different theories of religion, he thought it unlikely that any of them had it completely right or wrong. So, which do you believe? Some chose the religion of their childhood, and then some changed or converted several times during their lifetimes.

The scientific community certainly had proven the theory of evolution, but how incredible was it for that to have been random? He, being the optimist, liked to believe there was something out there that gave a crap about us, though truly unlikely to think that each and every prayer was heard by some guy in a white robe sitting on a cloud watching over each and every one of us. Reality constantly proved that prayers often went unanswered by a benevolent being, but it had also been proven that the power of optimism and positive thinking were very real.

Yet, most humans since the dawn of civilization had seemed to conjure up a god theory, no matter where or when they existed. Was it just to answer the questions of the unknown for peace of mind and to dull the fear of death and the unknown? Or was it motivated by a Creator who allowed us each to gravitate toward the theory that made us more comfortable with the hope that each person would select some form of religion to encourage civilized order in the world? Or maybe the grand architect of the universe was just karma.

Brandon liked the notion that there was a grand architect of the universe, and he said his prayers every night to the Christian version. However, he also was aware of the flaw in that aspect of human nature, evidenced by the fact that over time more humans had probably been slaughtered fighting over religion than reasons of territory, food, power, or even survival. Which brought his thoughts back to the overpopulation question. Knowing that no one was going to change womankind to limit production, would Mother Nature solve the problem with some form of pandemic disease or disaster—or would another Hitler come along and give us a hand with nuclear war?

He shuddered to think as he watched his bobber floating lazily in the river. He popped another beer and asked Steve what she thought about the chances of humankind surviving their own devices.

Steve opened one eye, twitched an ear to detect the telltale sound of a fish on, and hearing none, resumed her doze. He was aware of the quote by Steven Hawking, something to the effect that the only way humanity would survive on earth was to figure out a way to survive off of it. He figured Stephen was probably right.

His philosophical musing brought him back to the thoughts, which brought him to the dock, namely, the phone calls. The most recent call was from his buddy, Jake Stone, who was a pal dating back to their high school football days. Jake had made a grievous mistake and married his high school sweetheart during college. Now, seven years later, he was looking to expand his horizons you might say. Brandon's theory was that men married for one of three basic reasons: lust, "true love," or to calm some real or perceived insecurity. The insecurities ranged from a need to replace one's mother, to financial security, to affirmation of one's sexuality or heterosexuality, or to just a cure for loneliness.

In Brandon's experience, the rare marriage based upon "true love" was the type his grandparents seemed to have, where after the lust and the insecurities wore off, they stayed together because they simply adored one another. The result seemed to be that guys who married for any reason besides "true love" seemed to find that after around five or six years, those reasons no longer seemed so important, and their priorities began to shift, hence the seven-year itch. Jake had probably thought he married Darlene because he was in love, but young hormones have the ability to cleverly mask the real deal like a duck blind, and decoys can ruin a bird's day. Jake wanted to go to happy hour tonight and "see what's happening." Brandon, the consummate single guy, was game, but he knew the evening would consist of listening to Jake relating how bored he was with his life and watching him flirt with any trolling women who strayed into his radar range.

Jake wasn't fooling around with anyone specific yet, but the writing was certainly on the wall that he was shopping.

All was not lost, however, as Brandon's prospects for the rest of the evening were dramatically improved by the first phone call of the morning. Genie had unceremoniously woken him up at six thirty. The ringing phone had jolted him awake, and startled Steve, who starting barking from the foot of the bed like the sky was falling, which further startled Brandon, causing him to fall out of the bed and conk his head on the nightstand. By the time he answered the phone, he was out of breath. "Hello," he rasped after seven or eight rings. "Hey, lawman," Genie said. "You sound out of breath. Did I interrupt something?"

"No, you just woke me from a sound sleep and scared the shit out of me and my dog," he replied. "I must have been dreaming about you, what's up?"

"Oh, nothing much," she said coyly. "I've been thinking about you too."

"That's a good sign," he said. "I've got some work to do that will take me to about seven tonight, and then I thought I'd come over and give you a tryout."

"You did, did you?" he said. "What did you have in mind."

"Well, how about we have a few pops and some snacks, then we take a nice hot shower, and then you give my pussy a shave, and then lick it until my head caves in?"

This was the moment when lust and love became difficult to tell apart. After he recovered his composure and cleaned the spilled coffee off of his shirt, he managed to say, "You are on, girlfriend. Meet me here at seven thirty, and I'll handle the rest."

"Ciao," she said and clicked off.

The irony was not lost on Brandon, and life was looking good. *There is nothing better than an aggressive woman who knows what she wants.*

His take on women generally was that they, for the most part, enjoyed sex just fine once they were having it, but they just didn't seem to have a chemically driven primordial need for it like men. God gave men the sex drive because without it, their penises wouldn't function, and the human race would die out. All women needed was a little lubrication, and they could fake the rest. Sure, some even had orgasms and stuff, and though he suspected there was such a thing as a nymphomaniac, he'd never met one. If he ever did, he'd probably marry her.

Women, he theorized, also married for one of three reasons, but lust wasn't one of them. Their motivation to marry seemed to originate from either "true love" and a maternal desire to have a family; a deep-seated insecurity that they need someone to take care of them financially; or some form of guilt or desire to escape home. It fascinated him to note how strongly many women were driven by guilt or codependence. It also amazed him how many felt the need to fix or change a man with problems or went for the bad boy because of the danger.

He laughed at the thought of how teenage boys would try to get into a girl's pants by telling them that physical harm could come to them if they weren't allowed to release the pent-up sperm. Single women tended to be very playful in the rack, but once they were settled into a secure marriage, they seemed to find exciting sex to be unnecessary, or at the bottom of the priority list, and they engaged in it much less frequently according to his married friends.

For the men, unfortunately, exciting sex never seems to leave the top of the priority list, and therein lies the rub. At least that was the way of things among most of his married friends. He read somewhere that men think about sex every ten seconds, and Brandon felt this to be an accurate assessment.

At that point in his musing, he almost failed to notice a tugging on his rod tip as a fish attempted to make off with his bait. His bobber was nowhere in sight. He reeled in the slack line and yanked back on the rod to set the hook, which invariably set Steve to whining, drooling, and pulling on her restraint.

"Get 'em on in here and let's get a look at that hog," he said in his best southern redneck voice as he reeled in a nice fat four-pound speckled trout. "Ah, dinner Steve girl, what do ya know?"

She whined appreciatively and strained to get a whiff of the beast. He unhooked the fish and dropped it into his cooler before she could grab it from him.

Brandon returned to his thoughts and fantasized about the evening's prospects.

Steve drooled and stared at the cooler as if she could both open and will her neck long enough to reach into it. She would eat that fish raw if he let her. She had done it before on several occasions.

He thought, *She must have some feral cat in her.*

CHAPTER 8

GRADUATION

Omar had also always been an optimist. He believed that optimists rode motorcycles without helmets, bought green bananas, and figured the golden parachute would always open over their heads. This, of course, was opposed to the pessimists who bought lots of life insurance, looked for their golf ball in the woods forty yards short of where it went in, and assumed that all new experiences would turn out to be bummers. That was probably why it has been said that inertia is the strongest force in the universe. His optimism prevailed as he exited I-95 and headed to the Ocean Center with forty-five minutes to spare. He parked his soon-to-be-replaced Toyota Corolla in the massive parking lot and jogged to the festivities as the hot April sun baked his black-clothed body. What the hell possessed him to wear black today?

He entered the Ocean Center looking like a sweaty Johnny Cash, and waded into the upper mezzanine walkway in search of his crew. The arena was well lit, and filling with guests while the graduates filled the floor in their maroon and gold caps and gowns.

Omar spotted Speed, Ronnie, Dump Truck, and the rest of their motley crew about halfway down the lower deck. "Boys!" he yelled

Several of the crew looked up, eyes brightening as they spotted Omar. "Yo, Pitch, come help me do hangover duty with these useless lumps."

They all slapped high fives or dabs and mumbled greetings.

"Man, Dump Truck, you look like shit," said Omar.

Dump Truck moaned. "Lay off me, man. Cooter got me drunk last night."

"And I'll bet he pissed in your pants and twisted your arm too?" Omar replied. "So, have you guys spotted the lovely Diandra yet?"

"Yeah, man. She's right down there glaring up at you," Speed said.

Sure enough, Diandra's expression revealed her open displeasure with his tardiness, but softened somewhat as Omar winked and blew her a kiss. Then he made an obscene gesture with his tongue, and she was forced to smile and turn around. He liked the view; Diandra was a statuesque beauty with a perfect bubble butt, legs that went on forever, and perfect posture. She wasn't as heavy up front as Wanda, but everything else was in perfect proportion. She had eyes that could swallow you and kept her hair short and tight in a bun to accentuate her face. Not to mention the softest most perfect kissing lips he'd ever tasted. She was a little nutty, but he could overlook that.

Graduation ceremonies are generally fun for the participants, but the audience was quickly growing bored and restless as the endless stream of youngsters paraded across to podium to receive their accolades. Omar knew better than to sneak out early—at least not before Diandra took her turn. He also needed to be there for the congratulatory hugs and kisses at the end of the ceremony. However, the two-hour process left the boys with ample time to sneak out to Cooter's car for a few pops during intermission. Speed fired up a joint, but Omar declined as he now had to be concerned with piss tests as the National League baseball draft neared. That didn't keep him from quaffing a few frosty, adult beverages with the boys. They were discussing their plans and prospects for that evening's festivities. It was going to be a target-rich environment for single men.

The evening after graduation typically featured private homes hosting raucous parties as well as several of the dorms on campus. Speed told Omar that he knew of several such parties, some of which he was invited to, and others not so much, but the prerequisite of an invitation had never stopped him from attending before. It was one of the benefits of being young and single in a college town, and Omar had no doubt that Speed took full advantage of that.

Speed said, "What say we start off this evening at the Theta Chi's party over on Madison."

"It will be fly, bursting with trim and free beer. I guarantold jew dat!" he said in his best Justin Wilson Cajun imitation.

Omar said, "It sounds good to me, Cher, but I got to run it by Diandra and make sure she doesn't have other plans."

"Shit, homey," said Dump Truck. "You the man with the plans—just tell the sister what's up."

"Hey, you know how it goes. It's her night, and if I want to get into that honey pot later, I gotta toe the line at least a little bit, ya know?" said Omar.

"Yeah, I hear ya. Just don't get all whipped on us. We don't get to hang wit chew much as it is," said Dump Truck, putting on his sad puppy dog face.

"It'll be cool," said Omar. "We'll be there."

At that, they tossed their empties in a bag and headed back into the Ocean Center.

Graduation seemed to take forever, and only Omar made it to the final curtain, the other boys having long since gotten bored and made their escapes back to the suds.

Diandra ran up to him afterward, her new tassel swinging off the cap that was perched precariously on her fresh hairdo, and her fresh face was all big eyes and a bigger smile. "Hey, ya big stud, do you believe I'm a college graduate?"

"Of course," he said as he hugged her tightly, cupping her ass in both hands.

She pushed away and slapped him lightly on the chest. "Watch those roving paws, you dawg. My parents will be here any minute."

"So, what's the plan, gorgeous? Are we gonna party tonight or what?" Omar asked.

"Why certainly … after I do dinner with my parents. Would you like to join us?"

He didn't relish the idea of hanging out with her family, but he would if he had to on this occasion. "I would follow you barefooted on a field of glass to the end of the earth just to smell your panties," he said, rolling his eyes lustfully.

"Just dinner would do nicely for now," she said as she grabbed his hand and pulled him to where she spotted her mother waving frantically.

Shortly thereafter, Omar and Diandra left the Ocean Center with her mom and dad and two sisters, all of them shouting questions at the same time at an overwhelmed Diandra, the graduate. Omar enjoyed being out of the spotlight for a moment, everyone seeming to forget that he was on the verge of becoming a professional baseball player—and probably becoming rich and famous as well.

Over dinner, Omar managed a quiet conversation with Diandra regarding the evening's festivities. "Some of the boys want to hit a few graduation parties tonight. What do you say?"

She said, "You know I have to take my parents to the dorm and show them around after dinner. Why don't you go with your friends, and I'll catch up later. You could meet me at my dorm around nine thirty or ten, and I'll sneak you up for a cocktail."

"Well, honey, by then, there will only be one kind of refreshment I'll be wanting," he said as he nibbled on her ear and breathed.

"We'll have to see about that," she teased, knowing full well he would get his wish that night.

CHAPTER 9

GENIE AND STEVE

Back in Daytona, Brandon reluctantly got up and carried his catch and equipment into the backyard for a quick squirt with fresh water. Steve, now unfettered, ran off in search of land-based prey, leaving him to his solitary chores.

After putting his stuff away and cleaning the fish, Brandon went for a three-mile run to stretch his muscles after two hours of sitting on the dock. Upon his return, and after a hot shower, he was feeling human again. He popped a Dos Equis and jammed a lime into the neck.

The phone rang as he was cleaning up the house in anticipation of a visit from Genie. "Whaaaats-aaaahhhpp" came the familiar greeting. He and his golfing buddies were still taken by the old Budweiser commercials, and the imitations never stopped.

Brandon replied in kind, and Marty said, "So whatcha doing? Having a Bud and watching the game?"

"Unfortunately, no," groused Brandon, "I'm cleaning house in preparation for a lascivious date with a high-flying nympho. How about you?" he asked.

Marty replied, "Well, as you know, this weekend, I am pilot in command, and I'm sitting in front of my computer checking the weather on DUATS. This week, I have selected a delicious track known as Jekyll Island, which has a nice little strip about a par five from three pristine eighteen-hole courses. I have a tee time for ten at the Oleander course, and if what the pro tells me is true, this spot may warrant a return visit or two."

Brandon said, "I've heard of it. Isn't it just north of Jacksonville … on the east coast?"

"You got it, my little white ball-chasing buddy; the flight should be no more than an hour."

"We'll shoot up the coast on the V-3 to Craig, and then it's just a bit farther north, and the weather looks great." Marty said.

"So, what time do you want us at the plane?" Brandon asked.

"I figure takeoff at eight should give us time for the ground fog to clear and leave enough time to screw something up along the way," Marty replied.

Brandon said, "That sounds great. I'm dying to try out my new Garmin 195 handheld GPS. I'll be there at seven thirty, God willing, and the creek don't rise."

"Well, just don't have too much fun tonight, big guy. You are my copilot tomorrow."

"There's no such thing as too much fun. I'll call the others, Ciao," said Brandon as he signed off. He quickly called Mike and Miles, the other members of the foursome, and left messages on their respective voicemails. The weekend was shaping up to be picture-perfect.

By seven thirty, the house was looking presentable, and he had made a run to Publix for fresh delicacies. For appetizers, he chose fresh raw oysters, Havarti cheese with dill, some fancy crackers, regular saltine crackers, and three pounds of shrimp, which he had to de-head, de-vein, and steam in Old Bay. For the main course, he had some Seabreeze seaweed salad, fresh asparagus with hollandaise, and a fresh tuna steak, which he intended to cook seared rare in sesame oil with soy and wasabi and sprinkled with sesame seeds.

He was chilling a bottle of Pouilly-Fuisse, which he liked to call "fussy pussy," and he also had a bottle of Patron Silver tequila in case Genie was in the mood for a shot or two. He had partied with her a few times, but he had never taken a meal with her and had no idea what her tastes ran to in the food arena.

When the doorbell rang, Steve started barking hysterically as she charged the door. She took her guard dog duties very seriously, though he knew she would probably never do anything about it if someone came in who shouldn't. His guest had arrived. Brandon tossed his ever-present cooking towel over his shoulder and answered the door.

Genie stood on the porch dressed in cut-off jeans, a pair of high-heeled "fuck-me" pumps, a low-cut yellow silk blouse, and obviously no bra, a package which left little to the imagination. He likee.

Her flaxen hair was held back with barrettes, and she was wearing red lip gloss and a very sexy smile highlighted by sapphire green eyes. Her cute little upturned nose was sprinkled with freckles. Around her neck was a gold chain holding a charm of a twin-engine airplane that resembled his Aztec.

"You look good enough to eat," he said as he swung open the door.

Steve rushed out for the first smell of this stranger, and Genie gave her a kiss on the nose and a pat on the ass before sashaying into the foyer. Steve obviously approved of Brandon's choice of companion this evening.

"What is his name?" she asked.

He replied, "*Her* name is Steve … it's a long story."

She laughed. "What a sweet dog."

"She has her moments, although kissing an Aussie on the mouth is taking a risk."

"I kissed you, didn't I?"

"You got me there," he said as he followed her into the foyer.

"I hope you're going to feed me first, lawyer boy. I could eat a rat's ass boiled in kerosene." She stretched up to kiss him deeply on the lips.

Brandon broke away and laughed at her raunchy expression. "For that kiss, you get dinner fit for a queen with a potty mouth." He put his arm around her and walked with her into the kitchen.

His kitchen was a modern chef's style of stainless-steel appliances including a Viking gas stove, a huge Sub-Zero fridge and freezer, a halogen tabletop range, commercial-sized granite sink, dishwasher, microwave, and food processor. He had all the gadgets in the form of under-cupboard space savers such as coffee and espresso maker, can opener, Bose stereo system, and a Phillips flat screen TV on the wall so that he could watch sports while cooking. All of this was framed in custom-made light oak cabinetry to surround the state-of-the-art Viking appliances. It looked like Emeril could walk in at any moment with his camera crew.

He knew he had guessed correctly on the menu shortly after she swept into the kitchen and began to ooh and ah over the food laid out for final preparation. "Yum," she said. "How did you know this was my favorite?" She batted her eyelashes seductively.

"Just a lucky I guess," he said. "I have some white wine chilling—or would you prefer a beer or something stronger?"

As he pulled out the bottle from the fridge, she said, "Fussy Pussy? I love it. Some of that immediately please!"

He smiled, shook his head, and poured them both a healthy glass. It was almost scary how much they had in common.

She took the wine and began to walk around the house, checking things out. He popped another bottle of wine from the rack in anticipation of it being required very soon, stuck it in the freezer, and followed her. He noticed that her eyes were immediately drawn to the picture windows at the rear, which were currently framing a beautiful sunset over the river. "Wow," she said. "This is gorgeous."

"As are you." He took her hand and led her out to the deck where oysters and shrimp sat in ice on a plate on the patio table. He balanced his famous homemade cocktail sauce precariously with his wineglass. Steve was prancing happily with her poor excuse for a tail vibrating in its attempt to wag. When Steve walked, her ass swayed like a runway model. Brandon swore that she knew when she was being made fun of because of it, and as a result, she liked to walk behind people to avoid ridicule. He suspected the real reason was probably that it was the best place to spot and inhale food items being dropped by careless humans, intentionally or otherwise.

His friends accused him of attributing far too much human understanding to his dog, but they dared not say that to his face. Steve assumed her favorite position under the table, again, in order to be in position should any food fall to the floor, or, as was usually the case, a benevolent human should deign to hand her a scrap or two.

Brandon and Genie relaxed in the comfortable patio chairs facing a descending sun over the river. It was a beautiful night in the seventies with a light breeze and few clouds. Brandon hoped there were enough clouds on the far horizon to make for a colorful sunset. That mixed with a little horizontal drill, and this could shape up to be the perfect evening.

"So, tell me what you like to do besides skydive," Brandon said.

She sipped her wine and snacked on a large prawn. "Oh, well, my degree from Stetson is in physical education, and I'm into sports of all kinds, but more so as a participant than a spectator. I like volleyball, golf, baseball, and all activities normally performed in a gym—or on a waterbed."

"I think I may be in love," said Brandon.

"Well, take it easy, lover boy," she said. "You ain't seen nothing yet."

He could hardly wait, he thought as he let a small shrimp fall to the waiting jaws of Steve down under who caught the morsel in the air and swallowed it without chewing. "How about family?" he asked.

She looked at him funny with those beautiful green eyes, her hair blowing gently in the afternoon breeze, and said, "Didn't we cover all this in the bar the other night?"

"Perhaps," he admitted, "but I'm a little fuzzy on the details of that particular evening."

She said, "Well, my big brother is a golf pro up in Jacksonville, and I have a younger sister who is a veterinarian in South Carolina."

A golf pro! Brandon was even more interested, but he didn't let on.

She said, "My folks live in Sarasota and are retired; my dad was in the navy."

"That's right," he said. "You've heard that we have old folks in Daytona, but their parents live in Sarasota."

She laughed and said, "You've got that right. The place is codger city, but it's pretty nice. What about you?"

"Pretty boring from a family point of view," he said. "My parents are both deceased, and I have no brothers or sisters."

"I'm sorry," she said. "What about pastimes?"

"Well, I play tennis, drive fast cars, and fondle women, but I have weekends off—and I am my own boss." His favorite line from *Arthur* got the desired laugh, and the conversation continued comfortably on into the night.

CHAPTER 10

THE FIGHT

On the other side of the river, not far from the Martin Luther campus, Omar, Speed, Dump Truck, Ronnie, and Cooter piled out of Omar's Buick and headed into the yard of a house on Lincoln Street from which emanated the unmistakable thumping of bass sounds of a party in progress.

They walked around to the back of the house from where the most noise seemed to be coming and found thirty or forty people congregating on a patio where a bar and stereo system had been set up. Not being from these parts, Omar didn't expect that he would know anyone, and he was content to hang out with his friends. It became quickly apparent that Speed and Cooter knew almost everyone.

"Hey, lookie here, it's the Tampa gang," someone shouted.

Speed acknowledged the crowd and said, "Word up" to someone who offered him a high five and a beer in that order. Speed introduced Omar, Ronnie, and Dump Truck to those within earshot who seemed interested.

The boys helped themselves to cups and took their turns at the keg at the invitation of a guy named Scooby who apparently was hosting this event. Scooby was a bookish-looking dude with glasses and a thin frame covered with preppy duds, kind of like Urkel without the suspenders, who was manning the front door. "You look familiar. Do I know you?" Scooby asked Omar as he walked in behind the others.

"Do you play ball?" Omar asked.

"No, but I follow our teams. Why, you?"

"Yeah, a bit ... baseball and football mostly."

"Oh, I know you. You're that dude from A&M who throws gas on the mound, the closer right?"

"Yeah," said Omar. "That would be me."

"Hot shit," said Scooby. "I've seen you pitch a couple times, damn near unhittable as I recall."

"I have good days and bad." Omar felt a bit uncomfortable as he recalled shutting down the Martin Luther team the last time he played here.

"Tha's cool," said Scooby. "What brings you here? You got kin in school?"

"Nah, my girlfriend graduated today," Omar said.

"What's her name?" Scooby asked.

"Diandra Wilson," Omar replied.

"Oh, baby. I be knowin' that number. She is hot!"

"Thanks," said Omar, blushing slightly.

"Where's she at?" Scooby inquired.

"She's visiting with her folks. I'll catch up with her later after I make the acquaintance of some fine local folks like yourself Scooby Doo. If you'd excuse me, I need to refresh my frosty beverage and check on my boys." Omar sidled up beside Ronnie and Cooter who were getting acquainted with two local sophomores and the keg.

The decibel level of the party increased, and more noise was coming from inside the house. Shortly thereafter, eight or nine young men burst onto the patio in various gang-type colors, all of them laughing and gesturing about in an animated fashion.

"Here comes trouble," said Cooter.

"Sup?" said Omar.

"That's a dude calls himself Mr. Justice and his crew. They got a gang they refer to as the Masons, though the only thing I know they have constructed are drug deals and trouble. Most of them have flunked out of school but forgot to tell their parents so they just hang out."

Mr. Justice had a doo rag, two gold teeth top front, and a scraggly beard. He was wearing a black wife beater that displayed a cluster of tattoos on his arms and shoulders, some ratty jeans hanging low on his ass, and untied basketball shoes. Upon spotting Cooter, Mr. Justice said, "Hey, boys, look what the cat dragged in: a bunch of losers from Tampa crashing our party. Who invited you, Coot?"

He smelled like weed soaked in beer, and Cooter backed away. "Who died and left you king, Justice." Cooter crossed his arms and flexed his considerable biceps.

"Don't mean nuttin'," said Mr. Justice. "I's just givin' you a little shit."

Cooter outweighed Justice by fifty pounds and was spoiling for a chance to clock him. "You and your boys play nice and I won't have to give it back," he said.

Justice waved off the threat and turned his attention back to his crew and the pack of girls who seemed to materialize at his side.

As the evening wore on, the party got progressively louder. More people showed up, and the spirits began to have their effect on the ever-loosening inhibitions of the participants. Dancing was happening inside, and Omar and the boys decided to partake since most of the girls present seemed to be inside.

Once inside, there were plenty of girls to go around. Ronnie and Omar began to get acquainted. Neither Speed nor Cooter nor Dump Truck were much for dancing, which bode well for the furniture in the room.

Teaching Dump Truck to dance would be like teaching an elephant to play putt-putt golf. They preferred to hang near the fringes and continue quaffing prodigious quantities of free beer. Mr. Justice and his crew were following the same plan on the other side of the room, which had become so loud that conversation became impossible.

Omar, being handsome and fit, had no trouble attracting the attention of the local coeds, and Ronnie was no slouch either. The two were dancing very close to two girls whose names had escaped them when Omar saw Ronnie began to fondle his companion's rather generous derriere with both hands while grinding his hips into her torso to the music.

Ronnie's dance partner seemed to be enjoying the groping.

Mr. Justice approach Ronnie from behind, cuffed him across the top of the head, and yelled, "Get your meat hooks off my girl's ass, you Tampa-grown faggot!"

Ronnie backed away with a look of stunned surprise. "What's your problem, asshole?"

"You my problem, nigger. I'll fuck you up if you touch her again."

Ronnie launched himself at Justice, wrapped him up across the chest, and began a tackle that carried them out onto the lawn before anyone really knew that a fight was happening.

Omar had seen the whole thing and immediately signaled to Cooter and the others as he began to push his way through the crowd toward the exit.

On the front lawn, Ronnie was getting the better of the fight, tattooing Justice repeatedly in the face as Justice screamed and tried his best to ward off the blows. After a dozen or so good haymakers from Ronnie, Omar extricated himself from the crowd, grabbed Ronnie, and pulled him roughly off his opponent before he killed him. Ronnie and Omar backed away as Justice sputtered and wiped blood from his mouth in the grass.

Cooter, Speed, and Dump Truck clustered with Omar and Ronnie as Justice's crew came out and picked him off the grass.

Mr. Justice's boys held him back as he tried to get at Ronnie. "I'll gut you, motherfucker. Let me go, niggas. This ain't over, boy. This ain't over—no way!"

Speed said, "Let's get out of here before this gets out of hand or the cops show up."

Omar swiftly agreed with the suggestion, and they hustled Ronnie toward the car as he and Justice shouted dire threats at one another.

Omar drove back to Speed's crib as they related their individual versions of what had just happened. It sounded like Howard Cosell doing the play-by-play after Mohammed Ali had just finished whipping an overmatched opponent, and they all had a grand laugh at Mr. Justice's expense.

Back in the house, they all grabbed beers from the fridge and plotted their next move. The night was still young, and there were surely more parties to visit.

Omar called Diandra's dorm, and her roommate picked up on the third ring. "Happy graduation. Who pray tell is this?"

"Hey, Shirl. It's Omar. What's up, girl?"

"Well, good-lookin', your main squeeze and I are chillin' and waitin' for our knights in shining armor."

"Let me speak to her then, and we'll see about that," Omar replied.

"Hey, babe," Diandra said.

"What's the plan?"

"Are you up for going to a club?"

"Sure," he said. "We just left a party somewhere near school, and Ronnie got into a bit of a scuffle with some guy who calls himself Mr. Justice, so we booked it back to Speed's crib."

"Oh, Omar, that boy is trouble. I hope Ronnie's okay."

"He's fine. In fact, does Shirly need a date tonight?"

"I believe she'd like that," said Diandra with a mischievous giggle. "Why don't you two come pick us up, and we'll go to the dance club over on Cyprus Street."

"You got it, gorgeous. See you shortly."

They decided that Omar and Ronnie would go to the dorms in Omar's car while the others gave them a head start. They would follow in Speed's car and meet them at the club. They would use the interim to have an attitude-adjustment session with the incredibly harsh bong.

Omar parked on Martin Luther Drive in the center of campus near the security office. Neither he nor Ronnie knew exactly where Diandra's dorm was located, but the campus was not large, and they didn't anticipate having a problem. They exited the Buick and headed down a side street between buildings. It was around ten o'clock, and the street was not particularly well lit. About halfway down the street, they heard an engine roar behind them, and as they turned, a large SUV came to a halt a few feet from them. Six or eight guys jumped out and approached them menacingly.

When they were within a couple of yards, Omar recognized Mr. Justice leading the pack. He was carrying a large knife and looking much more confident with his crew in tow—and two of them were carrying baseball bats.

They surrounded Omar and Ronnie, and Mr. Justice said, "I done told you this wasn't over, motherfucker. Now we goin' ta dance."

Omar felt two or three of the crew members grab his arms from behind, forcing him to watch as Mr. Justice and the others pummeled Ronnie with fists and bats.

Ronnie traded blows with them for several seconds, but he had no chance against the angry gang members who were stabbing and pummeling him. He was left writhing on the ground with blood coming from his head and mouth.

Omar struggled and tried to pull away, but they held him tight.

Ronnie soon stopped moving and held his stomach while curled in the fetal position as the blood drained from his mouth, face, and stomach.

As he watched his best friend dying on the asphalt, Omar yelled, "Let me go, you bastards!" He'd never been so mad and scared all at once. He wanted to kill them, but he knew his friend desperately needed his help.

Mr. Justice kicked Ronnie in the stomach for good measure, spat on him, and whistled for his crew to release Omar.

They retreated to their vehicle, laughing and high fiving all the way. As the thugs hooted and hollered their victorious retreat down the street, Omar dropped to the ground and clutched his bleeding friend into his lap.

"The bastard cut me, dude," Ronnie croaked.

"Where are you hurt?" Omar asked.

"The son of a bitch stuck me in the gut!"

"Can you walk?"

"I think so," Ronnie mumbled.

"We've got to get you some help and fast." Omar lifted his friend to his feet with one arm around his waist and draped Ronnie's other arm over his shoulder as Ronnie clutched his stomach with the other. Blood seeped out between his fingers and darkened his jeans.

Omar had left his cell phone in the car and couldn't call 911 for help, and there was no one else around. He began walking Ronnie back toward the street. In his panicked, adrenaline-stoked brain, he recalled seeing a security office on the street near where they parked.

The small security office was fifty yards away. Omar thought they would have a first aid kit and could call 911 after stopping the bleeding in Ronnie's gut. Stabilizing Ronnie was his only thought.

On the night of graduation—with all that was going on around campus—he never thought the campus security office would be unlocked and empty, but that is what they found when they struggled up to the entrance. The door was open, but nobody was home.

By the time Omar realized that help would not come in the form of campus security, Ronnie was beginning to weaken. Omar looked around in desperation and spotted the lights of a dorm across the street. It was much closer than his car, and Omar didn't know the way to the hospital. Ronnie had lost a lot of blood. He was barely conscious and was moaning softly.

"This way!"

They slowly crossed the street and reached the porch. The door was locked.

Omar sat Ronnie down against the wall, pounded on the door, and shouted, "Somebody help!"

As Ronnie clutched his stomach and groaned, the dorm house mother came to the heavy glass door and said, "What the devil is going on here?"

"Open up! My friend needs help."

"This is a girl's dorm, young man, and school policy does not allow me to let men inside after curfew!"

"Come on, lady! My friend is dying here."

She opened the door a crack and leaned into the opening to look down at Ronnie's inert form slumped against wall. "Stay right there. I'm gonna call the police." She rushed back into the hallway.

"Hang in there, buddy," Omar said as he crouched next to Ronnie.

Two black SUV's cruised up the street nearly adjacent to the dorm. Someone shouted, "There they are!"

The SUVs screeched to a halt.

Apparently, Mr. Justice was coming back to finish them off.

Just then, Cooter, Speed, and Dump Truck pulled up on the other side of the street after spotting Omar's car. As the gang exited the SUV's and ran toward the dorm like a band of screaming Indians, Omar's friends were in hot pursuit from across the street. Omar took one last look at Ronnie, who looked on helplessly, and stood to face the onrushing mob. Fortunately for Omar, the small porch was barely big enough for four people at once.

The first two gang members reached the porch just before Cooter and Speed, and one of them slipped a punch from Omar as the other one cracked Omar in the head with a pipe, knocking him to the ground next to Ronnie.

Speed and Cooter crashed onto the porch from the other side like a pair of angry bulls running the streets of Pamplona, and tossed the gang members to the ground, effectively stopping the charge of the others.

What ensued was a very loud and confusing melee with Cooter, Speed, and Dump Truck dealing and receiving punishment from the mob as they tried to defend their unconscious friends.

The house mother returned to the door as Omar regained his wits. Blood was streaming down his face, and she apparently decided to bend the rules. She opened the door and pulled Omar and Ronnie inside with the help of two girls who had come down to see what the commotion was all about. Once they were safely inside, Erma slammed and locked the door.

The house mother, Erma, was nearly as tall as Speed, and she probably outweighed him by a hundred pounds. Omar figured that few folks had the courage to mess with her to her face, and she had no trouble hauling Omar and Ronnie into the dorm.

Mr. Justice jumped onto the porch and began beating the door with a baseball bat. "Open up, bitch!"

Erma backed away from the door and shook her fist at the window.

Omar was stunned and confused, and he guessed was probably concussed by the pipe as shattered glass landed on them.

Omar was suddenly overcome by a terrific sense of dread. In his trauma-addled brain, he knew his life was about to end. He mumbled, "Gotta get away." The rest of the glass gave way and landed on him. Omar scrambled away from the window on his hands and knees.

Mr. Justice grappled with the inner door wire in a furious attempt to break in. His hands were dripping blood.

Omar shrieked and ran toward the stairwell at the rear of the foyer.

The heavy gauge wire mesh protecting the inside of the door wouldn't hold back Justice for long.

The squad cars with lights flashing and sirens blaring only added to his panic. The police attacked the mob with nightsticks and heavy flashlights, which ended the fight quickly. Those of Mr. Justice's crew who were still ambulatory scrambled off into the night, leaving their disabled brothers along with Cooter, Speed, and Dump Truck to fill the paddy wagons.

As Ronnie was being loaded into the first ambulance, Omar started screaming from the rooftop. In his confusion, Omar had stumbled up to the third floor and burst into the first room he found. Its occupant screamed and dropped her blow drier.

Omar ran to the window and began wrestling it open. He screamed to no one in particular and jumped out. He fell three stories to the ground and landed on his left leg, which crumpled unnaturally beneath his body.

Omar felt an excruciating pain in his ankle. His left foot was turned in the opposite direction, and bloody bones were sticking out. He passed out.

Two police officers ran to Omar's side and began rendering aid. The first cop looked at his partner and said, "What the hell possessed him to skydive out of that window? He's got a pulse, but its weak. Get those paramedics over here."

"You got it!"

The ambulance arrived quickly, and the paramedics whisked Omar away.

When Omar awoke in the emergency room, Diandra was holding his hand and stroking his head. His head was bandaged, and his left leg was killing him. When he saw that his bandaged foot was still pointing at an unnatural angle, he thought, *Oh my God, my career is finished.* He passed out again.

Dr. Gaines, a middle-aged, athletic white guy in a white jacket, said, "Are you family?"

Diandra said, "No. I'm his girlfriend. His family is in Tampa."

Omar thought, *Girlfriend? Wanda's gonna kill me.*

"As you can see, he's going to need emergency surgery. How old is he?"

"He is twenty-two … about to graduate from college."

"Okay then, he's an adult. If you could assist the nurse with as much of his information as you have, I'm going to prep him for surgery."

"He's going to be a pro baseball player," she said through her tears. "Please take good care of him."

"I will. Don't you worry."

Omar knew he would never play competitive sports again at the college or professional level. He'd be lucky to walk in the Gasparilla Parade, and if he was really lucky, perhaps he could play in a good old boys' bowling league. He would never be able to do anything that would require full-speed running, especially if the treatment included a fusion of the ankle joint, which he knew from past teammates with similar injuries was a likely outcome.

CHAPTER 11

AFTERMATH

Brandon awoke to a strange licking sensation on his mouth. As he struggled to regain consciousness, he smiled and said, "Not again, baby. Didn't we just do this?" As he realized it was not Genie administering wet kisses, he yelped, "Yuck," wiped his mouth, and pushed the dog away.

Steve wagged her stump of a tail and barked.

Brandon looked over at the other side of the crumpled bedding to find it was empty. "All right, all right," he said as he hauled his naked body out of the rack and let Steve out the back door. *That dog will lick anything,* he thought, *even a mouth that tastes like monkey crap.*

The bright sunshine streaming in felt like needles invading his brain, so he dragged the curtains shut and headed for the kitchen. He noticed a trail of his clothing leading from the living room to the bed and considered that to be a good sign, but he had only a vague recollection of the end of the evening's festivities. Genie was not to be found. When he had the coffee maker doing its thing, he leaned on the counter and spotted a piece of paper. Scrawled in lovely cursive writing was a note from Genie: "Had to run, gotta jump today, lover. I had a great time. See you soon. Hugs and kisses, Genie." Brandon smiled and tossed the note in the junk drawer. It was six thirty, and he had a very important golf date. He walked into his bedroom, turned on the Weather Channel, cranked up the volume, and hit the shower.

By 7:25, he was rolling into the parking lot of the private aviation section of the Daytona Airpark. It was called Daytona International now, but the only thing international about it was the host of foreign students who were enrolled in the local flight schools. Marty was sitting in his Lexus talking to Flight Service on his cell phone. Brandon hoisted his clubs and golf shoes from the back of the truck and walked over to his buddy's car. Marty acknowledged him with a wave as he spoke to a weather briefer and filed their flight plan. It would be an easy flight up the coast with nothing but puffy white clouds in the way. Both Brandon and Marty were instrument-rated pilots, so that would not be a concern.

As Brandon waited, Mike and Miles pulled in and parked next to Marty. "Yo, fly boys, whaaats aaahhhhp?" yelled Mike.

"Same old," said Brandon. "Looks like another shitty day." Brandon looked up at the blue sky.

"Too true," Miles said as they unloaded their golf bags and shoes.

Mike was a notorious slob, and his trunk looked like a fast-food wrapper depository, as did the back seat of his late eighties Buick LeSabre.

Brandon looked at the car and smiled. "Mikey, you need for that crap can to get hit by lightning cause its trade value is less than your golf shoes."

"Hey, don't rag on my baby!" Mike replied. "She's all I got in this world, and she's a classic!"

"I'm just glad we're not driving to golf today." Brandon grabbed his bag and headed out to the ramp.

Marty turned off the phone and hopped out of his shiny new Lexus GS 400. He had all the toys, and you could tell within moments of meeting him that he was a fervent believer in the adage that he who dies with the most toys wins.

Neither Mike nor Miles were licensed pilots, but they often liked to ride in the right copilot's seat and take practice at keeping the plane flying straight and level. Today was Brandon's turn in the front, and he liked flying Marty's "like-new" 1957 five-seat, twin-engine Piper Geronimo. Brandon owned a single-engine Cherokee Six, which was very similar to fly and could carry more payload than Marty's twin. Brandon's plane, in fact, had six seats, but with full fuel and large passengers, it would be a stretch to fill it to capacity. Four guys and their golf bags with the rear seats removed was a perfect fit.

They gathered up their stuff and headed out to the flight line.

Marty said, "I filed IFR because of the clouds, but it should be a piece of cake."

"Okay by me," said Brandon.

The only hassle about flying under instrument flight rules was that sometimes the controllers would jerk you around near busy airports like Jacksonville to keep the corridors clear for passenger jets and low-flying military traffic.

The boys piled their clubs in the back of the plane, and Brandon mounted up with Marty who sat in his pilot's left seat with Brandon filling the copilot's right. Mike and Miles were as tight as teen jeans squeezed in back with all the golf clubs. Marty had completed the preflight inspection of the plane including checking to make sure the four fuel tanks were topped off and the oil levels were where they should be on both engines. The engines were each two hundred-horsepower continental upgrades from the original 180s, and the power difference was significant.

Marty flipped on the master switches, the two fuel pumps, one at a time, and yelled, "Clear prop" out the left window. He set the mixtures to full Rich and the propeller controls to full, and cracked the throttles. Then he turned the left ignition switch, and the corresponding propeller began to turn. It caught quickly, and he throttled back to 1,000 rpm and listened to its even purr. Then came the often-reluctant right engine's turn. He turned the right ignition switch, and the propeller turned once and stopped.

He repeated the process three more times without success. Marty yelled, "If you don't start up this time, I'll cut off your dingo balls." He increased the throttle on the left engine to give the right more battery juice. On the fifth attempt, the right engine coughed to life—and all was well with the world.

Brandon, as copilot, would be working the radios during the flight while Marty acted as PIC or pilot in command. While they liked to act like real airline pilots at all times, there really was nothing much to it as long as everything went as planned.

Brandon checked the Airport Terminal Information System for wind, barometric pressure, active runway, etcetera, and then obtained their IFR clearance from Clearance Delivery. Then he switched to ground control and received permission to taxi the aircraft. Marty taxied the plane out to runway seven right, the shorter of Daytona's two east-facing runways, and performed the obligatory engine run-up, steering check, gauges, and switches check. Everything checked out normal, so Brandon radioed the tower and informed the controllers that N804VG was ready for takeoff. The controller replied, "804VG, you are clear for take-off, maintain runway heading until reaching 1,500 feet, and then contact departure control on 125.8 and turn on course when advised."

"Roger that, Tower, 804 Victor Golf is rolling," said Brandon, and Marty advanced the throttles to full. At around eighty miles per hour, the little twin clawed its way into the sky, and they soon left Daytona in their rearview mirror.

Their course would be along what was called a "Victor airway" in the business, which is in effect a corridor or slice of airspace with a slot reserved for their plane alone. The heading would be 347 degrees, or basically slightly left of due north. They would be using a previously assigned transponder code, which would tell the traffic controllers their heading, altitude, and speed over the ground. They would also give the pilots a heads-up if any other traffic approached their flight path. Unpressurized civilian aircraft such as this one generally flew at lower altitudes below twelve thousand feet since they weren't carrying supplemental oxygen, and if they were on instrument flight plans, they would be instructed to fly at a round number of thousands of feet as opposed to those flying under visual flight rules, which were supposed to be at a designated number of thousands plus five hundred feet.

The system of rules of the road was designed to keep midair collisions from happening, but it wasn't perfect, so it was advisable to keep a constantly moving eye on the sky during flight. Of course, this was not possible when flying in clouds, so the system had rules that prohibited pilots who were not flying under instrument flight rules from flying in the clouds. Brandon always instructed all passengers to point out any other planes, no matter which direction they were headed. The flight proceeded as planned, and they landed at the tiny Jekyll Island strip forty-five minutes later without incident. A courtesy golf cart was dispatched from the hotel. It was almost like being in the 1920s again. The cart was driven by an elderly gentleman whose southern manners were exceeded only by his sense of humor. He wore tweed kickers, a green and brown argyle sweater over a pink collared shirt, golf spikes and a Gatsby newsboy hat. He called himself Bannister, and he treated the boys like visiting royalty and deposited them on the clubhouse steps free of charge. Brandon tipped him a ten spot which he graciously pocketed.

The course turned out to be as nice as advertised, and it had large, well-manicured fairways hinged by huge towering pines that had to be hundreds of years old. The boundaries were also dotted with magnolias and oleanders, which were in bloom and gave the boys the impression of playing in the Masters sans crowds. After a day of old cliché's, "Nice putt, Alice, does your wife play too?" "Never up, never in," and "Nice read, dickhead," the round was complete. Mike and Brandon had been a team against Marty and Miles, which was usually the tactic because the nonflying partners were free to quaff beers all day, and it wouldn't be tolerable to the pilots for them to play as a team nor fair to the partiers to have to play the nondrinkers for money.

The match almost never resulted in more than five or ten bucks changing hands, and that was usually spent at the snack bar or the cocktail trough. After refreshments, the boys hailed the courtesy cart for the return trip to the short airstrip, piled their stuff in the plane, and took off for the return trip, ragging one another all the way home about a missed putt or scoring opportunity during the round. Life was good—much more so for some than for others.

CHAPTER 12

THE WAKE UP

Omar awoke in the postoperative recovery theater of the Halifax Medical Center. He was alone, and his head hurt immensely. He had very little recollection of what had happened or where he was, and he was very sleepy. He closed his eyes for a little nap and soon was dreaming of flying from tall buildings like Superman.

His next moment in the sun came in the intensive surgical care ward, where surgical patients go to stabilize before being brought to a private room. Nurses flitted about, and there were other patients hooked up to all sorts of tubes and beeping monitors. He was scared shitless, and he also had begun to experience the onset of a throbbing pain in his left ankle. He looked down at it, and all he could see was wrapping gauze sufficient to encase a twenty-eight-pound turkey. "Oh my God," he said to himself. He whispered, "Nurse!" His throat was as dry as a Dean Martin martini.

A nurse came over and put her hand on his head. "How are you feeling, sweetie?"

"What happened to me?" Omar asked.

She took his hands in her other hand. "You've had quite a fall, and Dr. Gaines had to repair your leg."

"It's not broken, is it?"

"I am afraid so—broken and dislocated—but I'll let the doc give you the particulars. You need to get some rest ... you have visitors who will be allowed in shortly." She left him in increasing pain and anxiety over the extent of his injuries.

The bruises on his face and arms ached, but they were nothing worse than what could be experienced after a normal football practice. His left ankle, however, was sending pain impulses to his brain the likes of which he had never imagined could exist. It felt as though his entire left leg was exposed meat from the knee down, and several sadistic invisible people were sticking him with hot pokers in the tenderized areas. The pain seemed to come in waves, and during the peaks, tears would stream down his cheeks. His knuckles turned white as he grabbed the side rails of the hospital bed. His teeth clenched tight enough to bite a Louisville Slugger in half at the barrel end.

During one particularly bad session of pain, a younger doctor with curly light brown hair and an athletic build entered the room. "How ya doing, champ?" he asked while feeling Omar's pulse and counting the seconds on his watch.

"You tell me, man. This leg is killing me. Are you my doc?"

"Yes, I am, big guy. My name's Doc Gaines."

"You don't look much older than me," said Omar.

"Why thanks, Omar, but it just so happens I am ten years your senior and have been a board-certified sawbones for over two years now."

"Then tell me, Doc, how long is this going to keep me off of the mound, 'cause I've got the draft coming up in a couple of weeks, and I don't want any of the pro scouts to see me like this?"

"You are a left-handed pitcher, correct?" Dr. Gaines asked.

"That's right," Omar said, "and a damn good one."

"Well, I am very sorry to say that I do not believe that even with the most optimistic of outcomes here will you be able to pitch again. I'm so sorry, son, but this is your new reality, I am afraid."

"No!" Omar yelled. "You are wrong—you gotta be!"

Dr. Gaines said, "I am sorry, Omar, but your ankle was fractured in several places and completely dislocated, and all the connective tissue was torn apart, including your Achilles tendon. I had no choice but to fuse the ankle in order to save the foot. To do otherwise would have been too risky for the nerves and the blood supply to the foot. In fact, for a few minutes, we seriously considered amputation—and I haven't ruled it out as a distinct possibility if any infection sets in. And you certainly won't be able to run or pitch with the level of immobility you will have."

Omar looked incredulously between the doctor and his ruined foot, shaking his head as the tears ran down his face. "It can't be—all those years of practice, the training, all that talent, I was a sure thing! You don't understand, Doc. You can't let this happen—you just can't!"

Dr. Gaines held Omar's hands and said, "I'm sorry, Omar, but I don't think you would have liked amputation. At least this way, you will probably be able to jog again, and your arm is still strong, so there should be opportunities for you in coaching, but I'm afraid your sports-playing days are over."

Omar continued crying and shouting, "No!"

Diandra walked into the room, went straight to him, and held him close.

Over the next two weeks, Omar would go through the hell of rejection from all the scouts who had encouraged him over the years. The word spread fast through pro baseball about his injury, and no one recovered from a total ankle fusion to do much of anything more aerobic than a Stairmaster at the local gym. Omar was a superior athlete, but he wasn't stupid, and the more he came to realize that his dream was lost, the madder he became. *This shouldn't have happened*, he kept thinking over and over. When Ronnie came to visit, they agonized over what they could have done to have prevented the tragedy. Ronnie was already ambulatory and healing nicely, and Omar could tell he was truly crushed by what had happened to his friend and idol.

Diandra had been very supportive, though he could see in her eyes that she was feeling the loss as well, having been rather set on becoming the wife of a very rich pro athlete—and all the excitement and glory that went with it.

Wanda, on the other hand, was another matter. He called her from his cell a few days after the incident, and her first reaction was that she was pissed he hadn't called sooner. Then, when he told her why, she said, "So, what does that mean for your pro ball career?"

He said, "It means I won't be having one, babe."

She was silent for a moment, and then she said, "Well, it was fun while it lasted. Good luck, dude." She hung up.

He couldn't believe she had dumped him outright over the phone when she learned he was no longer on pro baseball's most wanted list. He slipped into a funk of depression that would soon become a more serious problem than the injury.

Even his mom and little brother had cried when they first saw him. He saw the disappointment in their eyes when they realized the dream was really over for them all. His mom sat on his bed and presented him with a box of her homemade cookies. He failed to generate even a passing interest in food. She encouraged him and told him how special he would always be to her, yet he remained inconsolable.

Ronnie got out of the hospital ten days before Omar. After about a week, when Speed and Cooter were taking him through his therapy exercises to keep the rest of his body from shrinking in atrophy, Ronnie said, "Man, you ought to sue that damn college, cuz. If they'd a had a damn security guard working where he was supposed to, none a this woulda happened."

"I heard dat!" Speed said. "You need to take this damn school to court, man."

Omar wasn't thinking about suing, but he was getting madder every day.

That night, Omar had a vivid dream. He was pitching for the Chicago Cubs in the bottom of the seventh inning in the World Series. His team had a one-run lead, with the bases loaded, two outs, and the batter was Aaron Judge of the New York Yankees. The count was full, and as he released the ball, he pushed off with his left leg for full extension. At the top of the release, his leg collapsed, causing the pitch to sail wildly by the catcher for ball four. As Judge trotted to first, the player who had been on third base scored.

The catcher reached the ball at the back of the backstop, whirled to see that the player from second was also coming home, and reared back to whip the ball to Omar who should have been covering home to prevent the winning run from scoring. Instead, Omar was lying prostate in front of the mound, he couldn't move to cover the plate, because his left leg was like jelly, and try as he might to crawl, with the crowd cheering him on, he couldn't move an inch. He awoke screaming, "Help me!" In his darkened hospital room, he was sweating, shaking, and crying profusely. He was alone—and the dream was his new reality.

CHAPTER 13

RETAINER

Brandon had read about the riot in the *Daytona News Journal* several weeks ago, and the injuries to several students, including a rather notorious athlete from Tallahassee named Omar Steele. It was seemingly just another senseless piece of violence in the world, and he didn't give the incident a second thought.

It was a balmy October day the following fall when he headed into the office as he always did after a mild two-mile jog with Steve. Although some days she came to the office with him, he had several court appearances and didn't want Steve distracting the girls all day while he was away. Dog lovers can't resist a fuzzy face, and Patty was a card-carrying member of the Humane Society.

When he stayed in the office all day answering calls and mail without depositions or hearings to attend, Steve would sit quietly at his feet all day with the exception of one or two trips to water the lawn. His office was a small commercial building near the beach, which backed up to the Oyster Pub, which was practically his office cafeteria. He shared his space with a nefarious divorce lawyer whose name should have been Simon La-greed. He was a heartless shark who always represented wives, and he liked to call himself "The Housekeeper." His name was James Cardell, but his friends called him Jessie for reasons that should be obvious by now.

They each had a secretary—Jessie's was Rhonda—and they shared a voluptuous receptionist named Tyson. Brandon had found her working at a biker bar named Froggy's during the infamous Bike Week the previous spring. He was attracted to her obvious attributes, but he also liked her cutting personality. She had learned how not to take any crap from anyone, which was an accomplishment with that crowd, and he was impressed. He could teach her how to answer the phone, and the rest was running errands, opening mail, making coffee, yada yada. How hard could it be? Plus, she was like having a Playboy playmate to look at every day. Definite eye candy. So far, Brandon had resisted dipping his pen into the company ink, but he hadn't been sorely tested yet. One could hope.

All three girls were used to the perversions of both Brandon and Jessie James, and they could dish out the harassment as well as they received it. Brandon had laid down the law, and they all were made to understand there was a time and a place for such things—and the time did not include times when clients were present. There was an old sign he had found somewhere in the bowels of the building: "Sexual harassment will not be reported; however, it will be graded." Brandon figured that sign would have been funny back in the nineties, but in the age of the #MeToo" movement, it was probably not a good idea to hang it on the wall.

Brandon came in the back door to his office and plopped in his chair. "Coffee made yet?" he bellowed toward his secretary's space. He hadn't mastered the use of the intercom button on the phone yet, much to Patty's chagrin, and she usually had to interrupt a phone call to respond. "Yes, your highness," she said sarcastically. "High tea is served." She brought him a steaming cup of coffee.

He said, "Just the way I like my women: hot and strong."

She ignored the remark and handed him last night's arrest reports, a stack of phone messages, and yesterday's mail. He flipped on his computer and waded through a pile of junk emails from solicitors and a few cute jokes and pornographic cartoons sent by friends. When first becoming email literate, he apparently opened several solicitations out of curiosity, and he had now found his way onto every email direct marketing mailing list known to man. It would take months to delete himself from ads promising a larger penis, larger breasts, Russian wives, get-rich-quick schemes, mortgage loans, contests, and debt reduction. For every site he blocked, ten more seemed to find him.

He kept hoping that some rich heiress would call for help with her billionaire husband's estate or a tragically injured person from New York or somewhere else would find him on the web and make his career with a huge personal injury case. No such luck today—it was just the usual drivel. He had to be at morning court today for what he liked to call breakfast club, where all the criminal defense lawyers lined up for monthly pretrial conferences. The hearings were held on a first come, first served basis of court appearances for criminal defendants in misdemeanor court. These mostly involved driving under the influence and small-time drug possession cases and were opportunities for the defense attorneys to plead with the prosecutors for palatable plea agreements so their clients could avoid the time and expense of a trial. Brandon loved to try cases, but they were costly and time-consuming affairs with uncertain outcomes riding on the whim of six people without the clout or imagination to get themselves out of jury duty. It was also each attorney's opportunity to actually do something for the client to justify their fees because happy clients referred more clients and didn't file grievances.

The cases that were not ripe for trial or a plea got continued or rolled over to the next month's round of Let's Make a Deal. The cases that had previously worked out deals either entered plea bargains at the pretrial or passed it to a special plea day, and those that didn't do either were continued or announced "ready for trial" whereupon they began a ride of anywhere from one to twelve months on the judge's limited trial docket before they actually got to see a jury trial. Each week in criminal court, the judge set aside Monday for jury selection, and the other four days usually saw one trial per day. Four cases at best would thus be disposed of when there might be eighty or more on the trial docket in any given week that were "ready for trial." Ultimately, after a jury verdict was rendered, the client got a sentence of less than a year in jail—or none at all, depending on their record of prior offenses.

Of course, some clients were found not guilty, and those often skipped happily from the courthouse, usually to the nearest watering hole for cocktails to celebrate a narrow escape from the claws of justice—only to risk the same peril on the way home that very evening.

Brandon had once represented a client who was charged with DUI after drinking twenty plus beers at a beach volleyball party. He was so drunk that he stopped his car on a four-lane road and put on the emergency flashers until a cop arrived. When the officer approached the driver's side window, his boy held out both wrists and said, "Take me to your leader." The officer obliged. The next day, after spending the better part of sixteen hours in the pokey, this young man's roommate picked him up from jail and took him to a hotel bar that was hosting a party called "Drink Till You Drown." His roommate swore to him that he would stay sober, so Brandon's recalcitrant client could go ahead and drown his sorrows over the previous evening's misfortunes.

Unfortunately, when they attempted to leave, it became apparent that the designated driver had lied about his abstinence plan when he passed out while attempting to start the car. Brandon's hero then slid his gelatinous butt to the side and began his own heroic efforts to extricate them from the hotel parking lot's numerous obstacles in the form of parked cars. After striking seven or eight, who's counting, the local gendarmes returned Brandon's client to his rightful cocoon lovingly referred to as the Brig. Brandon was able to extricate the young man from purgatory with a minimum of hassle in order to facilitate his entry into the army just in time for the Gulf War in Iraq. Brandon often wondered whether the boy had gotten himself blown up or whether he survived only to wind up in the Betty Ford Clinic or some such. All's well that ends well, Brandon figured.

One of the calls on his desk was from a law school buddy named Jack Temple from Tallahassee who he hadn't heard from in some years. They had played some intramural football together for his law school team, which called itself the "Hosebags," a term of endearment purloined from the show featuring guys from the "Great White North." They actually had a talented squad that finished in the semifinals of the entire university tournament of 160 some teams his third year on the strength of some pretty strong athletes from various undergraduate football programs.

He gave Jack a call and got past his secretary quickly.

"Hey, you old hosebag, how the heck are ya?"

"I'm good. How have you been, hosehead?" Brandon replied.

For several minutes, they tried to outdo the other with jabs of verbal abuse while butchering Canadian accent.

Finally, Jack said, "Brandon, I've got a case I want to refer to you in Daytona. It's a really good injury case with an impressive plaintiff who may well have lost a pro baseball career as a result of his injuries. It's going to be a negligent security claim against your local college. Do you have any conflicts?"

Brandon replied that he had never represented the school and had no conflicts of interest.

Jack said, "The bad news is that liability is going to be difficult, and the law firm they have hired to defend it is one of the biggest defense firms around. Ever since I filed suit, they have been running little old me ragged going back and forth between Tampa, Tallahassee, and Daytona for hearings and depositions. I don't even want a referral percentage fee; I'd just be much obliged if you'd take it off my hands. If you make a fee, you can pay me for my costs and time … whatever is fair."

Brandon knew that lawyers who referred injury cases to other lawyers normally expected to be paid a referral fee of up to 25 percent of the net attorney's fee. Brandon was always skeptical of cases sent to him by other lawyers who do personal injury work because they tended to be dogs, but he trusted Jack, and the case sounded interesting.

"All right, hoser," Brandon said. "Send me the file and make arrangements for the client to come and see me. I'll take a look at it. If it's a go, I'll send you a stipulation for substitution of Counsel."

"You got it," Jack said, and he rang off.

Brandon pondered the call, *Things that make you go hmmm.* He liked cases with big damages, big coverage, and challenging liability. What he didn't like were cases with no coverage or no damages. You could only turn a sow's ear into a silk purse if you had some silk to work with.

A couple of days later, a potential client named Omar rang up Brandon's office, and requested an appointment to discuss his injury case. Patty set it up. On Friday morning, Omar limped into Brandon's lair and was escorted into his office by Patty.

After seating him, Patty winked at Brandon and gave him a thumbs-up before exiting demurely. She obviously liked what she saw on first appearance. Omar was casually dressed in sweats and certainly looked like an athlete. He was a light-skinned black man with a well-defined musculature. He stood about six foot one and probably tipped the scales at around 215 pounds. He walked with a noticeable limp. Brandon started off by shaking hands and offering Omar a soft drink, water, or coffee, which he politely declined.

"So, Mr. Steele, it's very nice to meet you. Let's dispense with the small talk and tell me about your case," Brandon said. He had reviewed the file Jack had sent and was aware of the particulars, but he wanted to hear it from the horse's mouth.

Omar said, "Well, it all started harmlessly enough when I was down here last spring for graduation. My girlfriend was graduating from Luther, and I was down for that. We hadn't hooked up yet that evening, so I was hanging out with some friends from Tampa. We went to a party not far from campus, and one of my boys got in a scrap with a local gang member. It was a one- or two-punch affair that we broke up quickly. We didn't think much of it, and we left the party and went over to campus."

"What was your friend's name?" Brandon asked.

"Ronnie Short," said Omar.

"Was he from here?"

"No, he's from Tampa. He came over for the party with his brother."

"Okay, so, go on. What happened next?" Brandon asked.

"Well, after that, Ronnie and I left and went looking for my girlfriend's dorm on campus, but we really had no idea where to look. So, we were walking down an access road between two buildings when a black SUV drove up, and five or six dudes jumped out and surrounded us. This guy they referred to as 'Mr. Justice' was the guy Ronnie decked back at the party, and he started talking trash to us. I could see that there was going to be trouble, but before I could make a move, two of the goons grabbed me from behind and held me by the arms. Then this Justice dude pulled out a blade and started waving it at Ronnie. Ronnie tried to defend himself, but one of the other dudes pushed him into this Justice who stuck him in the belly with the knife. Ronnie went down and got pummeled, and then they kind of panicked and let me go. They all got back in the truck and hauled ass. I went to Ronnie on the ground and checked him out. He was conscious but bleeding pretty bad from the stomach. It didn't look good. I stuffed my shirt into the wound area and told him to hold it there. Then I helped him up, and we started looking for help.

"We walked out to the street and up to a little office with a security sign in the window. I banged on the door, but no one was there. So, we walked across the street to a dorm that had the porch light on. I sat Ronnie down on the porch and pounded on the door. An older lady who was apparently the house mother came to the door, but she wouldn't open it. I yelled for her to call an ambulance. She screamed when she saw the blood all over my hands and disappeared back down the hall. About that time, the SUV returned and stopped on the street. They had apparently gone to find more of their boys and were back to finish the job on us. I tried to protect Ronnie, but Mr. Justice rushed me and clubbed me over the head with a pipe or something. I was out like a light."

Brandon continued taking notes.

"Apparently, at about that same time, our friends Cooter and Speed showed up and got to the porch in time to pull Justice off of me before he could kill me. I don't remember any of this, but apparently while Cooter and Speed fought with the gang boys, someone pulled me into the dorm and shut the door. I apparently came to as Justice was trying to break down the door to get in at me. When I saw him, I must have freaked out and ran up the stairs to the third floor. I was dazed and confused and convinced they were chasing me, so, apparently, I barged into a girl's dorm room and proceeded to jump out her third-floor window to escape. I fell three floors to the ground and landed on my ankle and busted it to shit and then on my head, knocking myself out again. The cops had arrived by then to break things up, and the next thing I knew I was in the hospital recovering from surgery. My memory is pretty sketchy about the whole thing."

Brandon had read the complaint, which alleged that the college failed to man the security office with a single security guard on the night before graduation when there were sure to be many parties, and many drunken students looking to cause trouble. What he didn't know as yet was why? The college had answered with a general denial of all claims. The defense attorney was a very experienced trial lawyer named Bob Knight from Orlando. He worked for a large firm that was going to do its damnedest to exonerate the college on behalf of its insurance company, American National, which carried a ten-million-dollar liability policy. So far, Brandon liked what he saw. Omar was a very good-looking, articulate young man, he looked you in the eye when he spoke, he was relaxed and easygoing, and he had suffered tremendously both in terms of pain and the loss of his career.

Brandon also saw two huge problems right off the bat. First, on the question of liability or fault, it was going to be difficult to overcome the fact that no one pushed Omar out that window. He jumped of his own accord, so how could the college be made to answer for that? Second, the loss of Omar's baseball career was going to be viewed by a court as speculative at best since he hadn't even been drafted yet, and there were scores of athletes who were drafted to play baseball but never made it to the lucrative world of the Major Leagues. He explained these problems to Omar, and Omar understood. "I know Mr. Michaels, but this didn't need to happen, and it would have been easy enough to prevent if they had taken minimal precautions."

"I agree," said Brandon. "Perhaps we can prove liability if we can discover a smoking gun in the security guard issue. What about damages? How are we going prove you would have made it to the show?" This was key, and he watched Omar closely since his answer to this question could end up being the linchpin to the whole case.

Omar responded, "I guess we'll never know for sure, but you could call the scout from the Cubs who was recruiting me, my coaches, and some of the other players I know who have made it."

Brandon asked, "Such as who?"

"Well, there's Gary Sheffield and Marquis Grissom for starters. Gary and I go back to Little League together, and Marquis played with me at A&M. They're both doing really well in the pros."

"Do you speak to them often?" Brandon asked.

"Sure do, I have both on my speed dial right here." He held up his cell phone. Sure enough, both were in his contact list of favorites.

"Okay, Omar," Brandon said. "I'll take your case, but this would be a risky case to try, and the day may well come when they offer a settlement, which is in your best interest to accept, and I expect you to follow my advice at all times, okay?"

"Sure, Mr. Michaels. You're the boss."

They spoke some more, mostly about football and Omar's therapy, and the hour was up before they knew it.

"Okay, Omar. Go see Miss Patty, and she'll have some documents for you to sign. I will be handling this on what we call a contingent fee basis. That means that I will be paid a percentage of your recovery, specifically 40 percent, plus I will advance all costs, so this won't cost you a thing unless we win. There may come a time, however, when they offer a formal settlement in the form of an offer of judgment, and if you don't accept it, and we don't get a verdict greater than 25 percent above the offer, you could be responsible for all the defense fees and costs. But don't worry about that yet—I'll tell you all about that when the time comes. For now, you get on with your rehab and keep in touch with me. Fair enough?"

"Sure, Mr. Michaels." Omar shook Brandon's hand and retired to the front office to sign documents.

"Oh, and start making a list of all those folks who you think could help out on damages, talk to your ballplayer friends and prepare them for this, plus call everyone you know of who saw anything at all—and get me addresses and phone numbers for each and every one of them!"

"Okay." Omar turned back for a second. "I guess I better make a list."

After Omar left, Brandon went into Patty's office where she was holding court with Tyson and Rhonda. "Well, girls, what do you think?"

They all started bubbling over at once.

"Hold it, girls. Get your hormones in check and tell me your thoughts one at a time."

Patty said, "I'll tell you what, boss. That boy is one large piece of man candy, and if you get one or two single women on the jury, it's all over."

"I'll second that thought," Tyson gushed. "He is a dreamboat who could float in my canal anytime he wants."

Rhonda laughed and punched Tyson's arm. "You slut puppy!"

"Me?" Tyson said. "I saw you checking out his ass on the way out—so don't go acting all goody two-shoes with me, girlfriend."

"Busted." Rhonda slinked back to her desk.

Brandon could see that not much constructive work was going to get done for the remainder of this day, and he went back to his desk. He knew this case would be an uphill battle, particularly against Bob Knight, but maybe he could coax a six-figure settlement out of them instead of putting ten million at risk. Time to get to work. He logged on to the computer and started writing a list of interrogatory questions to serve on the college in an attempt to elicit a picture of negligent security on their part. What were the names of the security personnel? How many were on duty that night—and where the heck were they? How many calls were made by the local cops to the campus in the past twelve months, and for what types of crimes or disturbances? He would also have his investigator look into the backgrounds of all the players, including Omar, to see who had a record of violent behavior or other skeletons in their closet. He would also have to gather up all the medical records on Omar going back to birth, if possible, as well as his history of sports accomplishments. He was starting to look forward to developing this case.

Brandon's low budget investigator was a local homeless man named Mr. Lee. Mr. Lee lived somewhere in the woods not far from Brandon's office in a tent that was apparently very well equipped with the comforts of home. Brandon didn't know his first name, but he did know that Mr. Lee was a former ROK Special Forces operative and was one tough son of a bitch. Brandon had represented him a few years ago on a court appointment due to a conflict in the public defender's office. Mr. Lee was then called Lee, no known first or middle name. He was charged with murder initially for killing a man with one punch. The man was attempting to rob Mr. Lee while he slept in his wooded abode, and unfortunately for the robber, Mr. Lee became aware of his presence. One punch later, the man was dead. Mr. Lee should have just buried the guy, but instead, he turned the body in to the police. After calling in a Korean interpreter, Brandon was able to establish that self-defense was the issue, and detectives were sent to the camp to investigate. They found the robber's shopping cart full of items apparently stolen from other homeless people, and he had on him several knives and a loaded .22 caliber pistol in his pocket. He never had a chance to use it, but fingerprints established that he and it had a long criminal history together.

Brandon was ultimately able to convince the prosecution to drop the charges to a misdemeanor assault beef, and Mr. Lee pled to probation. Part of the terms of his probation was that he was required to find a job, so Brandon hired him as his investigator. Since he didn't know how to drive, Brandon bought him a nice road/mountain bike and a cell phone and required that he always show up for work in clean clothes. He had been working on a loaner laptop with Rosetta Stone's English for Koreans, and his English was getting to where Brandon could nearly understand him. He also began to call him Bruce for obvious reasons. Bruce was eternally grateful to Brandon, and he soon became a valued and trusted employee. Brandon and Jesse had even installed a bath and shower in the third office in the building, and they let Bruce move into it.

He was supposed to stay clear of the office during office hours, which suited him fine as he used that time to work and pursue his hobbies, whatever the heck they were. At night, he would return to the office to sleep. Brandon felt it was a win-win situation; he got a reasonably priced investigator, and the partnership got the best security alarm in town. Woe be the poor fucker who tried to break into this office!

CHAPTER 14

GONE FISHING

Later that night, Brandon sat on his dock cradling a Corona in a foam hugger and watching his bobber. The sun was setting over the river, and it would have been terribly peaceful were it not for the rumble of Harleys cruising over the bridges to the north. It was Biketoberfest week in Daytona, the biannual pilgrimage of nearly a half million bikers who invaded his fair city every spring and fall to show off their chrome-covered bikes and leather costumes. He had a Heritage Softail in the garage that he would get out on in the next day or two when things heated up. Brandon enjoyed riding the Harley, especially in the spring and winter months when it wasn't too hot. A few years back, he had made the trip to the other Harley Mecca known as Sturgis, South Dakota. Sturgis boasted a bike week almost as large that had started the year before the Daytona event fifty plus years ago. Sturgis was older, Daytona was bigger, and both claimed to host *the* premier biker rally in the US.

Sturgis was a very different place from Daytona. It was a much smaller town in a more western and wild setting. It also was a locale much more suited to long rides. Brandon had gone to Sturgis with friends and spent three wonderful days riding to places called Devil's Tower, Crazy Horse, Deadwood, Lead, Mount Rushmore, the Black Hills, Wall Drugs, and the Badlands. His crew had ridden more than six hundred miles in three days on the Harleys. This was in addition to the 4,400 miles of driving to get there and back. It was a fun-filled seven days in which many miles were covered without incident—other than his new tattoo on his upper arm designed after the FSU Seminole spear. That was obtained through the use of much liquid courage.

Both events sported tons of vendors peddling trinkets, clothing, and enough beer to float a battleship. Brandon wasn't as prone to riding the Harley during Daytona's bike week due to the fact that much business was generated by new DUI clients and more importantly, personal injury cases. Motorcycle crashes were frequent during bike week, and they tended to produce more significant injuries than car wrecks. While this was unfortunate for the bikers, it was lucrative for the lawyers.

Brandon often marveled at the thousands of people who invaded his town every year. He was certain that the earth was going to punish humankind eventually for the overpopulation and pollution that was draining its precious resources. It was going to take some ballsy world leaders to someday mandate a zero-growth birth rate or a sterilization program on a vast basis. He felt that more likely a huge plague of some sort would take care of the problem if humanity didn't.

Just then, he noticed that his bobber was no longer visible. He reeled in the slack, which was considerable since he had left his bail open while he spaced out, and a fish had nearly taken all of the line from his reel. When it came taut, he yanked back to set the hook. At that moment, the reel began to sing as a huge tarpon broke water some eighty yards out into the channel. Steve jumped up and strained at her leash, whining and drooling as she looked out into the river at the splashing tarpon. This was what she lived for, and the leash was thwarting her most primal urges.

Brandon's excitement was short-lived as the tarpon took to the air again in spectacular fashion, spinning on its tail and shaking its great head. Just then, the twenty-pound test line snapped at the leader, and Brandon fell back to the dock, spilling his beer all over himself. "Damn, Steve, girl, did ya see that?" he yelled. It was obvious that she did as she was still quite agitated.

The tarpon jumped again as if to say "See ya, sucker" and vanished into the darkening water. Brandon had never actually landed a tarpon, mostly because they were so infrequent in these waters that he was never properly rigged for one. He told himself that one of these nights, he was going to have to haul out some heavier tackle and rig a steel leader on fifty-pound test line just in case. "Well girl, that's enough excitement for one night. What say we repair to the lair and watch a game on the big screen?"

Steve wagged her nub and accepted a pat on the head as he unhooked her harness. She hazarded one backward glance into the river, no doubt imagining that tarpon as her prize, and then followed her beloved master. The happy fisherman went inside as darkness came upon them, and a legion of Harleys growled in the distance.

CHAPTER 15

BACK TO REALITY

Omar returned to Tampa where he was once again living at home in the shadow of his doting mother and all-too-controlling father. Everyone seemed to know what was best for him, and they couldn't wait to make their opinions known. He was trying to rehabilitate his shattered ankle, but it was slow and painful going. He really didn't see the point since there was no way he would ever pitch again—or even run fast for that matter. He had run a 4.3 forty-yard dash during last year's football season, his most successful as A&M's quarterback. Were he not so focused on baseball, there was an outside chance he could have found a place in the National Football League. He was too small to be the prototype QB, but his speed and athletic ability would have allowed him to convert to cornerback or wideout with no problems. Besides, Doug Flutie and Russell Wilson were shorter QBs who hadn't done so bad, right? And Michael Vick was no giant.

Now, instead of intense workouts with teammates followed by the joyful camaraderie of belonging to a team, he was relegated to living at home and learning how to walk again. His day started with breakfast and a long soak in the hot tub to loosen up the soft tissues that had stiffened during the night. Then he spent an hour on the treadmill, limping along while holding on to both support bars with sweat dripping off his nose and shooting pains coursing through his lower leg. Next, he would do upper-body work on the universal gym his dad had installed in his room with his ankle elevated and iced. He would watch a ball game with the sound turned down and try to read a book at the same time to keep his mind from dwelling on his predicament.

Lou had called from the Cubs organization soon after the injury to express his condolences. He was very disappointed—as was Omar—when he confirmed that he would have gone high in the first round of the draft. His signing bonus alone would have set him up for life.

If only he had stayed in Tallahassee with that callous bitch, Wanda, none of this would have ever happened. They say all things happen for a reason, but for the life of him, Omar couldn't figure out what possible good could come from this. Because of this, he had missed his own ceremony while he was in the hospital, he hoped he was officially a college graduate, but was a bit concerned he had not received a diploma. His degree was in physical education, and he thought that the least he could do was try to find a job teaching high school and maybe get an assistant coach's job. He spent the afternoon putting together a resume of his athletic and academic achievements to circulate to the local high schools in hopes of finding work. He also sent off a request to the college inquiring as to his status as a Graduate, and also the status of his diploma in the event he was a graduate. The way his luck was running there was probably some snafu keeping him from graduating.

The therapy took on a new significance as his plan formulated in his head, the thinking being that nobody would hire a coach who was crippled. Effective coaching required being able to demonstrate the techniques being taught. With this goal in mind, he pushed through the painful exercises and fought off the constant bouts of depression.

Brandon had given Omar the task of gathering up documentation of all his sports achievements. He wanted old programs featuring Omar's statistics, newspaper articles, trophies, and anything else that would tend to portray him as a successful athlete destined for greatness on a Major League diamond. There was no shortage of information available since Omar had been playing sports his whole life, and on every team, he was invariably the star player. Most of his accolades came from baseball and football, but he was no slouch at basketball and track in high school, and he had lettered in all four sports for four years in a row. A rather large filing cabinet at home was filling up with stuff from his past. There were many fond memories in that stuff, but reading through it only caused his depression to worsen.

Dump Truck was a big help and also served as moral support. He had always worshipped his older brother's more talented friend, and now he had become his right-hand man and chief gofer while Omar convalesced.

Brandon told Omar that Bruce Lee was out looking for witnesses to the fight. Most of them would likely not want to become involved, but Brandon said that Bruce could be painfully persuasive.

CHAPTER 16

PREPARATIONS

Some weeks later, Brandon was in his office going through the mail and reading the answers to interrogatories supplied by the college. They had revealed that Dean Mathews was the head of security, and it also included a list of all the security guards in the college's employ at the time of the incident. Brandon instructed Patty to set them all for depositions in which they would be placed under oath and be asked to divulge things such as where they were supposed to be on the night in question and who was not at their assigned post. He also had received his requested information from the Daytona Beach Police department showing all 911 calls to addresses on the campus during the twelve months prior to Omar's injury. Joe Cline's investigation was proving to be invaluable in developing the liability theory of a dangerous campus with inadequate security personnel.

It was unbelievable to him that there were 286 calls to the police department from persons in distress or reporting drug deals, prowlers, burglaries, vandalism, and other calamities on campus in that twelve-month period. The school was definitely in need of an attentive security force, an area that seemed to be lacking in the budget figures he had subpoenaed. Also scheduled for depositions were the house mother and the girls in the dorm who had witnessed some or all of the proceedings that night.

Brandon decided to focus his discovery efforts on the liability side of the equation, mostly because if that didn't pan out, he might not ever get to the more-expensive-to-develop damages side. He had obtained the medical and hospital reports that would continue to come in as Omar went through the recovery process. He would wait until the doctors finished with Omar's care before taking any of their depositions. Brandon liked to take videotape depositions of doctors for presentation to the jury because doctors hated to come to court and typically charged a thousand bucks or more for every hour of testimony. Also, nearly everyone liked to watch TV, and it was a good way to break up the monotony of a trial by simply popping in a videotape and letting the jury watch it.

While discussing the case on the phone, Brandon had explained to Omar that the defense in any personal injury case was entitled to have the plaintiff examined by a doctor or doctors of their choice in what was called an "compulsory medical exam." These exams were often far from independent, however, because the defense doctors were expected to be extremely conservative, often disputing the plaintiff's doctors and calling into question whether the plaintiff was hurt at all. This was especially true in soft-tissue "whiplash" cases where there were no real visible injuries. Unfortunately, no one had yet developed a test to objectively measure pain, and juries were often loath to award money damages to people who looked just fine when the case went to trial. Depending upon the type of injury, the CME doctor would most often be an orthopedic surgeon or neurologist. If brain damage were alleged, they may also enlist the services of a neurosurgeon and/or psychiatrist.

Brandon wasn't concerned about the defense having Omar examined by their orthopedic surgeon because the ankle fractures showed up beautifully on x-ray—as did the pins that were used to piece the bones back together. Any doctor the defense selected would have to be a total crook and completely unbelievable to try to tell a jury that Omar was as good as new. The defense had scheduled him to see an orthopedic surgeon in Deltona named Haas who had a reputation for finding no permanent injury unless the plaintiff was missing a limb—and even then he would only grudgingly concede a minor permanent impairment. He would also try to discount the functional aspects of every disability. Brandon had no doubt that Haas would testify that Christopher Reeves, RIP, the former

Superman actor turned quadriplegic had made a miraculous recovery should he be asked to render his opinion.

The exam was set for Monday, and Brandon invited Omar to spend the weekend before with him. He wanted to get to know Omar on a personal level, which would help develop the case and flush out the names of persons who would best be able to portray the differences in Omar's life since the injury. They would need "before and after" witnesses, which as the term implies were folks, preferably not loved ones, who had known him before and could testify as to the changes in his life brought about by the injuries. Brandon thought the best way to get to know someone was by going fishing with them.

When Omar arrived on Saturday morning, the boat was loaded and ready to go. Omar pulled into the drive while Brandon was finishing putting the rods and reels and tackle in the boat. He had already loaded up a cooler with beer, sodas, and sandwiches.

Omar walked up and yelled, "Hey, Mr. Michaels, how are you?"

Brandon turned and said, "Hey yourself, but if we're going to spend the weekend together, you can start by calling me Brandon."

"Okay, Coach. Brandon it is. What's the plan?"

"Well, I thought we'd go wet a line and get to know each other a bit. Do you like to fish?"

"I've never really done much of it, but I like to eat it."

"Well, it might not be a bad idea for you to develop a taste for more sedentary amusement, my friend." Someone once said that a man should strive to make enough money to allow him to fish all the time, or failing that, to be so poor that he had to. Brandon was neither, but it was one of his favorite things to do. "Put your bag in the house, and we'll hit the road. I've got everything you'll need already in the boat."

"Okay." Omar went into the house to stash his stuff.

As soon as he closed the door, Omar was greeted by a fuzzy barking machine. Steve had been awakened by the door closing and was attempting to protect her home from an unknown intruder.

From outside, Brandon yelled, "Shut up, Steve. It's okay."

"Hey, boy." Omar bent down and extended his hand for examination.

Steve walked forward tentatively and sniffed at the proffered digits. Dogs can detect a person who loves animals, and the nub of her tail began to revolve.

Omar patted her roughly, stowed his bag in the hall, and returned to the driveway.

Steve followed close behind.

Brandon hopped down from the boat and said, "I see you've met my vicious guard dog."

"Yeah. What's his name?"

"*Her* name is Steve!" Brandon said.

Omar had a curious look on his face as he said, "A girl named Steve? Is that like a boy named Sue?"

"Actually, I named her after Steve Nicks, the singer. I always had the hots for her."

"Cool," said Omar. "Is she going fishing?"

"She wouldn't miss it for the world," Brandon said. "Let's go." Brandon opened the truck door, and Steve bounded in without being told.

Omar got in on the other side, and Steve sat in the middle, keeping a wary eye on Omar. She nuzzled his hand with her snout in an effort to be petted. There was no such thing as too much attention for her.

The drive to Oak Hill was pleasant on that early Saturday morning.

Omar said, "I don't think I have ever seen so many motorcycles. I have heard of bike week, but I had no idea it would be like this."

All the way down US-1, there were hundreds of bikes on the road and parked adjacent to seemingly every bar in town.

"Yeah, it's a big deal here," Brandon said. "These bikers are a blend of hard-core bikers and yuppie wannabes who spend between fifteen and fifty thousand bucks on a bike, dress up in leathers, apply fake tattoos, and act out a fantasy for one week out of the year."

"I noticed you had one in your garage," Omar said.

"Yep, I fall into the latter category, although I do have a real tattoo." Brandon lifted his shirt sleeve and showed off the Indian spear he had tattooed on his right upper arm.

Omar smiled. "A hard-core Seminole, no doubt."

"You got it, bubba. I bleed garnet and gold."

Brandon pulled into the bait store in Oak Hill and bought three dozen pigfish for the live well, and they were off to the launch.

Gus was smoking a large cigar next to the launch when they pulled up. He was wearing a set of denim overalls that looked like they had seen use in Mr. Ed's stall.

"Hey, old man," Brandon yelled out the open window.

"Hey, ambulance chaser," Gus said with a smile. "How's my buddy?"

Brandon opened the door, and Steve ran to Gus for her customary greeting and a treat.

With Steve occupied and introductions made, Brandon backed the trailer into the water effortlessly. Launching the Hughes was a piece of cake, especially when one has done it hundreds of times. He parked the truck on the side of the gravel road and said, "Where are they biting?"

Gus said, "I heard the school was over on George's Bank yesterday, but no one has come in with a report yet today." He normally didn't divulge such information, but Brandon was a longtime customer, and Gus knew he obeyed the rules and didn't keep more fish than was allowed. Gus generally hated Yankees and any other asshole who killed more fish than they could possibly eat.

"We'll give it a shot and let you know," Brandon said.

"Nice to meet you," Omar said.

"Don't fall in," Gus said as he walked back to the air-conditioned shack, he called home. It was stifling hot, and the sun was a blazing orb in the blue cloudless sky.

Brandon sat at the controls and tossed Omar a hat. "I don't know if dark-skinned folks get sunburned or not, but you better wear this just in case, and there is some sunscreen in that tackle box."

Omar grinned and put on the hat. "Yassa, boss, I be wearing the boss man's hat."

Steve assumed her position in the bow, and Brandon idled the boat out of the narrow channel and into the river. Once they were through the no-wake zone, he cranked up the powerful Yamaha outboard, and they were quickly on plane and zooming across the water at forty miles per hour.

It was too loud to speak, so Omar held his hat with one hand and the gunwale with the other with white knuckles. Omar was an athlete of many talents, but Brandon did not know that swimming was not one of them. He was wearing a life vest and clutching it tightly, so Brandon was not worried.

Omar watched the bottom of the river streak by with tearing eyes, and Brandon guessed that he was certain that they would hit some submerged obstacle and be tossed to their deaths.

After several minutes, Brandon slowed the boat and began to scan the horizon for a telltale redness in the water or a large number of tail fins piercing the calm water. Redfish liked to feed on crabs and other delicacies found on the bottom, and in shallow water, their head-down position often left their tails exposed.

When Brandon spotted the school, he shut down the engine. He dropped the trolling motor into the water and began slowly creeping toward the area where the school was heading. When he had the boat on an intercept course, he dropped the anchor and whispered, "Sit still, and I'll fix your rig. You do know how to cast and set a hook and shit, right?"

Omar nodded.

Brandon unclipped the leader and hook from one of his Shimano rigs and hooked a pigfish through the tail. Once pierced, the little fish grunted its displeasure. It was this grunting noise that would hopefully attract a hungry redfish. He handed the pole to Omar and pointed in the direction he wanted Omar to cast. "Yonder."

Omar released the bail, reared back, and whipped the rod forward, causing the little pigfish to be hurled through the air and land some forty yards away.

"Tell me about your path to greatness on the ball field," Brandon said. "Were you always good—or did you have to work at it?"

Omar was modest by nature, but he loved talking about sports, especially the ones he played, and for the next hour, he brought Brandon up to speed on his football, baseball, and track career.

Brandon was impressed to say the least. Be that as it may, they were still fishing. "Now, reel in your slack, and every so often, twitch the rod tip up to pull the little critter out of the grass. Otherwise, he will hide in the grasses, and the fish might miss him."

Omar nodded and followed directions.

Brandon had rigged up his own rod and tossed it out to the left of Omar's. He set the pole down in a rod holder and hooked up Steve's leash to her chest harness.

"Why'd you do that?" Omar asked.

"You wouldn't believe me if I told you," Brandon said.

Omar shrugged and stared at the area where his bait was waiting to become breakfast for a much larger fish.

Brandon asked, "So, what's next? What are you going to do with your life now that pro sports is off the table?"

After a few seconds, Omar said, "Man, I have no earthly idea." A single tear flowed down his cheek.

Brandon gave up the questioning for a minute and decided to wait for a bite.

They did not have to wait long before Omar's rod suddenly bent over double. He hauled back to set the hook, and the reel suddenly began to scream as the fish took line off the spool at will.

Before he could recover from the shock of the strike, Brandon had one of his own hooked. Brandon said, "Omar, these redfish are very strong, and on light tackle, they will put up a valiant fight—so hang on when it runs."

Steve was straining at the leash in an effort to assist in the recovery of the fish.

Brandon's fish ran toward the boat and went under it, causing him to walk around to the other side, crossing under Omar's line in the process.

Omar appeared to be gaining on his fish after recovering much of the line expended in its first run. Any feeling of triumph he may have had was short-lived as the fish, upon seeing the boat, took off again, stealing nearly a hundred yards of line before Omar could stop it.

Brandon's fish was somewhat smaller than Omar's, and he brought his fish to the side of the boat. With the rod in one hand and the net in the other, he skillfully netted the fish and brought it into the boat. It was a beautifully golden redfish with spots on its tail that looked like eyes.

Brandon extracted the fish from the net, pulled the hook free from its jaw, and held it up for Omar to see and for Steve to sniff.

The dog barked a challenge at the fish and lunged at it with teeth bared.

Brandon pulled it back before she could sink her teeth into it and laid it on the measuring board. The fish measured thirty-two inches—too big to keep.

Omar was too busy struggling with his own version to pay much attention. "Nice fish. We gonna keep it?"

"No, it's too big." Brandon gently laid it in the water, holding it by the tail. He moved it back and forth in order to get the water flowing through its gills, and it promptly squirted out of his hand and swam away to locate its school. This fish had grown in excess of the length allowed for keeping. Theoretically, it was safe forever, but it would probably be a while before it sampled another pigfish.

Omar was still struggling with a monster. After twenty minutes of fight, he and the fish were substantially exhausted. He brought it to the side, and Brandon maneuvered it into the net. It was so big that the tail stuck out of the top of the net after its nose had reached the bottom. Brandon removed the hook and measured it. It was forty inches long and quite thick, probably twenty or more pounds.

Omar gasped. "Wow! I ain't never seen a fish that big outside of Sea World."

Brandon said, "It's a beauty. How about you release it?"

Omar bent down and grasped the head in one hand and the tail in the other. His legs were shaky as he turned toward the side and began to lower the fish toward the water.

The fish began to struggle mightily, and the combination of Omar's momentum and the fish's struggles caused him to lose his balance—and both fish and angler went over the side into the water.

Brandon was momentarily stunned, Steve started barking, and Omar freaked out and screamed for help. Fortunately for Omar, the water was only two feet deep, but Brandon watched him for several seconds of thrashing in panic before he finally realized he was sitting on the bottom with his chest out of the water. Seeing that Omar was unhurt, Brandon fell into the bottom of the boat in a spasm of laughter.

Steve alternated barking and licking Brandon's face while he coughed and sputtered and tried to ward her off. He was beginning to regain control as a dripping, muddy Omar peered over the gunnels and looked at Brandon with a look of utter disapproval. He had a weed hanging off the top of his head, which made him look like Little Richard.

The apparition set Brandon and Steve to howling again, and it was several minutes before calm was returned to the boat.

"Well," Brandon said, "it's probably fair to say the school of reds has been thoroughly spooked. Sorry, Omar, I couldn't resist. That was just too fucking funny."

"That's okay," Omar said. "I certainly deserved it."

"Well, let's dry you off a bit, have a beer and a sandwich, and discuss your case for a while."

"Sounds good," Omar said. As Brandon began to prepare the refreshments, Omar dripped his way back into the boat.

CHAPTER 17

SKYDIVE

The next day, Brandon had a date with Genie at 8:00 a.m. sharp. She wouldn't tell him what she had planned, and that had him a bit worried—but in a good way. He got up at six, let Steve out to forage for critters and do her daily thing, and did thirty minutes on the Stairmaster while watching the news. He hated all networks—they were all biased as hell—but he could tolerate Fox. Brandon finished his workout, showered, and changed into his normal weekend attire of cargo pants and a golf shirt. His closet was bursting with golf shirts from all over the continent due to his habit of picking one up every time he played a new course. Some still had the tags on them as they had never been worn.

The doorbell rang promptly at eight, and he went to get it with two cups of coffee in hand. Genie was standing on the porch all bright-eyed and eager. She had her flaxen hair in a ponytail, a Miami Dolphins hat, tight jeans full of holes, and a pink T-shirt that said: "24 hours in a Day … 24 beers in a case … Coincidence? I think not." The low-cut shirt revealed excellent cleavage, which was his favorite attribute.

"Hey, flyboy. Aren't you sweet?" She gave him a big, wet kiss and grabbed the fullest cup of java. "So, are you ready for today's adventure?" She flashed a devilish grin.

"I'll try most anything once—as long as it's heterosexual."

She laughed. "I don't think that will be a problem today."

"So, exactly where are you shanghai-ing little old me today?" Brandon asked.

"You'll see soon enough," she said.

"Okay." Brandon went to the back porch and whistled for Steve.

Seconds later, Steve bounded in with filthy paws and a distinct odor of old, dead seafood.

"Whoa, cowboy," Brandon said. "Stop right there!"

Steve stopped in her tracks on the mat and stood there whining with her nub revolving like a turnstile. The dog was obviously dying to run to Genie for a rub and sniff, but she would have to wait until Brandon cleaned off her fur.

Genie was finishing her coffee at the kitchen table, and came over to Steve's mat by the door. "Hello, girlfriend," Genie cooed as she scratched Steve's ears.

After toweling off his dog, Brandon grabbed a backpack for his necessities and took Genie by the hand.

Steve started hopping about in anticipation of a ride.

Brandon said, "You're staying here, old girl. I want you to hold down the fort and stay out of the garbage and the river."

Steve whined, but Brandon knew once she figured out that she was not going, she would curl up on the cool tile in front of the sliding doors where she could pout while keeping an eye on the backyard to ward off any intruders.

Brandon walked out the front door, locked it, and followed Genie to her jeep, admiring her backside the whole way. She caught him looking as she turned quickly to jump in, and he was pleasantly surprised that it seemed to make her happy that he noticed. He figured she knew she had a great ass, and she obviously went to great pains at the gym to keep it that way.

They headed out to the west across the bridge for US-92, otherwise known as Speedway Boulevard.

"So, beautiful, where are we headed?" Brandon inquired.

"We're going to a perfect spot," she said.

She didn't seem inclined to elaborate, so Brandon sat back and thought about Omar's case. He chuckled to himself as he recalled Omar's dunk in the water.

"What's so funny?" Genie asked, and he told her the story. She loved it, and they both shared a laugh at the conclusion. Brandon was not under any illusions about Omar's case; he knew he had liability problems and a formidable opponent. There was no doubt about the damages, however, as Omar had definitely been a man about to make some serious money before this life-altering injury. The problem was that even if he got past the inevitable motion for summary judgment on liability and got the case to trial, he was afraid the judge would rule that his lost future income claim was too speculative to present to a jury. He wanted to call to the stand several ballplayers who knew of Omar's talents to predict his marketability and earning potential, but that was something the court would probably not allow under the rules of evidence. *Unless there is some other way!*

After doing some internet research, Brandon learned that there were thousands of wannabe Major League ballplayers who got drafted but never made it to the show. Many languished in the minors, riding on buses, staying in cheap hotels, and making barely minimum wage. Those outnumbered by at least a factor of ten the ones who didn't make it past the first year at all. It was a very low percentage of them who actually saw the big leagues, and some of those didn't stay there for long. The odds were certainly against Omar becoming another Nolan Ryan or Roger Clemens—or even the next great closer like John Smoltz with the Braves or Mariano Rivera with the Yankees—but there was no doubt he had the raw talent and basic skills necessary to have a chance. That chance would likely include a hefty signing bonus. Omar also had a talent scout with some clout in the name of Lou Pinella from the Cubs—who he said would surely be willing to testify.

As Brandon strategized, Genie turned off of US-92 just before reaching Deland. At first, he thought she was taking him the highway patrol station, but he shortly recognized that they were headed for the Deland Airport.

She pulled up into a dirt lot and parked alongside several other cars. "We're here," she said and jumped out of the jeep. He followed her up to the first building, which had a colorful mural painted on the side with the name "The Perfect Spot" painted over a picture of skydivers under canopy with a jump plane flying away overhead. The Perfect Spot was a restaurant sandwiched between the Skydive Deland parachute-packing building and the offices of the skydiving outfit. There were several people about, most of them younger than Brandon, and most of them wearing colorful jumpsuits. Many of them recognized Genie and called out to her.

"Excuse me for a sec," she said and went to get hugs from several of them.

At first, Brandon thought, *This is cool. She's brought me here to watch her jump.* He had a sneaky suspicion, however, that her intentions were not that innocent. Brandon sat on a bench on the deck next to the restaurant and watched as ten or twelve of them came swooping down from the sky for landings in the grass nearby. They all made picture-perfect landings on their feet, immediately turning around, and letting their square chutes fall to the ground to be quickly scooped up and returned to the hangar for repacking. They were a uniformly happy-looking bunch, which was understandable having just survived jumping out of an airplane and returning safely to the ground.

Brandon believed, like most pilots, that no one should jump from a perfectly good airplane while it was flying just fine.

Genie snuck up on him from behind, wrapped him up in a bear hug, and started chewing on his ear. "So, are you ready for my surprise?" she asked playfully.

"I'm afraid to ask," Brandon said.

"Well, if we're going to be an item, you are going to have to have a taste of my lifestyle."

"I've already tasted you," he quipped.

She poked him on the side. "That's not what I meant."

He wriggled away from her probe. "Certainly, you don't mean for me to go up in one of those death traps and jump, do you?"

"That is exactly what I have in mind, and before you get all defensive, hear me out. I have purchased for you what is called an AFF jump. It stands for accelerated free fall."

"I was thinking more along the lines of absolutely fucking foolish," Brandon said.

"In the old days, beginning jumpers had to do several low-altitude static line jumps where the parachute is attached to a line in the plane, and as soon as you exit the plane, your chute opens automatically."

"Like with airborne army troops," Brandon said.

"Exactly," she said. "Then one graduated to short free falls where the jumper opened her chute with a rip cord. It took up to twenty jumps before a student got to make a sustained free fall from above ten thousand feet. We have pioneered an accelerated method whereby the student makes her first jump from thirteen five accompanied by two jump masters who make sure the student is stable and that she correctly pulls her own chute at a safe altitude. Then he or she flies their own canopy to the ground."

He looked at her skeptically.

"It's perfectly safe—I assure you. Plus, I will personally select the best jump masters for you, and best of all, I will jump with you on the same load!" *Yee-haw*, he thought. *I must be out of my friggin' mind.* "Is this at all negotiable?" he asked. "I'll do anything, cover you in whipped cream and bring you many orgasms or fly you to dinner at the place of your choice and wine and dine you to death?"

"Oh, me thinks you'll do all that and more after you experience a real free fall," she said. "Besides, it cost me nearly three hundred bucks, and I've already paid for it—so there is no backing out, buster."

He knew she would not take no for an answer and followed when she dragged him into the office. He had to fill out several forms, basically guaranteeing that his estate would not sue the school, the instructors, the pilots, or the lawn man should he become road pizza, and then he watched a film showing how it would unfold. He had to admit that it looked very exciting on TV. For an extra seventy-five bucks, a cameraman would come along and film the whole thing. *Great*, he thought, *they will have a permanent record of me soiling myself and screaming at the top of my lungs like a schoolgirl as I plummet to my demise.* Brandon figured he would opt for the video so that in the event he survived, he could prove to his buds that he actually did it, which was probably the real reason that most first timers paid the extra bucks for the video.

Genie led him to the student room in an adjacent hangar where the various equipment was stored for use by fools such as him. She introduced him to Nikki, his primary instructor, a compact woman from Iceland with a ready grin and a slight accent. She was a foot shorter than Brandon and told Brandon that she had made more than twelve thousand successful skydives.

Genie said Brandon's course of instruction would take at least a couple of hours, and after assuring him that he was in good hands, she gave him a rousing kiss and skipped out of the classroom.

Nikki selected the biggest jumpsuit for Brandon along with a plastic helmet and some flimsy goggles. She then selected a big black parachute, which she said was a three hundred, which had something to do with canopy size-to-weight ratio. The final piece of the puzzle was an ingenious device called a Cyprus. It was a small rectangular silver metal box which would be activated on the ground, and in the unlikely event that he became incapacitated for some reason, and was rendered unable or unwilling to pull his main chute, it would automatically sense the speed and low altitude and fire the reserve at 750 feet above ground so that his prostate form could safely come to earth whether he knew it or not. That was the theory at least.

Nikki assured Brandon that she and another master jumper would be falling with him at all times with a hold on either side of him. One of them was tasked with pulling the main handle (they weren't called rip cords anymore) in the event that Brandon wigged out completely and was unable to do it himself. The other was in charge of making sure he remained stable and didn't assume the fetal position and tumble out of control.

Brandon began to have serious reservations about this point in the proceedings.

Nikki instructed him on the proper use of the chest mounted two way radio they would use to guide his descent, and how to don the helmet and goggles.

"Are you sure this helmet is for real?" Brandon asked. It was a very flimsy plastic thing that would be sorely insufficient for football.

"Yeah," she said.

"It's only to protect you if we bump heads or something like that."

Brandon thought, *Oh, now I feel much better. I figured it was just a bucket to hold my brains in after the impact.*"

"That too," Nikki said with a wink.

They spent the next couple of hours going over the procedures for exiting the aircraft, the free fall itself, and the basics of flying the canopy with the toggles, the flare, and the landing. The experienced jumpers all landed right in front of the skydive shop, but the rookies and tandem jumpers landed in the middle of the field where there was much more room for error. Since it was an active airfield, jumpers also had to be sure to stay out of the way of other airplanes flying in the airport traffic pattern, taking off and landing. The dos and don'ts began to mount to a scary level, but Nikki assured Brandon that it would all come together.

When they finished the instruction phase, Nikki instructed Brandon to chill out while she put him on the manifest for a load. She assured Brandon that they would jump from the Skyvan first since that plane was the easiest to exit.

Brandon wandered around the classroom and looked at photos of various jump scenes while he waited. Before Nikki returned, the door burst open. Genie was wearing a very tight pink jumpsuit and was obviously excited. "How's it going stud?" she asked.

He said, "Great. I'm a nervous wreck."

She laughed and said, "You'll do great. I just finished my second jump today, and the sky is fine."

"You just jumped?" he asked.

"Yeah, you didn't think I would be sitting around waiting for you, did ya?"

"Well, you should have told me so I could be worried," he said.

"There's absolutely nothing to worry about." She gave him a hug and a kiss.

Nikki walked in and said, "Hey, none of that in the classroom, you two. We're on lift 12." She pointed to a small TV screen hanging from the ceiling, which displayed the next two lifts with jumper's names. Sure enough, Brandon's was on the second one.

"You have twenty-five minutes, so we best start suiting up," Nikki said.

"I'll see you outside." Genie slapped Brandon on the ass and trotted out the door.

Brandon donned a black and green jumpsuit with patches on the chest and shoulders. He felt like an Airborne Ranger as he climbed into the parachute after giving it the ten-point check to be sure everything was in place. The leg straps got pretty confining for his "boys," but Nikki assured him that tighter was definitely better. He ran the chest strap through the radio and snapped it tight. Then he put on the goggles and helmet, and Nikki checked him over to make sure there was nothing loose that would beat him to death during free fall.

They were set with fifteen minutes to spare, and Nikki led Brandon out to the practice area where they would go over the exit procedure. Genie and twenty other skydivers were standing around.

Nikki introduced Brandon to Vlady, a friendly Belgian dude who was even bigger than Brandon. He would be Brandon's backup in charge of the pulling of the handle for the chute if Brandon freaked out and couldn't do it himself.

Brandon would practice reaching backward with his right hand and touching his drone chute handle while bringing his left hand in toward his head in a salute in order equalize the reduced drag of his right arm reaching for the handle. He was told to do this three times and then look again at his altimeter and then back to each dive master for another thumbs-up. After this process was complete, he was told to just stabilize and enjoy the ride, looking at the altimeter every few seconds until he noticed that his altitude was nearing six thousand feet. At that point, he was to fixate on the altimeter until it hit 5,500 feet, wave off the guys with both hands, reach back, pull the drone chute handle, and toss it as far as he could.

The drag or drone chute would then unhook the main chute, which would pull the main chute from the pack and, hopefully, open it correctly. Then, he was told to count to three and await the jerk of the chute opening. After that happened, assuming he was still conscious, he was to look up and make sure the main chute had opened fully and properly—and then he was on his own to fly the canopy to a proper landing in the center of the airport. *Nothing to it. Right?* Brandon was as nervous as a whore at confession. His hands were clammy, his head was sweating, and his mouth was absolutely dry, but he tried to maintain a game face as he stood there with twenty other maniacs waiting for the Skyvan. Hell, several of them were woman, and he refused to be afraid. At least not noticeably so.

Moments later, his prayers for a disabled aircraft went unanswered, and a squat-looking twin-engine airplane that looked like a boxcar with wings taxied up to the loading area. The jump masters waved Brandon forward first. Since he would be the last to exit the plane, he was the first to enter. The whole rear of the craft was an exit door whose bottom lifted up to allow entry and exit from a standing position at the rear of the plane.

Brandon mounted up with helping hands and bent over for the walk to the front of the empty cargo plane. He sat with his back to the pilot's area, which had a bulkhead separating the skydivers from the two pilot's seats. The mission had only one pilot, Charlie, and he sat in the left seat waiting for the plane to load with both engines turning at high idle. Brandon sat with his two instructors by his side, and the other jumpers squeezed in similarly in three rows with their backs to the knees of the jumper behind them all the way to the exit ramp. They all snapped in seat belts to their harnesses, which were required until the plane reached an altitude of one thousand feet.

The door was lowered, and the plane moved off with an ever-increasing level of noise. As the plane became airborne, Brandon could see its shadow out of the starboard window. He flinched when all the jumpers yelled and raised their hands when the plane became airborne.

Nikki thankfully distracted him at that point by making him recite the order of tasks that he would be performing on his jump. Upon reaching one thousand feet, everyone undid their seat belts and removed their helmets and goggles. This was a welcome event for Brandon since his goggles were fogged and rapidly filling with sweat.

Upon reaching 10,500 feet, the pilot leveled off, and the rear door opened.

"What's going on?" Brandon yelled over the din of engine noise.

Nikki said, "The teams jump here for relative work practice. This is competition altitude."

Brandon was relieved; since he was going out at 13,500 feet, he had some time before his suicide attempt.

Genie was seated in front of him to his left, and she reached back and pinched him. He guessed it was to see if he was breathing. *Barely.* Brandon smiled weakly, wiped the sweat from his forehead, and winked at her—or at least he *thought* he did. He would have liked to have said something courageous, but at that moment, he realized that his teeth were stuck together. Just then, after the plane had leveled out, the engine noise quieted some.

A green light came on next to the cargo door, and the closest dude opened it up all the way. The noise level increased dramatically, a howling wind rushed into the opening, and the temperature in the plane immediately dropped by twenty degrees. The jumpers began leaving the plane in groups of four, each group accompanied by a man with a camera affixed to his helmet to record their work on video. Each exit caused Brandon heart palpitations he knew would leave permanent scarring.

One minute, they were all holding onto a bar just inside the door, and then someone nodded—and they were gone. After three teams left, there were only five of them left in the plane: Brandon, Genie, Nikki, Vlady, and the cameraman, Gus. The green jump light changed to red, and plane began to climb again. No one bothered shutting the cargo door. Brandon thought he was nervous before, but now he was really shitting bricks.

When they reached altitude, the plane leveled off again.

Nikki had Brandon stand up on wobbly legs, and she checked his rig again to make sure everything was in place.

Genie gave him the skydiver's good luck shake, which was a hand-to-hand swipe with a snap and a finger point, and then she winked.

Vlady bid him to turn and face the front of the plane. They would walk backward to the exit point in order to exit the plane facing forward. Brandon suspected this was also to keep him from looking down at the ground nearly three miles below through the gaping maw of the cargo door as much as it was to ensure a proper exit. He would have asked and confirmed this, but his lips were stuck to his teeth, which were still stuck to each other. If every orifice were this dry, at least he probably wouldn't piss or crap himself. What a comforting thought.

Unbeknown to Brandon, as he shuffled backward with Nikki holding firmly to his left side and Vlady to his right, Genie and Gus were hanging out of the rear of the plane on either side, waiting for him to get ready in order to give him room. He thought his mother would turn over in her grave if she saw this. They reached the back, and he saw the light turn green out of the corner of his eye. Brandon thought he was going to pass out, but he knew his manhood would not tolerate turning back now.

Nikki and Vlady gave him a thumbs-up, and then over the roar of the wind and the engines, he said, "Up!" while squatting down, then "Down!" while standing up, and before he knew it, and without consciously moving, he was flying through the air.

Brandon made himself arch, the rushing air cleared the fog from his goggles, and he began to relax. There was no sense of falling or dropping; he instantly felt like he was flying. He thought, *Holy shit, this is very cool!* He looked under his left arm and saw Nikki giving a thumbs-up and then under his right for the same from Vlady. He was surprisingly stable falling through the air, and he checked his altimeter and saw that it was moving, but he really had no idea what it said. He looked at the horizon, it was simply beautiful, and he looked down and saw the clouds below approaching. He remembered passing through some puffy clouds at around five thousand feet on the way up, and he marked this for future reference as a likely place to pull the handle. Then he did the practice reaches for the handle and found it on three attempts.

Nikki was somehow able to convey congratulations over the din of noise in his head. He had declined earplugs, and the wind rushing through his ears at terminal velocity made hearing anything else impossible.

Gus floated down in front with his camera mounted on top of his helmet, and Brandon couldn't resist screaming for the camera with his tongue extended like a wild man. The wind had apparently blown his lips apart. During the jump, he never saw Genie because her slight frame didn't allow her to fall as fast as the boys, but she was watching from above.

Nikki compensated for the weight difference by wearing a twenty-pound weight belt.

Vlady didn't have a problem keeping up, and the three of them fell as one. After what felt like five seconds, Brandon felt Nikki tugging on his left arm, and he pulled it in for another look at the altimeter. The big hand was spinning down and pointing generally at the six. This was his cue, so he waved his arms, reached back with his right hand, and yanked the chute handle. Nothing happened! As he received another quick jolt of panicked adrenaline, Vlady tore the handle from his fist and tossed it away. He had pulled it perfectly; he just forgot to toss it. Now he knew why first-time jumpers are closely supervised on the first go. The handle was attached to a small bag or drone chute that inflated and pulled the main chute out of the opened container. It opened quickly to say the least.

Just as Brandon chided himself for his stupidity, he endured the biggest jolt of his life as the chute blossomed, and he heard a loud grunt as he slowed almost instantly from 120 mph to about thirteen. It nearly took his breath away, and it suddenly got very quiet; the only sound he could hear was his screaming balls, which were being strangled by the harness between his legs. He looked up to see a full canopy, but the lines were twisted. He recognized the situation from the classroom discussion and reached up for the lines and twisted like a kid on a swing set who twists his seat around and around, and soon he was sitting under a properly opened canopy with straight lines and sore balls. He released both riser handles from their moorings and held onto them for dear life.

As he grabbed the risers and pulled them loose from the Velcro holding them as his radio chirped with a voice from below: "You're looking good, Brandon. Let's see you maneuver the canopy some—make some turns to get the feel." He didn't want to do anything to upset the perfect canopy, but he felt it was necessary, so he pulled on the left riser and began a nice gentle turn to the left. He looked about and could see the ocean and the Daytona Beach in front of him. He could even see runway 7 left in the distance, some fifteen miles away, upon which he had landed his plane hundreds of times. He pulled the right toggle, turned to the right, and saw the Deland airport looming four thousand feet below. It was incredibly beautiful and peaceful under the canopy. He could also see other canopies open below him and flying majestically. Once past the terrifying part, it really was a breathtaking and beautiful experience.

The voice said, "Now, practice a flare by gradually pulling all the way down on both risers."

He complied and felt himself being lifted, and it suddenly felt like he had stopped moving altogether. He quickly let the risers back up, and he got his first true feeling of falling as the chute dipped and began to fly again. He looked at his altimeter, and he was still more than three thousand feet up, so he relaxed and looked around, really beginning to enjoy the ride. His balls had crawled up inside somewhere, and were no longer crying out, so it was actually quite pleasant.

He spotted the triangular area that was his intended landing spot. The wind sock in the middle was surrounded by white dash marks that formed a circle around it to aid pilots in spotting it. He began to calculate a downwind leg for landing with fifteen hundred feet to go according to the instructions from his guardian below on the radio. He saw other chutes below from others in his load who were all landing over by the jump school. He also saw one chute heading in for a landing where he was headed, and he correctly surmised it was Nikki.

He turned for the base leg at five hundred feet or so and saw the jump plane landing on runway 5 in front of him. The plane was actually going to beat him to the ground although he never saw it after the exit until now. The windsock was hanging limp so he couldn't really be sure if he was landing into the wind as he turned to the right and began to track for it. A pickup truck was parked near it; two people standing next to it were looking up at him. As Brandon neared the ground, he remembered his instructions to look at the horizon and not directly at the ground.

The guy on the radio said, "Keep your legs out for landing," and he extended them as far as the very tight harness would let him. He was heading right for the circle around the windsock, and he pulled down both risers when he figured he was about ten feet off the ground. Unfortunately, the circular dashes around the windsock were concrete blocks, and with no wind to slow his flare, he landed right on one of the blocks with his right foot. His ankle turned under as he skidded to the ground on his butt. Brandon ignored the sharp pain in the ankle and leaped to his feet as his parachute collapsed to the ground.

He was in some pain—but much more overcome by great feeling of relief and the sheer excitement of having survived. In fact, Brandon already felt a growing itch inside, and perhaps a little devil sitting on his shoulder shouting like a kid fresh off his first roller-coaster ride saying, "Do it again, do it again!" He folded up his chute and carried it over to the truck.

Nikki and the radio guy congratulated him on his good fortune. Nikki said, "Great job, Brandon. I knew you could do it."

He was grinning from ear to ear and needed a beer in the worst way. He was still coursing with adrenaline, and he had a horrible case of dry mouth.

Ben, the truck driver, said, "That circle around the sock is only for guidance. It ain't a target."

Brandon nodded, but neither Ben's sarcasm nor his throbbing ankle could dampen his joy. The truck returned them to the jump school area, and Brandon returned his chute to the packing room. He went back to the classroom to debrief the jump, and Nikki and Vlady gave constructive criticism, which he took like a man.

Genie ran into the room and gave him a big kiss as he finished the debriefing. "Well, how was it?"

"It was scary as hell, but I think I actually liked it. However, I don't think my right ankle is going to allow me a repeat performance anytime soon." He explained how he had twisted it on landing.

Vlady, a paramedic, checked it out and pronounced it a minor sprain. "Nothing a beer couldn't cure."

Genie said, "Well, I think this calls for some suds then."

Brandon said, "Hear, hear!" He shook hands with Nikki and Vlady, gave them a twenty to buy themselves a beer at day's end, and limped out of the classroom to the bar for a beer or six. He thought of Omar's broken ankle, and he was glad his injury was not in the same league.

He had apparently passed a threshold with Genie. She was holding onto him tightly in a show of affection that she had heretofore not displayed. This bode well for his evening plans for the horizontal drill. Brandon felt he was definitely deserving of some TLC after his near-death experience.

As they were driving back to Daytona, Brandon's cell phone rang. "Yo."

Omar said, "Hey, man. I just got off the phone with Marcus Jones, and he wants to testify for me."

"You mean the pitcher for the Braves?"

"Yeah, he and I pitched together my freshman year. He's seen my stuff—and now he's in the show. He said I had definite Major League potential, and he wants to help!"

Brandon was impressed. Having a current pitcher from the Braves testify on Omar's behalf would certainly have jury appeal. "That's great. Where and when?"

"He's giving me their schedule and his cell number, and he said anytime they are in Atlanta, just call him up. He'll meet you in a conference room at the hotel or something."

"Okay," said Brandon. "I'll set it up tomorrow."

"Keep me posted," Omar said.

"You got it, champ. See ya." Brandon smiled as he put the phone back on its hook. *This will shake up old Bobby Knight,* he thought. His thoughts returned to the gorgeous woman by his side, and she seemed to love it when he talked about legal stuff.

CHAPTER 18

REHAB

Omar was back in Tampa. He was trying to rehab his shattered ankle, but he was finding himself more and more depressed. Wanda had apparently moved on in light of the fact that Omar no longer had professional ballplayer potential. Diandra was still his girl in Daytona, but after graduation, she had found a teaching job in Orlando. The distance was creating a rift in their relationship. Omar didn't really have anyone on the line in Tampa to play with of the female persuasion, and being out in the clubs on crutches had only garnered him the occasional one-night stand pity fuck, so with Wanda out of the picture, he decided to approach the idea of moving in with Diandra. He was crazy about her, and lord knew he needed help.

His mother was driving him crazy with her constant "mothering," and he felt he really needed to get away. Plus, in Orlando, he would be closer to Brandon and could help develop his case. He had to admit, for a white dude, Brandon was cool. He hoped he knew what he was doing because basically Brandon had his future in his hands at this point. He often toyed with the idea of trying for a really high-profile plaintiff's lawyer like Johnnie Cochran or F. Lee Bailey—or even the TV lawyers who were constantly filling the airwaves with "Have you been killed or injured in an auto accident? Call us!" In the end, he decided to stick it out with Brandon. They had become friends, and he trusted him.

He knew Brandon had his best interests at heart, and he was certainly familiar with the system in small-time Volusia County. They had discussed this very thing, in fact, and Brandon assured him that the high-profile lawyer from out of town was often at a disadvantage with the judges and treated like a bully by local juries. The other option had been to try filing the case in federal court in Orlando, but there were no federal questions of law at issue and no diversity of jurisdiction between parties from different states, so that wasn't really an option.

Omar called Diandra that evening and got her on the first ring. "How are you, baby?" he asked.

"I'm fine, stud. The real question is … how is your ankle?"

"Well, I ain't gonna be no track star, but it's coming along well enough."

"So, what's up?" she asked.

"Well, I was thinking about coming over to stay with you this weekend." Omar tested the waters.

"That's great, honey." She had just finished fixing up her new apartment, which was not far from her work in Winter Park, and Omar had not seen it yet. "How long can you stay?"

He decided to take the plunge. "I was sort of thinking that we could give a try at living together for a while, sort of a dry run for the future."

"Are you serious? That would be great! I could possibly get you a coaching job at the high school where I'm teaching. I'm sure they could use a good assistant football or baseball coach with your talents."

"Let's take it one step at a time, babe. I can still barely walk—and only for short periods of time without major pain." Truth be known, he had still not given up completely on making a comeback, unlikely though it was.

"Whatever you say, baby," she said. "When are you coming?"

"How about tomorrow?" said Omar.

"That's perfect. I get out at around three and can be home by three thirty. I'll leave the key under the mat, and you come when you can and make yourself at home. I'll send directions to your email."

"It's settled then," he said, "I'll see you tomorrow, and I promise you won't be sorry."

"Ciao, baby," she said. "I love you."

"Ditto," he said and hung up the phone. He had the chills in anticipation of living with this fine woman and felt truly blessed that she was still hot for him in spite of his disability and diminished prospects for a successful future. Sure, he had lots of girls around the state who had a thing for him, and he had always enjoyed playing the field, but with this life-changing injury, he felt like he needed help and stability more than anything else, but at only twenty-two, marriage still seemed a long way off.

That night, he said, "Ma, Dee and I are moving in together. She's going to get me through this mess."

This was greeted by complete silence.

"Say something, Ma."

"You know you are always going to be my baby, and I only want the best for you, but I was hoping you'd let me mother you a bit!"

"You can, Ma, but we won't be far from your house—and you can visit as often as you like."

She didn't seem impressed, but she went along.

The next day, he loaded his stuff into his car and made the trek up I-4 to his new digs. He was unsure how monogamy was going to pan out for him, especially since he knew Diandra would be all set to blow it into a full-on pre-engagement arrangement, but he felt it was high time to give it a shot. He wasn't committing just yet, and Diandra was a hottie who had always seemed to worship the ground he walked on. Who buys a pair of shoes without trying them on anyway?

Living in Orlando, with most of his friends in Tampa, would not be so bad. It was much closer than Tallahassee—and *way* closer than Chicago. He would also be close to his lawyer in Daytona, which would be handy when meetings and stuff became necessary. He was going to need a job soon since he had no visible means of support, and that was terrifying. Coaching was always something he thought he could be good at. With as much time as he spent playing sports, how hard could it be to coach it? He just was not quite ready to throw in the towel on his dreams. He dedicated himself to working harder at rehab than he had ever worked before. Being an athlete had always come easy to him, and while he trained some in the gym and did some running, most of his athletic prowess was God-given. He thought, *God giveth, and God taketh away—or better yet, man plans, and God laughs.*

Omar rolled into Orlando, and after some brief confusion, he was able to navigate his way to Diandra's apartment complex. Since she lived on the first floor, he wouldn't have to hump his shit up a bunch of steps on crutches. It was a bitch getting around on those things, and he couldn't wait until the day he could get around without assistance. Maybe he'd get him one of those cool canes with a skull on top and a chrome tip.

Diandra greeted him warmly at the door with a hug and a long kiss, and then she pulled him into the apartment. "Oh, you poor baby. You hand me those crutches and have a seat on the couch. I'll go out to the car and get your stuff."

He gladly obliged, and while doing so, he noticed the aroma of meat cooking in the kitchen. "I think I could get used to this," he said as he reclined on the couch and flicked on the TV, which was already set on ESPN.

Diandra returned to the apartment with his two large suitcases and set them by the door. "What the hell you got in those things, anyway, rocks?"

"No baby," he said. "It's just my stuff, you know. I didn't want to have to go all the way back to Tampa anytime soon."

"Let me get you a beer and some food. I made one of your favorites: Brunswick stew. I hope you like it." She scurried into the kitchen and soon reappeared with a tray on which was a steaming bowl of stew, several packages of saltine crackers, some Tabasco sauce, and an icy mug of beer. She set it on the coffee table in front of him and sat down on a chair.

He had found a baseball game on the TV, and all was well with the world.

"You relax tonight, stud, because tomorrow, I'm taking you to the school. We're gonna get you hooked up with a trainer and a regular schedule of physical therapy to get that ankle back into shape. If you think you're moving in here to get fat and be waited on hand and foot, you've got another thing coming."

Suddenly, his vision of paradise took on an ominous overtone. He smiled between bites and mumbled, "You got it, sugar britches. Now come here and give your daddy some sugar."

She snuggled up next to him and appeared to be watching the game, but he felt her checking him out from time to time with one eye.

CHAPTER 19

THE CASE BUILDS

On Monday morning, Brandon was interviewing a newly court-appointed criminal defendant at the jail. It seems that this genius had been a suspect for rape, but the police had not been able to obtain sufficient evidence for a search warrant, and he wasn't admitting anything. To make matters worse, the victim was unable to pick him out of a lineup due to his unremarkable features and the fact that the crime occurred in a very dark place. The cops were fairly certain they had their man, and they devised a brilliant strategy to collect a DNA sample to match with the sperm taken from the rape kit. They sent him a letter informing him that he had won a sweepstakes, and all he had to do was return the official-looking document in the enclosed self-addressed and stamped envelope to claim his prize. This he did, not being one to turn down easy money.

Unfortunately, he obliged the police by licking the envelope in order to seal it and voila! His DNA was matched to the semen left in the victim, and he was now wearing an orange jumpsuit—and was none too happy about it. Brandon had a tough time keeping a straight face during the interview, especially when the perpetrator mouthed his new favorite mantra: "Man, it just ain't fair. Who'd a thunk the damn Publisher's Clearinghouse would fuck me? If you can't trust them, who can you trust?"

"Life's a bitch," Brandon replied.

"It sure is that," said the client. "It's a fuckin' communist plot is what it is."

Brandon thought, *You just can't coach stupid.*

After concluding the interview and giving the dimwit instructions not to talk about his case to anyone in the lockup, Brandon left the branch jail and returned to his truck. He always took an especially long breath of fresh air when he left that place. His client would no doubt be entering a plea in his case as they had him dead to rights—and he had no alibi. His address would soon be changing from the branch jail to a state correctional facility operated by the Department of Corrections with shitty food and no air-conditioning.

Upon returning to the office, Brandon said hey to the staff, grabbed his phone messages, and dropped into his comfy leather chair to read his mail and catch up on returning his phone calls.

One of the first papers he dealt with was the motion for independent medical exam filed by Bob Knight, which asked the court to appoint Dr. Haas to examine his client on behalf of the college. No surprises there. He would agree to it, but he would also send along a court reporter to take down every word that was said and to record the amount of time the doctor actually spent with Omar. Invariably, doctors hired by the insurance companies hated this practice because it took away some of their intimidation factor, but the rules allowed it. All plaintiffs who placed their personal health at issue were required to submit to an exam paid for by the defense in order to make sure they weren't completely faking the injury. Most of the doctors who did that sort of thing would say the plaintiff was unhurt or exaggerating their claims—no matter how bad their injuries. That's what they were paid for, and Dr. Haas was notorious for it.

There was a phone message from his professional "high dollar" investigator, Joe Cline, who was working on digging up dirt on the college and tracking down witnesses. Unlike Mr. Lee, Joe actually had a professional investigator's license and could actually testify in court on matters he dug up. Joe reminded Brandon of Magnum PI without the rugged "Tom Selleck" good looks. He picked up the phone and called Joe on his cell. "It's me Joe, Whatcha got?"

"Hello to you too," Joe said. "And how are you today, Counselor?" Joe always busted Brandon's balls for his lack of phone manners.

"I'm fine, Mom," Brandon fired back. "Give me some good news for a change."

"I've got good news and bad news," Joe said. "The bad news is I'm having a hell of a time tracking down the alleged security guards who were supposed to be on duty the night of the attack. I don't know if the bastards are hiding them or if there is just normal turnover, but they are in the wind."

"What's the good news?" Brandon asked.

"That is the good news too," Joe replied.

"How do you figure?" asked Brandon.

"It's looking like of the eight guards who were supposed to be on campus that night, only two were working, and I could only locate the one with amnesia. Seems he can't remember where he was between ten and eleven that night".

"At first I thought he was stonewalling me on the advice of their attorney, but the more I pressed him, the more I believe he was somewhere he shouldn't have been and doesn't want to admit it for fear of being prosecuted."

"He was probably in one of the girls' dorms doing the nasty with a coed," said Brandon.

"Bingo," said Joe. "How'd you know"?

"That is good news," said Brandon ignoring the obvious question. "Let's set him for a deposition and see how he does under oath. I have a request to produce and interrogatories coming due any day now, which should tell us who the players are. It will be interesting to see if they provide any current names and addresses for these rabbits. You keep digging, and I'll be in touch."

"Yessa, master," Joe said good-naturedly as he hung up.

Interrogatories and requests to produce were the standard first steps in any civil litigation wherein the parties shared information and disclosed defenses, witnesses, and exhibits that were intended for use at trial. Any question or request that might lead to admissible evidence was fair game, and Brandon had sent quite the laundry list of questions and answers to Mr. Knight. Of course, the defense goes by the same rules, so Brandon had his paralegal working on a similar request and set of questions that they had received from the defense. After this exchange, the lawyers would be setting depositions in order to question the witnesses under oath and sending out subpoenas for records to nonparties who may have information germane to the case. The defense would be gathering up every medical record Omar had ever generated along with his school transcripts, arrest and driving records, athletic statistics, and tax records.

Being a plaintiff in a personal injury lawsuit opened one up to all manors of intrusion into one's personal life. That was the nature of the beast, and Brandon hoped that Omar had no skeletons in his closet that he had forgotten to tell him about. His day ended, and he completely forgot to tell Patty to set up the deposition of the ballplayer Omar had told him about on the car phone on Sunday afternoon. *Oh well, never do today what you can put off until tomorrow.*

He locked up the office, got in his truck, and headed to the grocery store for beer and bait in anticipation of a quiet evening of contemplation on the dock with Steve.

The following day, Brandon sauntered into the office after his morning run. It was already hotter than hell outside. Welcome to Daytona Beach.

Tyson handed him his mail and said, "Hello, good-looking."

"You are too cute for your own good, you know that?" he said.

"You don't know the half of it, big boy," she said.

He laughed and went back toward his office.

Patty was banging away on the computer and didn't even look up as he dropped the mail that didn't interest him on her desk. "What's up today, oh efficient one?" he asked.

She stopped her typing and pulled out his big red calendar. "You have a hearing at ten, two new clients after that before lunch, and then a bunch of criminal pretrials at one. Then, at two thirty, you have the Brown mediation over at Church's place."

"Another shitty day in paradise," he said as he headed into his office. The Brown mediation involved a hugely fat woman, Sheila Brown, who had sat in a chair at the Slenderella Slim shoe store. When it collapsed, it fractured her tailbone and knocked her back out of alignment. He couldn't imagine the effort it took for her chiropractor to try to sling that mess back into shape. She was pushing three hundred pounds easily at probably five feet two inches tall. She was as wide as she was tall and had a face that would leave one to believe she had some rhino blood in her line. She also had kids, and he shuddered at the thought of making that happen. A turkey baster was the only method he could come up with that was humanly palatable.

Brandon had time enough to prepare a mediation summary for the mediator before his ten o'clock hearing. He punched the intercom and said, "Patty, I need you to schedule the deposition of a ballplayer named Marcus Jones in Atlanta." He rattled off the potential dates and the name of the hotel where the players stayed while visiting. "Clear the potential dates with Mr. Wonderful, Bob Knight, first, or he'll raise hell."

"You got it, chief," she said.

He hung up the phone and cranked up his computer.

Brandon liked doing mediation summaries because he could use his initial demand letter for the main body and prepare it in minutes. In personal injury cases, he typically would send a demand letter to the insurance carrier after the client finished their medical treatment. The demand letter set out the facts of the case, his theory of liability on why it was the defendant's fault, and covered the damages such as past and projected medical bills, loss of wages, pain and suffering, inconvenience, and loss of the ability to enjoy life. He would attach any accident reports, photos of the scene or the client in a cast or their bruises or scars or whatever, along with the medical bills and reports documenting permanent impairment ratings, and wage loss documentation, if any, and then ask for money.

In larger cases that justified the expense, he might also include an economist's projection on loss of the ability to earn income in the future, a vocational rehab specialist's opinion regarding various options open to the plaintiff for retraining and reemployment, a day in the life video, and computerized accident reconstruction. Since the latter went for about ten grand a pop, only the six-figure cases warranted the expense because all dollars spent on preparation came out of the recovery after the attorney's fee percentage was deducted. He usually gave the insurance carrier thirty days thereafter to open settlement negotiations, and in about 60 percent of the time, the cases would settle without the need to file a lawsuit. The cases that didn't settle were usually the ones where there were problems with proving liability or causation or the plaintiff had stars in his or her eyes and felt they weren't being offered enough money.

In Brandon's experience, many insurance companies were used to dealing with TV lawyers who tried to avoid litigation, and they would settle their cases for a fraction of their worth in order to avoid the time and expense of filing suit. Often, the insurance carriers would test the case first, trying to steal a cheap settlement from a lawyer who was not a litigator. Unfortunately, most clients didn't know any better, and they went along with a low settlement obtained by their non-litigious or inexperienced attorneys. Whenever Brandon figured he was getting jerked around, he simply filed suit. He had to build a reputation as a lawyer who was not afraid to go to trial; otherwise, the carriers would never take him seriously. Unfortunately, that would require either trying a lot of dog cases or risking leaving some good money on the table to take some decent cases to trial in hopes of bigger verdicts.

Once a lawsuit was filed and the defendant was served with process, it was out of the hands of the insurance adjuster and into the hands of a defense attorney like Bob Knight. Some of them were okay guys or gals who were generally overworked, and when it came time to mediate the case before trial, they'd convince the adjuster to cough up a decent settlement. They didn't like to lose any more than Brandon did. Others, on the other hand, like Bob Knight, took it as a personal affront that any plaintiff's lawyer would have the balls to sue one of his clients, and it seemed to Brandon that he tried to teach each and every one of them a lesson by playing hardball. He knew it to be a fact of life that most trial lawyers had big egos and type A aggressive personalities. Given a big enough expense account, some of them loved a good fight. Unfortunately, for a solo practicing plaintiff's attorney like Brandon, they only got paid when they won, and the defense attorneys were paid by the hour—win or lose.

Bob Knight acted like every dollar sought was a dollar coming out of his children's college fund. Brandon never understood that mentality in defense attorneys since the money wasn't theirs, and they got paid by the hour, either way. Granted, it was a shitty hourly rate, but there was very little risk for them, and they all had ways to inflate their bills with extra hours and unit billing to overcome the paltry eighty or one hundred bucks an hour they were getting paid by the insurance carriers.

Fortunately, today's mediation was against one of the former defense guys, Brad Banks, a generally nice, cooperative guy, who was no problem to work with. Brandon felt lucky because he knew it would be a cold day in hell before a guy like Bob Knight would allow Slenderella's carrier to pay a dime to his rotund client with the fractured ass. He sent the summary over to the mediator, Mr. Church, in the fax, and then he went to court for his ten o'clock hearing, which the usual bullshit motion was "to dismiss" filed by a defense attorney stalling for time. Then he wanted to prepare Mrs. Brown for the two-thirty mediation. He had taken this case early on in his private practice when he was taking anything that walked or crawled into his office in order to build a practice, but he wasn't proud of it. He was looking forward to the day when he could be much more selective, but he always finished a task he started, and this case needed to be settled and finished soon.

After a quick Rasta chicken salad at his favorite eatery, the Ocean Deck, he went back to the office to meet Mrs. Brown. She waddled into his office wearing something brown that must have come from a tentmaker.

"How are you today, Mrs. Brown?" He offered her his hand.

She gave it a limp shake with a moist paw and began to tell him in her raspy voice about how her butt "be hurting something awful."

He commiserated with her for a while, and then he explained how the mediation would go and what to expect. He tried to lower her expectations by explaining the obvious problems with proving that the store had any knowledge that the chair she destroyed was unfit for normal customers. One thing in his favor was the fact that the store specialized in outfitting large-sized customers, and they certainly should have known that their chairs needed to be particularly sturdy. He had an expert lined up who would state that while the chair's width would accept an ass the size of hers, it was only designed to support someone under 250 pounds. He was concerned that he would not be able to make this claim with a straight face at mediation. He could always argue that if a 375-pound NFL lineman sat in it, his relatively small ass would certainly fit since most of the bulk was above the waist, but there would no doubt be a similar result. They would then be facing a very serious lost wage claim from a disabled NFL player!

It became obvious early on that Mrs. Brown's settlement interests centered around a new car she had in mind, which naturally bore no relation to the facts of the case. However, after considerable coaxing, Mrs. Brown agreed to follow his recommendations at mediation, and he gave her directions to the office where it was to be held.

Brandon threw on a coat and tie, grabbed his file, and headed out to a chorus of moos from the giggling girls in the office. Mediation went as expected, with Brandon extolling the virtues of Mrs. Brown and her case and her grievous injuries, followed by the defense attorney's presentation of all its obvious weaknesses. He made his usual outrageous demand and was led to a separate office to caucus.

Mr. Church was the consummate professional, and he took it upon himself to prepare Mrs. Brown for the worst in the hopes that something better would be forthcoming—and she would feel herself lucky when she chose to settle. He emphasized the weaknesses in her case and explained how she could end up owing money to the defense attorneys when it was all said and done.

Mediation went as expected, and after three hours of haggling back and forth—with Brandon on the phone squeezing the doctors to reduce their outstanding medical bills and the adjuster on the phone to his superiors explaining why he needed more money that had been reserved on the file—the case settled. Mrs. Brown got twenty thousand dollars, a third of which would go to Brandon for attorney's fees and costs, and another approximately one-third to her doctors for unpaid medical bills. Her share came to around $7,500 and was tax-free money that she dearly needed to set aside for a Weight Watchers' program, but more likely would use for the down payment on that new car. Brandon had seen plaintiffs use their settlement money for everything from breast implants to exotic vacations to hair-replacement procedures.

After thanking the defense representatives and Mr. Church and seeing Mrs. Brown off, Brandon returned to his quiet office to drop off the file and change into his after-work attire. The girls were gone for the day since it was after five, and he locked up and went next door for a much-deserved libation or three with the usual happy hour crowd. As expected, it was a meat market populated by all the usual suspects with the occasional group of tourists in the mix.

Brandon chatted up the bartenders as they were a good source of referrals, especially DUI clients. *Blessed is he who busts my client,* Brandon thought. He pulled out his Dictaphone and recorded a memo for Patty to remind her to set up Omar to come in and go over his answers to interrogatories with him. Brandon liked to handle this part of the case personally in order to make sure no stone was left unturned. He also knew that Omar was scheduled to be examined by the defense doctor tomorrow, and he couldn't wait to hear how that went. The rest of the evening was uneventful, and Brandon made it home at the wheel of his truck with no strange women in tow.

CHAPTER 20

THE DEFENSE BUILDS ITS CASE

The next day, Omar reported dutifully to the office of Dr. Haas in Deltona at 2:45. His appointment was for three o'clock. He was still walking with a cane and in considerable pain.

Finally, after reading every magazine in the waiting room and making small talk with gorgeous blonde court reporter sent to take down everything that was said during the exam, a very abrupt nurse came out and said, "Follow me." Without further ceremony, she walked back through the door into the clinic.

Omar held the door for the court reporter and her suitcase on wheels and limped in after her. The nurse showed him into an examination room that was going to be a stretch to hold all three of them. The nurse handed him a robe, told him to remove his pants, socks, and shoes, and left. Adjacent to the little room was a bathroom; Omar stepped inside to change while the court reporter set up her equipment.

When Omar came out, an older gentleman in a white coat was flirting with the reporter. The doctor had a stethoscope around his neck and pens in his pocket. As the reporter smiled politely at some joke he found to be terribly funny, the doctor said, "Oh, there you are. Come over here and sit down, young man. Let's get a look at you."

Omar noticed the blonde was taking down his every word with her stenograph machine. He hoped she'd gotten down the doctor's stupid joke as well. Omar sat on the table and tried to keep his backless gown from sliding off his ass. It was the only thing between his skin and the frozen exam table.

"I understand you have a small ankle problem," the doctor said.

"You could say that again," said Omar.

The doctor pulled up a small stool and began turning Omar's ruined foot over in his hand, bending it this way and that while Omar struggled to hold in his cries of pain. "Does this hurt?" the doc said as he twisted it inwardly.

"Yes!" Omar yelped. It felt like the doctor had inserted a hot knife into his foot and then twisted it nearly off.

The doctor grunted. After thirty seconds of critical viewing, the doctor said, "Well, it looks like Dr. Gaines did a really good job with this. Sonny, you should be nearly as good as new after a few more months of physical therapy."

"I beg your pardon?" said Omar. "You mean to tell me I'll be able to play ball again?"

"Oh, hell no, but you should be able to walk with almost no limp at all. Besides, baseball is a child's game." Dr. Haas winked at the reporter and walked out of the room.

Omar thought he heard the doctor say, "Cha-ching" as he went down the hall.

The court reporter looked at her watch and went back to typing for a few seconds. "Eighty-five seconds—that's longer than he usually takes."

"Is he always that compassionate?" Omar asked.

"I think he was Stalin's gravedigger in an earlier life."

"Why the heck did I have to get picked for him to examine my ankle?"

"Hmm. Tell Brandon I'll type this up and get it over to him later in the week." She checked out Omar's backside as he went to the bathroom to put his clothes back on.

"Will do," he said. When he came out, she was gone—and the office was apparently closed. He let himself out and limped to his car with his cane, all the while failing to notice the nondescript van on the other side of the parking, lot which contained a private investigator who was filming his every move. Brandon hadn't bothered to warn him about the standard defense tactic of surveilling plaintiffs after an CME because he knew there was nothing fake or exaggerated about Omar's injuries. Perhaps Bob Knight was expecting him to turn a few back handsprings as he left the doctor's office. Brandon would turn this invasion of his privacy against the defense when the time came.

Omar drove carefully back to Diandra's apartment because it was very difficult to drive with a right foot that had all the flexibility of a frozen turkey. Thank god no one ran out in front of him or made him take evasive action. He hadn't been cleared to drive yet by Dr. Gaines, but he had no other way to get to the CME with Diandra at work. Unfortunately, Brandon had warned him that defense attorneys loved to score points with the jury by exposing the injured plaintiff's unwillingness to follow doctor's orders. It couldn't be avoided today since he had no money for a cab and no credit card to call an Uber. He was getting tired of being constantly broke.

When he arrived safely at the apartment complex, it was getting dark. He limped up to the mailbox to check the mail before going in. The box contained a cardboard roll mailer addressed to him from his college. He opened it up under the dim light of the mailbox hut. Inside was his college diploma. He had missed graduation, but he hadn't really noticed while he was in the hospital. He smiled sadly and thought, *At least they can't take this away from me.* He hauled out the rest of the mail, mostly bills and solicitations, and limped up to the apartment.

Diandra wasn't home yet, so he sat on the couch in the dark and silently cried. He was not unhappy with how the living arrangements were going with Diandra. He still thought about a few other girls, but so far, he was happy with her. What he was not happy about was the pain and the agonizingly slow recovery, and he was feeling terribly sorry for himself. He did not notice the guys with the surveillance camera sitting in a van outside who had missed this emotional part of his evening.

How did it come to this? Just a few short months ago, I was a world-class athlete with pro scouts drooling all over me and girlfriends in seven cities. Now, I'm just another crippled black dude with no future. He wanted to kick somebody's ass, but even that would probably not go well. *Maybe*

I could make the Special Olympics wrestling team. Nah, I'm too old for that. He poured himself a tall glass of scotch and sipped it until he fell asleep on the couch with the TV blaring in the dark. He didn't hear her come home, but he felt it when Diandra draped a blanket over him after cleaning up the spilled drink on the carpet. He let her go to bed alone. He wasn't feeling like snuggling and hoped she wouldn't mind.

The next morning, Omar rode to school with Diandra. Apparently, she had caught on to his sullen mood, and she didn't even mention his having slept on the couch or the fact that he smelled like booze. Omar knew he needed something constructive to do, and he definitely was sick of sitting around. Dr. Gaines had given him some exercises to do with his ankle, and he could certainly work his upper thighs, torso, shoulders, and arms. His right calf was significantly atrophied from lack of use as was the rest of his formerly solid body.

Diandra's school had a fine weight room, and she had secured permission for him to use it. Part of the deal included his helping the athletes with their workouts a couple of days per week for no pay at first. It was a foot in the door to a possible paying job and a relief from the pit of depression and boredom he was slowly sinking into.

Diandra showed him where to change into his sweats and gave him a quick tour of the facility. It was nicer, newer, and better equipped than the one he had used in college. The gym had the usual basketball setup, with a locker room and showers adjacent to it. On the other side was the weight room with free weights, Nautilus machines, and other various apparatus. On the other side of that was an Olympic swimming pool with diving boards off one side of the L-shaped deep end. There was also a sizeable Jacuzzi and a steam room. Since it was only eight o'clock, he had the whole place to himself.

Diandra gave him a chaste kiss on the lips and pat on the ass and said, "Okay, stud, you get some exercise, but don't hurt yourself. I'll come get you for lunch."

"Okay, sweet cheeks." He tried his best to be cheerful as she trotted off to her class. His normal workout in his playing days was two hours. He wasn't sure how she expected him to kill four, but he had a book and was up for it.

Omar found an empty locker, took off his street clothes, and hung them up. He pulled on a jock for the first time since his last baseball game, a pair of sweatpants, and an old A&M T-shirt. Getting his socks and sneakers on was still a chore, and the right one would not lace up tightly as it was still very swollen. He decided to start from the bottom up, and he climbed onto a leg press machine that was used to work both the calves and the upper thigh. He used to be able to push this machine up all day long with the full 250 pounds of weight on it. He started with a mere fifty pounds, figuring he could move that with his left leg alone if he had to. The doctor had cleared him for light weight training, and it was taking all his concentration to keep it light yet forge some benefits from the process.

As soon as he placed both feet in on the platform, his right ankle sent shooting pains up through his leg. The pain brought tears to his eyes, and he quickly lifted his right leg off the platform. He managed to push the platform up with his left leg, but it wasn't as easy as he thought it would be. He was amazed at how weak he had become in such a short period. The right leg would support almost no weight, so he let the platform back down and slowly climbed out of the machine.

Omar decided to start at the top and work down. He spent the next two hours putting himself through a grueling workout on his shoulders, lats, chest, and arms. He finished the upper body workout with a low back routine and set of stomach exercises in various positions. By the time he finished, he was soaked in sweat, but he felt somewhat pumped up for the first time in months. He sank into the Jacuzzi and pondered just how sore he was going to be for the next couple of days.

He met Diandra for lunch in the spacious school cafeteria. Everyone knew her and seemed to take the opportunity to say hello to her as an excuse to check him out. The school was predominately white, and obviously rich, but that was cool with Omar since he had always gotten along with everyone.

After lunch, he limped his way back to the gym for the 1:15 weight training PE class. The lifting coach, John Douglas, was a huge dude, probably six three with arms nearly as big as his waist. He looked to be of mixed descent, a light-skinned black man like Omar, and probably in his early thirties. He wore gray sweatpants and a shirt with the school logo on it.

Omar shook his hand and introduced himself, "Hey, Coach, Omar Steele."

Coach Douglas wrapped his huge mitt around Omar's and said, "Good to meet you, son. I'm sure you can be of some use around here. From what your girl tells me, you are quite an athlete, and obviously no stranger to the weight room."

"I guess you could say, I was …"

"Hey, cut the crap, no whining in my weight room. You're gonna be fine if I have any say in the matter. First, let's teach these young miscreants how to pump some iron, and we'll deal with you later."

Omar didn't tell John he was already pretty spent from the morning session.

The boys were young—but eager to learn. Most of them had heard of Omar from the school rumor mill, and they were anxious to grill him about his nearly getting drafted to play real ball in the show. Now was just not the time.

After the afternoon classes cleared out, John said, "Let's take a look at that ankle."

Omar was not too sure about that idea. "Why?"

John said, "I used to play some ball myself, linebacker for the Pittsburgh Steelers, until these gave out." He then pulled up his sweatpants above his knees and showed several old scars on both sides of each of them. "I've blown out most of the ligaments in each knee at one time or another, and I am no stranger to rehab. Both of these will need total replacements before I'm forty, but for now, rehab is what keeps me walking. Now, hop on up here and let's get that shoe off."

Omar sat on the bench, pulled off his right shoe and sock, and slid his sweats up to his knee. His ankle was swollen and sporting some angry scars with earthworm-like keloid scar buildup across the sides and top of the foot which were typical for African Americans. Such scars were typical for African Americans.

Coach Douglas took the foot gently in both of his huge paws and began to massage the foot. He pulled it this way and that, always stopping before the pain became too much, and looked into Omar's eyes each time to see where the pain began. He felt Omar's calf muscle and compared it to the other one. "Did they have to fuse it?"

"Yeah, it was broken to shit, and there are still screws and pins in it too."

"Well, that's a shame," said John. "There isn't much we can do with the flexion or extension of that ankle, but we can work the foot and calf in other ways. I'm going to help you learn to walk differently, using different muscles, in order to do so with any degree of normalcy."

"Okay, Coach," said Omar as a tear slid down his cheek.

"Hey, shit happens, and we move on," John said. "Nobody plays ball forever."

"I know, but it's hard, man. I've been playing ball basically for nearly twenty years; it's all I ever wanted. So, when you get that close to your life's ambition—only to have it all taken away from you in an instant right before you had a chance to start—it's devastating."

"That it is, brother. That it is." John pulled Omar's pant legs down and helped him put his sock and shoe back on. "Let me show you a few easy exercises to do that should get you on the right track."

Omar followed John to the Nautilus section of the gym.

By the end of the day, he was spent. Diandra drove, and Omar tried not to fall asleep.

"Well, how was it today?" she asked.

"It was good—much better than watching game shows on TV all day—but I'm gonna be one sore puppy come tomorrow."

"Well, why don't we get us some Chinese takeout and go back to the apartment? I'll give you a massage, and we'll see what happens."

"That sounds good, baby." Omar would have loved to get laid, but he didn't know if he had the energy.

An hour later, he fell sound asleep in the middle of his massage. Diandra watched TV and ate Chinese food alone. He was already treating her like a wife, and she was not happy about it. Omar sensed this, but he didn't really know what to do about it. He'd always been all about me—and this humbling experience was exposing some of his flaws and weaknesses.

CHAPTER 21

SKYDIVING

Brandon was sipping coffee and reading through his stack of mail. He quickly came upon a notice of taking deposition from Bob Knight. The deposition of Omar was going to take place one week later at the court reporter's office in Daytona. It was scheduled for all day. Brandon groaned at the thought of sitting through an all-day grilling of his client by the ever-intimidating Mr. Knight. He would have to prepare Omar well for this one, and he buzzed Patty and scheduled Omar for a two-hour conference the day before. Then he phoned Omar's place and left him a message to call so he could be sure to clear the whole afternoon and next day for this ordeal.

On a paperwork-only day, he was dressed in khaki shorts, a golf shirt, and running shoes. He spent the day dictating deposition summaries, sorting through mail, and returning phone calls. He worked through lunch and then cut out early, leaving the girls to their tasks. He decided to head out to the drop zone to see if Genie was around. He hadn't heard from her in a couple of days, and he was beginning to feel lonesome—and a bit randy.

Arriving at the drop zone around four, he grabbed a Diet Coke and sat out on the outdoor patio. He saw Pedro, another instructor that he had met and partied with in recent weeks, and waved him over. "It's Brandon. How are you doing, Pedro?"

"Hey, Brandon," Pedro said as they shook hands. "I'm okay. What's up?"

"Not much. Have you seen Genie lately?"

"Yeah, as a matter of fact, she's up right now with nineteen of her closest friends doing a big way." He pointed to the sky.

Brandon looked up in the sky and squinted, but he couldn't see a thing.

"Hey, when are you going to jump again with us?"

Brandon had thought about finishing the accelerated free fall course, a total of six sections, which would then allow him to jump on his own with Genie. What he hadn't counted on, however, was doing it today, and he caught a quick rush of adrenaline just thinking about it. "I don't know."

"Why not now?" Pedro asked. "We've got plenty of light left to get you on a load before the end of the day—and I haven't got anything to do right now anyway."

"You really think we have time?"

"Sure, come on." Pedro grabbed Brandon by the sleeve and hauled him off the bench. "You go drop a blank check with the desk and tell them to put you on a forty-minute call. I'll meet you in the classroom."

Brandon did as he was told, and before he knew it, he was wearing that old green jumpsuit, and lying on the demonstration table as Pedro took him through the skills he would have to demonstrate in order to complete AFF level 2. Pedro took him through the safety procedures again and fitted him with a rig, helmet, and goggles.

On this jump, he would again be assisted by two instructors, and Pedro had grabbed Vlady to be his second. They would exit the plane as they did the first time, but the instructors would let go of him once he stabilized and fall next to him while he ran through a group of exercises that would demonstrate that he had situational and positional awareness. He had to check his altimeter periodically, wave off at the correct height, and pull his chute-release bungee. He would still be wearing a two way radio on his chest strap to talk to the guy on the ground guiding his canopy flight. When he was finally ready, his rig was properly fitted and checked. He exited the classroom with Pedro and Vlady and walked to the mockup of the plane to practice the exit. This time, he was much more excited than nervous.

As the other jumpers for this load started walking out, he noticed Genie wearing her outrageous pink jumpsuit with gold trim. It fit her like a glove, actually like body paint, and what a body it was. He couldn't stop staring at her.

She spotted him and ran over. "Brandon, you nut, what are you doing here?"

"What's it look like, sweet cheeks? I came out to observe, and while you were off risking your hide, Pedro shanghaied me—and here I am."

"This is just great!" She gave him a large kiss on the lips. "I'll shadow you on the way down and take pictures." She whipped out a portable camera from the pocket of her suit.

"Great!" Brandon said. "Now my terror will be documented for all the world to see."

She told him all about the group jump she had just completed, and he understood about half of what she described.

Twenty-two jumpers lined up on the tarmac as the twin-engine Otter jump plane swung into place next to them. Vlady rolled the steps over to the plane and motioned Brandon to enter first. The noise of the engines was deafening, and the prop wash nearly knocked him over as he crossed behind the spinning blade. The smell of kerosene jet fuel was nauseating as well. The cargo door on the side of the plane was open, and Brandon hauled his ample girth up the steps and into the fuselage.

The plane was empty except for brown seat belts attached to the floor at two-foot intervals on both sides. It was somewhat quieter inside, but not much. Brandon sat down with his back to the bulkhead, and Vlady sat next to him and showed him how to run the seat belt through his harness and snap it on. They would all wear their belts until the plane reached one thousand feet of altitude. Pedro sat down directly in front of Vlady, and the rest of the jumpers began settling in as well. Genie squeezed comfortably between his legs, and all was well with the world.

As soon as the last jumper climbed in, he kicked away the platform, pulled down the clear plastic cargo door, and sat with his back to the rear bulkhead. As soon as he sat, the plane surged forward. Brandon was used to taxiing a plane out to the runway, going through an engine run-up, and a series of preflight checks before beginning the takeoff roll. Not so this craft—as soon as they were rolling, the plane careened onto the runway and accelerated. The plane lifted off quickly and climbed out at a steep angle. The jumpers all hooted and clapped as they felt the plane leaving the ground, and Brandon watched his precious earth receding in the window next to his head. He had the same butterflies as the first time, but not so bad, and his mouth hadn't dried up, which was nice.

One thousand feet was reached quickly, and as if on some unseen signal, everyone disengaged their seat belts and took off their headgear. Brandon was wearing a soft leather helmet that was designed to soften any head butts which might occur in the air, but it would certainly not prevent him from becoming a dead duck in the unlikely event of a terminal velocity impact with the ground.

Genie was practically sitting in his lap, and under any other circumstances, he would have found her positioning to be very pleasant. The engine noise was so loud he had to yell to be heard, and small talk was out of the question. Everyone basically sat quietly with their thoughts during the ascent to 13,500 feet. Some, Brandon included, said a silent prayer. Others just seemed to be resting or taking in the views. At ten thousand feet, the folks nearer the exits began replacing their headgear and goggles, and then they helped each other stand up and get into position. Equipment checks were performed quickly. Someone farted and managed to pollute the entire aircraft with a smell that would have gagged a medical examiner, and everyone groaned or bitched and covered their faces or closed their helmet covers. Brandon made a face and tried to ignore it.

Brandon's palms were sweating, and his teeth were sticking together. As they neared the desired altitude, someone near the back opened the cargo door, and the temperature inside the plane dropped considerably but the air quality simultaneously improved. Brandon hadn't even noticed this phenomenon on his first jump. He was told that awareness was a very good thing in this sport, and he took comfort in the chill. Jumpers began checking each other's gear and exchanging the skydiver's shake, which he recalled as something like a rub across the palm, a bang of knuckles, a snap of the fingers, and a point to the person shaking with you. Brandon managed the ritual with everyone he could reach.

Genie turned and gave him a quick hug and kiss.

Brandon never closed his eyes because he noticed the red light near the door turn green at that moment, and people began to dive out of the plane into the slipstream. Exiting the Otter was a little different than the Skyvan where one basically just walked out the back end of the plane, which was opened like a garage door. The Otter had a cargo door in the port rear side, which was made of clear plexiglass with aluminum ribs that was easily slid open from the inside. A side exit required one seeking stability to exit sideways, facing the front of the plane, which allowed the jumper's forward motion to bleed off as one began to fall downward. It was hoped that he wouldn't tumble backward and assume the fetal position, so Vlady and Pedro kept a tight hold on him as he neared his turn at the door.

When Brandon's turn came, Pedro stepped completely out of the plane and held onto some unseen handle on the side of the fuselage with one hand while holding onto Brandon's left side with the other. Vlady held his right side and shouted the count: one … two … and with three, Brandon felt himself exiting the plane. He held a firm arch and faced forward while looking up and trying to spot the plane disappearing as he fell.

Fear was quickly replaced by exhilaration, and Brandon felt his body stabilize as he maintained a fully arched, spread-eagle position. He was quite comforted by the fact that Vlady and Pedro had a firm grip on him until they let go. While they were no longer holding him, they maintained very close contact an arm's length away, and he didn't waver from his stable position.

As instructed, Brandon experimented with moving his arms and legs to feel how this affected the flight of his body. Curling his legs in caused him to drop back, while straightening them out caused him to move forward. Simply twisting his hands allowed him to turn from side to side. Vlady made a circle motion and backed off a little, allowing Brandon to turn his hands and complete a 360-degree rotation.

Upon returning to his original position, he found himself looking into Genie's eyes as she fell right in front of him and snapped his photo with her helmet camera. It was very exciting, but a quick glance at his altimeter told him it was nearly time to pull the ball and open his chute.

Vlady and Pedro came close again, grabbed his sides, and signaled him to pull, which he did, and they quickly disappeared from view as he was yanked upward by the opening canopy. A perfectly open canopy is a beautiful sight indeed! He reached for his front risers and pulled his brakes loose from their Velcro holders. He spun to the right just in time to see Genie, Vlady, and Pedro's chutes opening below him.

The ride down was beautiful—and so was his landing in the large center of the grassy airfield between the runways near the waiting pickup truck. Genie and Pedro were already on the ground when he landed, and he could hear her yelling at him as he neared the ground. He executed a perfect flare by pulling the toggles all the way to his waist, and he landed on his feet as easy as stepping off the bottom step. The chute collapsed to the ground, and Brandon looked around with a stupid smile on his face. He was hooked; that was all there was to it.

Genie yelled, "Look at him. He's like a butterfly with sore feet!"

CHAPTER 22

THE ENEMY CAMP

Bob Knight sat at his conference table surrounded by young associates and paralegals. It was their weekly case meeting wherein case developments and strategies were discussed. He had his game face on as he called out the case names and enlisted the reports of his minions as they described how their efforts to dismantle each and every case on their dockets were progressing.

When Omar's case was reached, Knight looked to Kevin Doyle and Monica Easton for a report. "What have you got on this dude? From what I've seen so far, there is absolutely no liability on our client. Do you see any way this kid gets a verdict in this case, Kev?"

Kevin was a young associate lawyer two years out of law school, and Monica was his paralegal sidekick. Kevin was a typical white, yuppie preppie: a clean-cut Stetson graduate and fraternity boy who had not yet tried a case by himself, but he was brimming with cockiness.

"Well, Mr. Knight, discovery is in, and I've completed my preliminary research on the plaintiff, and the news isn't good."

"Go on," said Knight.

"He's a graduate of Florida Tech with a degree in physical education. He was a Black College All-American in both football and baseball for the past two years. He has no criminal record and no record of significant previous injuries. He's been in athletics all his life, and he has excelled at every sport he has participated in. He lettered in baseball, football, and track all four years of high school and set records there that may never be broken. As a college quarterback, he also set several records, including most total yard and most touchdowns by a QB. He runs a 4.3 forty and throws ninety-five-plus fastballs. His pitching record is quite excellent, and it looks like he was a shoo-in for the draft before this happened."

"Well, that don't mean shit," Knight said. "If I had a dollar for every college athlete who washed out of the pros, I could retire. Any attempt by this Michaels to prove loss of prospective income will be speculation and inadmissible—not to mention we should get a directed verdict on liability. What about actual damages?"

Kevin said, "It was a nasty injury, completely disrupted the ankle joint with comminuted fractures repaired through open surgical reduction and fused by insertion of semi-permanent rigid pins. He will no doubt have permanent loss of use and function, will likely have a permanent limp, and certainly will never run or play competitive sports again. His medical bills so far total over thirty K, and he had no health insurance, so the bills are all outstanding."

Knight scratched his chin and said, "So, the kid never worked a day in his life, may end up with a degree in physical education or some shit, and has now become another out-of-work black kid about six months before he otherwise would have. He probably won't even graduate now, which will make him a likely candidate for membership in the Future Drug Dealers of America club. And if he does graduate, his best bet will be teaching PE in some Podunk elementary school." Knight chuckled, and his remark drew nervous snickers from around the table. Bob Knight thought every plaintiff was a money-grubbing malingerer or an outright fraud. He'd never met one who deserved a dime from *his* insurance carriers. "What about Michaels, Monica?"

Monica was a paralegal who had been assigned to research Omar's lawyer to see if he would be a formidable or even competent opponent. She was an intelligent and strikingly good-looking Greek girl with olive skin, black hair, and black eyes. She was medium height with a tiny waist and breasts too large for her petite body. There was rampant speculation around the office as to whether she had augmented her assets, but no one as yet had been able to get close enough to render an educated opinion in spite of numerous attempts. Kevin had been trying to get her to go out with him for weeks with no luck.

"Brandon Michaels is a white male, seven years out of Florida State Law where he was an above average student, but no superstar by any means. He's never been married and lives alone in a small house on the river with his dog. He probably has a little family money since the neighborhood isn't cheap, and he flies and owns his own plane. He spent six years doing insurance defense with a medium-sized firm where he compiled a pretty good record defending relatively small cases. He's been out on his own doing plaintiff's work and criminal defense for a little over a year with no big verdicts to his credit. He has a reputation as player with the girls and likes to party. My guess is he will be shooting for a quick settlement in order to boost his cash flow. Frankly, I can't see this case going to trial."

"Sounds good. You'll see, we'll offer him ten grand, and he'll jump on it," Knight said. "Kevin, what are your thoughts on liability and coverage?"

"There's the kicker." Kevin smiled broadly. "Like you, I don't see any liability. The guy jumped out of a third-floor window of his own accord while trying to get away from a riot of some sort. He injured himself in the fall and is probably lucky he didn't kill himself. Michaels is claiming negligent security, but I just don't see it. We might get summary judgment on that issue."

"Coverage?" Knight asked.

"Ten million," said Kevin.

"Well, let's see to it that this young shyster doesn't get any of *my* goddamned ten million. Kevin, do the research for summary judgment and keep digging on this black kid. See if you can hack into his juvenile record. There's got to be some drug use or dirt somewhere."

"You got it chief," Kevin said.

"And, Monica, check with your sources and see if this Michaels has any buttons to push. He's single, you said?"

"Yes," she replied.

"Well, why don't you pay him a visit, undercover if you will. Use your feminine wiles and see what you can dig up—see if he has any skeletons in his closet. Who knows? Maybe he's a fag." Knight erupted in laughter.

The others joined in, but Monica wasn't smiling. When order was restored, they moved onto the next case and pushed Omar's aside.

Monica went to the gym after work as was her habit three nights per week. She didn't really like to go to the gym after work since it was always crowded, and she found herself constantly fending off advances from muscle heads who thought themselves pretty. Since she was not a morning person, this was her only realistic chance. As she cranked away on a stationary bike with her headset playing jazz music, she reflected on her day. She wasn't crazy about being given the assignment of spying on the plaintiff's lawyer in the Steele case, but she knew some girls working in other defense firms in Daytona and had made some inquiries.

The initial report was that Michaels was athletic and reasonably good-looking. One of her court reporter friends reported that he was smooth in front of juries and could charm a snake into buying shoulder pads. She laughed to herself, thinking that this reference probably came from his sharing snake DNA on some level. Being single herself, she was intrigued and decided to take a ride to Daytona soon and do some digging on her own. It was an assignment that did not sound altogether unappealing—albeit a bit demeaning to be assigned to do so. Plus, it would not be the first time she had been tasked to torpedo the case of one of her boss's opponents. She figured it came with the territory, and she wanted to keep her job.

CHAPTER 23

DEPOSITIONS

Brandon was sipping coffee at his desk on a Wednesday afternoon and reading the *Florida Law Weekly*, a weekly publication featuring all the appellate decisions handed down by the various district courts of appeal and the Florida Supreme Court in the past week. It was a tedious chore that he never seemed to have time to get through every week. He was lucky if he skimmed the cases that seemed likely to have something to do with the type of cases he handled.

Almost every week, he found something useful in the endless stream of legal mumbo jumbo, which he filed away in his ever-expanding research files for use when the occasion arose.

Patty buzzed him and said that Omar had arrived to prepare for his deposition.

"Send him in," Brandon said, relieved that he could put down the heavy reading for the day before it put him right to sleep. He had been burning the midnight oil with Genie of late as her juices seemed to have been stirred by his interest in skydiving. He had completed the AFF course the previous day, and the celebration at the drop zone had left him a bit fuzzy. Luckily for Omar, Brandon had participated in hundreds of depositions, and he could do it in his sleep, especially since he wouldn't be asking the questions.

Omar strolled in wearing a menagerie of athletic apparel and sat in the chair facing Brandon as Patty studied his rear end approvingly.

Brandon caught her red-handed and said, "That will be all, Patty, unless my star witness requires a beverage." He winked at Omar.

Omar said, "I'm okay, Patty. Thanks."

Patty reluctantly exited, closing the door behind her.

"Well, how goes it?" Brandon asked.

"Okay," Omar said. "The rehab is coming along slowly, but I've been helping out at the school where Diandra works, and the coaches have been real cool about it. They say I might be able to get an assistant's job after the docs release me."

"That's great," Brandon said. "But let's not reveal that little tidbit to the defense attorney tomorrow if we can help it. We wouldn't want to make things look too rosy until the time comes, you know what I mean?"

"I got you," Omar said.

"Let me tell you, first of all, this won't be nearly as stressful as you may think. A plaintiff's deposition is 90 percent background and 10 percent facts about the actual case. Knight will ask you where you have lived, worked, and played."

"Everywhere?"

"Yep. He will be especially interested in every doctor you have ever seen, who your friends are, and what kind of trouble you have been in. It is as much a test of your memory as anything else, and most of it won't make any sense at all. Basically, the rule is that any question that could possibly lead to admissible evidence is fair game. The only thing he really can't ask about is what you and I discuss."

"You need to remember to always let him finish his question, think about the answer before giving it, and then answer truthfully. If you don't understand a question, by all means, ask for clarification before answering. Do not guess or speculate unless you are asked to, especially when it comes to times, dates, and distances. If he cuts you off, wait until he finishes what he is saying, and ask if you can finish or explain your answer if you feel you need to. However, try not to help him to expand upon his question or volunteer information he didn't ask for. We don't need to make this any easier for him than necessary. Waiting for him to finish his question before answering allows you to be sure of its content, and it allows me to interpose an objection if I need to. Remember that

'I don't recall' is a perfectly good answer—as long as you don't say it so often you either sound like an idiot or are hiding something."

Omar shifted in his seat.

Brandon said, "Most of the time, I will object to the form of the question and instruct you to answer if you understood it. This may cause him to withdraw the question and rephrase it anyway. If I instruct you not to answer a question for any reason, then don't answer it. If he and I get into a legal argument, wait until we finish and there is another question posed before saying anything. If at any time you think of something that you feel you need to run by me before answering, ask to take a short bathroom break. I will follow you out, and we'll talk in the hall. If your leg starts to bother you, and you need to get up and stretch, say so and go ahead and do so. I want him to see your discomfort if you are feeling any. And no matter what he does, do not let him piss you off or lose your cool.

"Make no mistake about it, this is your chance to showcase your cause, so don't be modest and try to downplay what you've been through. It will be largely based upon this deposition that Knight will report back to his insurance carrier, and his report will form the basis for what they are ultimately willing to offer you to settle this case. I want you to focus on the pain and rehab you have been going through."

Omar then asked the most common question of all, which Brandon had been dreading. "What do you think my case is worth?"

"Well, that's the million-dollar question, isn't it?" Brandon said. "I'm not going to lie to you, Omar. This case is going to be difficult, primarily from the standpoint of liability. There is no doubt you sustained a terrible injury that is going to have a life-changing effect on you. Your career as an athlete has been ruined, and the potential damages in the form of loss of income could be huge. The real questionable part is quantifying and proving the loss of your earning potential.

"There is no doubt you were a talented athlete, but the problem comes with predicting with any certainty what you might have earned as a professional baseball player, and Knight will fight me tooth and nail if I try to introduce speculative salary predictions. I haven't really decided how I am going to handle that yet, so let's put that issue aside for a moment. What I can say from my experience is what your injury is worth on its own from an insurance company's perspective. I have run some jury verdict research on the injury itself to see what type of verdicts have been returned around Florida in the past in cases involving young males like yourself with similar injuries. If we discard the loss of income numbers, the average verdict for this type of injury is around a hundred and fifty thousand dollars. That's assuming clear liability, which we certainly don't have in this case."

"Man, that ain't shit for what I'm going through."

"I know, but the reality is that there is probably a 70 percent chance in this case that the jury will find no liability on the part of the college, and if they do that, you get squat—no matter how sorry they feel for you. Let's just see how the deposition goes, and we'll talk numbers later. I have some tricks up my sleeve on the liability question that may motivate them to be reasonable in this case if you impress Mr. Knight tomorrow."

Brandon spent the next two hours going over sample questions with Omar and working out the kinks in his style of responding. By the time they finished, it was after five. The office was quiet as a tomb.

Brandon and Omar went next door to the pub for a beer before Omar got in his car and headed home. Brandon decided to hang out with the locals and have one or three more beers to decompress.

It was shortly thereafter that a nicely packaged brunette walked into the pub and sat at the bar a couple of stools away from him. Brandon was engaged in conversation with one of his colleagues and didn't even notice her entrance. She was wearing jeans with a very revealing low-cut T-shirt. She dressed like any other well-tanned tourist with nice cleavage, and it wasn't long before Brandon took notice. Shortly thereafter, his friend excused himself, and Brandon sat alone contemplating going home at the bottom of this beer when he noticed that the attractive brunette was giving him the smiley eyes.

By then, his tie was loosened, and his sleeves were rolled up, but he still looked like a lawyer to some extent. He smiled back and told Walter, the bartender, to put another drink for her on his tab.

Shortly after, she got up with her fresh drink, which looked like a sea breeze or some other girly concoction and strolled over to him. She smiled sweetly. "Hi. Thanks for the drink."

"No sweat," Brandon said. "We locals try to be nice to the tourists on occasion."

"How did you know I was a tourist?"

Just a guess based upon your lovely tanned skin, and the fact that I haven't seen you around." He tried his best not to let his eyes wander south to her ample display case.

She held his gaze while sliding onto the stool next to him, sipping her drink at the same time.

"My name's Brandon," he said as he stuck out his hand.

She took it and gave him a firm handshake. "Monica," she said shyly.

"So, where are you from?"

"I'm a student at the University of Michigan—down for a little spring break."

"You're here alone?" he asked.

"No, I'm with friends, but they're back at the hotel chasing boys. I needed a little space."

Brandon thought she looked a little old for a college girl, but he liked what he saw. If he wasn't currently in something of a relationship, he might have put the full-court press on this babe. Instead, he was just being friendly.

"So, what do you do, Mr. Brandon the local?"

"Well, I drive fast cars, I play tennis, and I fondle woman, but I have weekends off, and I am my own boss."

"Cute," she said. "I remember that line from Arthur. No, for real what do you do for work?"

"I'm a lawyer who represents the downtrodden and injured of the world in constant combat with ruthless money-hoarding insurance companies."

"Are you any good?"

"I do okay."

"Well, we have something in common then because I'm studying to be a paralegal." She leaned closer, inviting a closer look at her spectacular cleavage.

"Really?" he said as he finished his beer and signaled the bartender for another.

Monica reached up and fingered the lapel of Brandon's shirt and licked her lips seductively. "Tell me about some your most interesting cases."

Brandon smiled and reminded himself again that he was not going to pick up this girl. He took her hand in his, gave it a friendly pat, and placed it in her lap.

She reached over, grabbed his left hand, and inspected it for a ring. "You're not married, are you?"

"No, nothing so dreadful, but I am in a relationship, so I'm not available for calisthenics this evening—and I'd really rather not talk shop during happy hour."

"Is that a rule?" she asked.

"No, more like a preference."

"So, you have a girlfriend?" she asked with a pout.

Genie walked up and said, "He sure does, toots. So, why don't you take your big phony tits and go hit on someone else?"

"Easy, tiger. I was just making nice with the visitors." Brandon climbed off his bar stool and took Genie's hand. "I was just leaving anyway. It was nice meeting you, Monica. Enjoy your stay in Daytona." He dropped a twenty on the bar and steered Genie away from the catfight that was about to erupt.

"Thanks. Maybe I'll see you around." Monica turned back to the bar just in time to miss seeing Genie shoot her a bird behind her back.

"I leave you alone for one hour, and you're hooking up with a double-breasted, split-tailed, mattress-thrashing bimbo?" she said with mock anger.

"Hey, I can't help it if beautiful women find me irresistible."

"Watch it, Buster—or your next free fall may be your last." She pinched his ass.

"What say we blow this popsicle stand and go back to my place for some relative work?"

"You're on." She sashayed out of the bar ahead of him, giving him an irresistible opportunity to watch her lower half in motion.

"Do you want fries with that shake?" he called to her back.

She ignored him as he tossed a wink at Monica on his way out the door. Back at his place, Genie gave him several reasons to forget the dark-skinned beauty from the pub—but not before he had a fleeting moment of wondering whether he had seen the last of Monica.

After Brandon left with Genie, Monica returned her attention to the bartender and began grilling him with questions about Brandon, acting all the while like she was a starstruck nymphomaniac. How old was he? How serious was he about that woman? How often did he come into the pub? Where did he live and work? How long had she known him? Was he rich or poor? Did he ever pick up girls in the pub? What type of clients did he represent? She went on and on.

Wayne's responses were designed to be vague, but he still unwittingly provided her with a wealth of information from which to inquire further.

What she learned made her more intrigued than she had been when she was first given the task. Since she had already told him she was only in Daytona for the week for spring break, so she knew she had to work fast. She left the pub and headed to the Daytona Beach Public Library, which was open until nine. She had two hours to research the archives of the local paper for references to Brandon or his work. She preferred reading the actual papers over doing it online, but she could get a start here and finish from home.

Monica was able to fill in considerable background on Brandon as well as dig up a few news articles about the Steele incident from the local paper. She was able to discover the names of several witnesses to the incident as well as the names of some of the investigating officers her team had been previously unaware of. Specifically, she learned the names of the persons who were chasing Omar, the house mother, and several of the girls in the dorm, including Carol Brown, the girl whose room Omar had leaped from. Monica left the library just prior to closing, feeling very good about her efforts and results. She drove back to Orlando and fell into her bed—alone and fairly exhausted.

The next day, Bob Knight showed up at Brandon's office with Kevin and an insurance adjuster in tow, carrying his trial bag, promptly at 9:30 according to Brandon's Rolex Submariner. Brandon happened to be sorting mail at the front desk and invited them to have a seat in the waiting room.

Omar had been going over last-minute details with Brandon since eight thirty. His arrival was noted by a sleepy Monica who had returned to Daytona at sunrise and had set up surveillance across the street before eight. Monica knew that the deposition would take at least three hours, so after noting the entrance times of both Brandon and Omar, she went to the county courthouse to snoop further and question court personnel. She would return to her post between eleven thirty and noon to film their exit from the building. It was not that anyone suspected that Omar's injuries were not real, but he could be exaggerating the effects to enhance his level of incapacity in the eyes of the jury. If that was the case, such as his limp only appeared when someone was watching, she'd film the acting, but that was not going to happen in this case, so she mostly just watched.

Patty ushered Knight and Kevin into the library and offered coffee and soft drinks. The court reporter, Lisl Mahoney, had already set up her steno machine. She was a tall, attractive blonde with a great body who Brandon had known for years. Kevin made small talk with her while Knight studied his notes. He was wearing a cheap gray suit with a red power tie and had obviously not shaved. A few moments later, Patty entered with drinks, and Brandon and Omar followed shortly thereafter.

The deposition began at nine forty-five, and true to Brandon's predictions, Knight asked hundreds of questions about Omar's life history without mentioning the accident for the first two hours. Kevin took notes, and Knight and the adjuster studied Omar during his responses. Brandon took notes and, as usual, had little to say.

They broke for lunch at eleven forty-five, and Brandon took Omar to the pub for lunch.

Knight, Stan the insurance man, and Kevin met with Monica to compare notes over a quick lunch at a nearby Burger King. Knight sat down with his lunch and asked, "So, what do you think so far, Kevin?"

Kevin replied, "Well you certainly are being thorough with his background. This Steele kid has a very good memory and is very articulate."

"He's also fairly hot," Monica added.

Knight gave her a dirty look and said, "Meaning what?"

"Well, I'm just saying, he will certainly draw sympathy from female jurors, especially young ones."

"Don't worry, kitten. This case will never see a jury. By the time I'm through, they'll settle for ten grand and be happy about it."

Monica briefed Knight and Kevin with the results of her research. It filled in a lot of gaps in Knight's plan of attack when the causation questioning began after lunch.

The deposition resumed after lunch, and before long, Knight began his inquiry into the events of that fateful night. Omar's memories of the day of the incident were burned into his brain like a tattoo, and he could tell the story over and over with little variation. Knight was particularly interested in how much everyone had been drinking. Omar could only be certain about himself, and his total consumption was less than one beer as the first fight took place shortly after his arrival at the party.

Knight did not believe this, and he pressed Omar aggressively with questions. "Do you really expect me to believe that a young college kid like yourself goes to a frat party with a keg overflowing and only has one beer?"

Omar remained composed. "I can only tell you what happened, sir. You are going to believe whatever you want to believe, I suppose."

Knight didn't like that answer and kept harping on the issue until Brandon had to begin objecting that the questions had been asked, and answered, and the witness was being badgered. If it got really ugly, Brandon would have terminated the deposition and brought it to a judge to rule on whether or not the questioning was proper, but Knight backed off before reaching that level.

When Knight finally moved on to the stabbing incident, Omar was somewhat relieved since the tension in the room had been mounting. After Omar related the scenario up to the point in which Ronnie had been stabbed and the gang left the scene, Knight again bored in with questions: "Why weren't you stabbed as well? Why did the gang just drive away? Do you expect me to believe that no one saw this going on?"

The questions invited Omar to speculate as to what was in the minds of others, and he knew not to do that—and Brandon objected to every one of them. As hard as Knight tried, Omar would not allow himself to be baited. As instructed, he answered, "You'll have to ask them." Brandon was hoping Knight would ask the sixty-four-thousand-dollar question: "Why didn't you call 911?" The lack of personnel in the security booth was the key to Brandon's theory of liability. Knight skipped right from the stabbing to what happened at the sorority house. He was clearly frustrated with the lack of progress.

Omar testified that he vaguely recalled being dragged into the house and that his head was killing him. He remembered someone trying to get in the front door and suddenly being consumed with dread and the fear of imminent death should they be successful. He testified to remembering running, but not to where exactly, and he remembered a window, but not the act of jumping out of it. The next thing he could recall was waking up in the hospital in a great deal of pain and screaming for a nurse to call his agent to tell him he was okay, and then passing out again after someone injected him with something very warm and told him that he was seriously injured. Omar became very emotional and could not stop himself from crying.

Brandon suggested they take a break, and everyone agreed. Not that he didn't love seeing his client's outpouring of emotion, he did, but enough was enough. Brandon escorted Omar back into his office and got him a tissue and some water. "You're doing great, Omar. Just tell it like it is, and we won't have any problems."

"I'm sorry, Brandon," he said. "I just can't help getting upset when I think about my whole life going down the drain over this mess."

"Well, my friend, that is a big part of this. I want them to feel your pain—so just let it out when we get back in there. There's no shame in getting upset ... anyone would."

"All right," Omar said, and he composed himself for the final push.

When the deposition resumed, Knight shifted gears to the aftermath of the accident: what doctors had he seen, what instructions were given, did he follow them, did he try to rehab, what alternative careers had he researched, did he have plans to play ball, to teach, to get married, yada, yada.

By the time the deposition was finished, it was nearly five o'clock. Omar was wiped out, and Diandra showed up to drive him back to Orlando. He sat silently in the passenger seat with tears leaking from his eyes the whole way home.

Most of the ride was passed in an uncomfortable silence. During the hour-long ride, Diandra tried to engage him in conversation about other cars on the road, future plans, and rehab schedules, but he remained sullen and unresponsive. This attitude was getting old, and he know that she wouldn't put up with it forever. However, he just couldn't seem to pull himself from the funk and give a shit about anything.

After Knight, the adjuster, and his acolyte had departed, Brandon took advantage of an unbiased witness by grilling Lisl about her impressions of Omar. Court reporters were a good source of feedback if you could get them to talk to you, and Brandon and Lisl went way back. She was happy to oblige. "Well, first of all, Knight is an asshole."

Brandon laughed and said, "That's only his deposition face. I understand he's like a bee to honey in front of juries."

"Well, I would suggest you make this trial last several days to give the jury time to see his true colors. After that display, I wouldn't throw him a rope if he was drowning in poop."

Brandon recalled his days as a defense attorney when he had a senior partner with a nasty streak. The associates called him "Three-Day Jay" behind his back because everyone knew that if the case lasted more than three days, the jury would begin to dislike both him and his antics—and the plaintiff's chances for a good verdict improved dramatically. Brandon tucked this word of wisdom away for later use.

"I thought your client was very believable, very cute, and he certainly has gone through hell over this."

"Well, I sure hope the jury sees it your way," Brandon said. "I appreciate you being here today, Lisl. I always value your opinion."

"Thanks for the work, and keep those cards and letters coming." She winked at him, picked up her machine case, and headed for the door.

Brandon opened the door for her and saw her out.

Up the street, in Knight's car, Mr. Knight was prepping Monica for another run at Brandon. "He's sure to head next door for a beer after that day, and this is the perfect opportunity to get him to open up about this case. Ask him what he did today and get him talking."

"Sure, boss. I know the drill." She got out of his car and climbed into hers. As Knight pulled away, Monica removed her business attire and bra, and she donned a thin pink tank top, which left little to the imagination, and a short, tight black skirt, applied some very red lipstick, and pulled on her flip-flops. She figured it was the perfect spring breaker wardrobe, certain to incite the prurient interests of Mr. Michaels.

When she walked into the pub, Brandon was already halfway through his first Heineken, and he was shooting the breeze with Walt. She plopped down in the stool next to him and said, "Hey, you're Brandon, right?"

"Why, yes, fair maiden," Brandon replied. "What was your name again?" He remembered her name, but he didn't want her to think he'd given it a second thought.

"How soon we forget. It's Monica. Thank you very much."

"Sorry," he said, "You know what they say: the mind is the second thing to go."

"I wouldn't know," she replied with a pout.

"Let me make it up to you, Monica, and buy you a drink."

"Okay," she said, and her smile brightened considerably.

"Walt here makes a mean Long Island iced tea."

Monica had never had one, and she said, "Why not?"

Walt smiled, winked at Brandon, and turned away to attend to the mixing.

155

With his back to Monica, so she couldn't see what he was doing, Walt selected a tall glass and poured in full shots of tequila, vodka, gin, rum, and triple sec, and then he added a splash of Collins mix and topped it off with a splash of coke. By the time he shook it up and placed it in front of her, it looked just like a glass of iced tea—only it was 80 percent alcohol.

Monica took a sip and exclaimed, "Wow, that's really good."

"Nothing but the best for you, my dear," Brandon said. "So, what have you been doing with yourself on this fine vacation day?"

Monica took a large sip of her drink and turned to face Brandon. In the process, she squared her shoulders and let her skirt slip up higher on her shapely thighs. It was cold in the bar, and her nipples were erect and straining at the thin material of her pink top.

Brandon tried to maintain eye contact, and she was obviously loving every minute of his discomfort. Fortunately, she had a habit of looking away when she was thinking, and he had ample opportunity to enjoy the view undetected—or so he thought. Monica rattled on about a perfectly boring day at the beach, and Brandon noticed that she wasn't sunburned. In fact, she had zero tan lines, and he figured that she was either one of the few intelligent girls who used the proper amount of sunscreen, a long-sleeved shirt and hat at all times while at the beach, or a full-body tan that was the product of a tanning booth somewhere where it snowed at this time of year.

She quickly turned the conversation around and asked, "So, what did you do all day—free monstrous prisoners from the jail and sue little old ladies for their Social Security money?"

"Nothing so exciting," Brandon replied. "I spent all day sitting in on my client's deposition in a personal injury case … nothing that would interest you."

"Really?" She took a sip of her drink. "I love that stuff. What's the case about?"

Brandon knew that the report of the incident was public knowledge, having been in the paper at the time, but he was still not comfortable discussing specifics with a stranger this close to trial. However, she did seem interested, and he almost never passed up an opportunity to entertain young ladies, especially ones as perky as this one. Also, it was sometimes strategically helpful to elicit the opinions of laymen about the merits of a difficult case.

"Briefly, it's about a young man who was badly hurt at a local college when he was attacked by a gang. We're suing the college for lack of security. The injury cost him his career as a professional ballplayer."

"Wow! That sounds like it could be huge." She sucked her drink dry and licked the straw seductively.

Brandon signaled Walt for another round. He could drink beer all night with little effect, but he was interested to see how Monica would hold up after a couple of Walt's famous Long Island iced teas.

"So, did the gang beat him to a pulp right on campus?" she asked.

"Well, not exactly. Actually, they knocked him over the head with a pipe, and he was pulled to safety by the girls in the dorm where it happened. The real bad injury came later when he jumped out of a window on the third floor while trying to get away from the gang."

"Wait a minute," she said. "He hurt himself, you say?"

"Well, yeah," Brandon said defensively. "He was scared out of his mind at the time—and was not thinking clearly as a result of the concussion he got from the pipe."

"Well, how on earth is that the college's fault?"

Brandon was getting uncomfortable; she had gone straight to the crux of his case's weakness. Who exactly was this college girl? Brandon dearly hoped that the jury would not come to precisely the same conclusion. And certainly not so quickly! His bullshit meter was starting to ping. She was asking too many pointed questions, and he was getting suspicious.

After another drink and more boring stuff about the case, it was time to deflect this kid and change the subject when she asked for about the fifth time how it was the college's fault.

"Well, silly, if they had placed several security guards under the window with a trampoline, this never would have happened."

For some reason, this theory suddenly seemed explosively funny to Monica, and she erupted into peals of laughter. She leaned into Brandon as she convulsed hysterically, holding on to his shoulders and pressing her chest into his. He was both irritated with her amusement at his dilemma and terribly aroused by the contact. Fortunately, while crying, she also drooled all over his shirt, and when she finally straightened up and attempted to recover her composure, she looked very dizzy. She looked at his shirt and slurred, "Oops. I made a mess." She tried to dab his shirt with a wet napkin, which only succeeded in making matters worse.

"It's okay," he said. "Don't worry about it." He took her hands and placed them back in her lap.

Her makeup was running, and she lurched off the seat and headed for the ladies room.

As she stumbled away, Brandon noticed that her third iced tea was almost empty. He figured escape was the better part of valor, so he paid the tab, left Walt enough money and instructions to call her an Uber or a cab and left the pub before she returned. All the way home there was a battle between the angel on one shoulder congratulating him for leaving her there, and the devil on the other shoulder shouting, "You had her, you asshole. You should have taken her to Pittsburgh. Slap on the knee pads, baby!"

Brandon could have taken his time since it took Monica twenty minutes to clean herself up after hurling the contents of her stomach into the toilet. She looked into the mirror and barely recognized the hazy reflection she saw. "Some sexy spy you turned out to be." She tried in vain to fix her makeup, left the bar without speaking to Walt again, and drove to a 7-11 for a huge cup of coffee. She sat in her car and drank her coffee. She had forgotten to eat today, and the alcohol had gone straight to her head. Her plan was to get him talking about the case and then try to shake his confidence, all the while setting him up for a small settlement. Unfortunately, the plan had backfired, and now she had only herself to blame as she slowly and carefully navigated her way back to Orlando without catching a DUI.

The next morning, at the attorney's meeting, Knight would want a full report on this conversation, but unfortunately, Monica could remember very little of the content. She made up most of her report and tried to avoid looking at Mr. Knight through her bloodshot eyes. For the rest of the day, she stayed in her office doing paperwork through her hangover. Several times, she vowed to herself never to drink again. It wasn't the first time she had made this vow—nor would it be the last. The last time was a tequila bash after a football game ten years ago, and to this day, she could still not drink the stuff. She briefly wondered if there was tequila in her drink last night. The bottom line was glaringly apparent: her attempt to get Brandon to divulge anything helpful to the defense had failed miserably. She forced herself to report to Mr. Knight that Brandon was a decent lawyer and a decent guy with no apparent weaknesses that they could exploit. Knight didn't like that report one bit, and now had a decision to make on whether or not to have her assist at trial and blow her cover, or keep her away from the trial all together. Decision made, he turned to her, "Monica" I'm going to keep you here this week. If Brandon sees you both your cover and reputation will be blown, and reputation is like virginity, you can only lose it once." She acted disappointed, "But Boss? She Pleaded" He shushed her and left the room. Secretly, she was relieved.

CHAPTER 24

MARCUS

Several days later, Brandon boarded a Delta flight for Atlanta. Omar's old playing partner, Marcus Jones, was in town for a game with the Braves, and Brandon had scheduled a meeting with him followed by his videotaped deposition. Brandon knew that it would be very difficult to bring Marcus to the trial, and the rules of procedure allowed for videotaped depositions to be introduced as evidence whenever the witness was either an expert or lived more than one hundred miles from the jurisdiction.

After an uneventful flight, he took a cab to the Marriott Marquis downtown where the team was staying. He was an outfielder with the Expos and had graduated from college two years ahead of Omar, making it quickly through the farm system to the Major Leagues. Marcus was also from Tampa and had known Omar since high school.

Brandon found the conference room he had rented a few minutes early and had a chance to go over his notes. He had brought several newspaper articles featuring sporting events from both Marcus and Omar's past, which he planned to use to assist Marcus in his recollection of some of the more significant events.

Marcus walked in shortly after one o'clock in a jersey, jeans, running shoes, and an Expos hat as Brandon had requested. Marcus was very dark, stood five feet seven inches tall, and was built like a sprinter: lean and muscular, soft hands, and a ready smile. Brandon liked him immediately.

Brandon stood and extended his hand. "How are you, Marcus? It's a pleasure to meet you."

Marcus shook his hand firmly and said, "Nice to meet you too. How's Omar doing?"

"Have a seat," Brandon said. "He's doing as well as can be expected under the circumstances, I guess. Have you seen him since his injury?"

"No, I don't get back to Tampa very often these days. I'm kind of busy, you know? But I saw him at Christmas at his folks' place. I did speak to him on the phone when we were setting this thing up, and he seemed to be pretty depressed over all this."

"Yeah," Brandon said. "He's been through a lot of pain and disappointment, and it will probably get worse before it gets better."

They spoke briefly about how Marcus's season was going and the team in general before Brandon brought out the newspaper clippings and began going over some of his history with Omar. While they spoke, the videographer came in and began setting up. The court reporter arrived shortly thereafter, but Brandon barely noticed. He wasn't a huge baseball fan, but it was very interesting to interview a big leaguer about whatever he wanted. As it turned out, there were three guys from Omar's circle of friends besides Marcus who had made it to the big leagues, and they often got together over the holidays in Tampa to hang out and shoot the shit. Invariably, the conversation got around to who was making what in the way of money, and Brandon was very interested in the particulars.

It was incredible how much money athletes were being paid these days, and the numbers were increasing rapidly. The average annual salary of a Major League ballplayer was over half a million dollars, and the really good ones were making ten times that. Their preparation hour passed very quickly, and at precisely two o'clock, Kevin walked in wearing his best suit and carrying a leather briefcase.

Brandon and Marcus had taken their seats at the conference table, and the videographer was fitting microphones to their lapels. Brandon stood, shook hands with Kevin, and introduced him to Marcus. He could tell that Kevin was somewhat starstruck by the encounter, and he was surprised that Knight had chosen not to come himself. "Where's your fearless leader?" Brandon asked.

"Oh, he doesn't usually make it to depositions of before and after witnesses. Besides, he's in trial this week in Orlando."

"Lucky for you," Brandon said.

"Shall we get started? I know Marcus needs to head over to the stadium for batting practice."

"By all means," Kevin said as he took his seat.

Marcus sat at one end of the table with the video aimed at him from the other end. Brandon sat on his left, beside the court reporter, and Kevin sat across from him. The court reporter administered the oath, and Brandon began the deposition by explaining that it was a deposition to be used at trial in lieu of live testimony of Marcus so he wouldn't have to travel for the trial. He covered Marcus's early sports career with an emphasis on encounters with Omar on the field. Marcus was able to effectively establish Omar as one of the best athletes he knew. As a football player, Omar was all-state as a quarterback in high school and was also very good at the college level. He probably could have made it to the NFL had he so desired. He also ran track as a sprinter, but his real talent was baseball. Omar had a ninety-five-mile-per-hour fastball and was very accurate. He was a good hitter and was very fast on the bases. Marcus had no doubt that he was Major League material, an opinion he gave over Kevin's strenuous objection that it was pure speculation. Brandon added several questions dealing with Marcus's experience evaluating talent in his career in order to defeat the speculation objection at trial. Kevin got tired of preserving his objections as the questioning continued, and Brandon felt sure he had qualified Marcus to give an expert opinion regarding Omar's chances of making it in the big leagues.

Brandon turned the questioning to occasions when Marcus had seen or spoken to Omar since the accident. He described their meeting at Christmas when Marcus and the other ballplayers had met at a park to play hoops. Omar was there with his crutches and was unable to play. Marcus got a little teary-eyed talking about seeing Omar on the sideline cheering everyone on and trying to remain stoic about his inability to participate with his friends. He knew that he was one bad slide or hit-by-pitch injury away from being in Omar's shoes. He spoke of Omar showing them his swollen and bruised ankle and how depressed the whole thing made him. He said Omar was especially distressed about the lack of mobility the fused ankle provided and the difficulty he experienced just walking due to the pain. They had gone to a restaurant for lunch, and the players talked about their contracts and what they were buying with their newfound wealth: expensive cars and watches, houses for their parents, clothes, trips, bling, you name it.

After establishing the fact that salaries were a large part of these discussions in Omar's presence, Brandon got into specifics about what players such as Marcus and his friends were making. Kevin objected every time money was discussed. "I object. Salaries are inadmissible as speculative and prejudicial to the defense."

You're damn right it's prejudicial, Brandon thought. After the objections were recorded, he said, "You may answer, Marcus." And he did. The numbers were spectacular.

After Brandon had gotten what he wanted on the video, he rested. Kevin did a brief cross-examination that focused on the fact that Marcus had no knowledge of what Omar could have made specifically—and the fact that there were no guarantees in sports. He established the fact that hundreds of players—in fact, by far the majority—languished year after year in the minor leagues, never making it to the show. The deposition ended after an hour, and Brandon got the feeling that Kevin would be leaving the hotel feeling very good about his case.

That night, Brandon enjoyed his box seat at the game that Marcus had hooked him up with at will call. Marcus went three for four that night, and the Expos whipped the Braves 7–1. Brandon felt secure that he had hit a home run in his case. After the game, Brandon hopped a cab to the airport and took the eleven o'clock flight back to Daytona.

The next day, Brandon called Omar and reported his good feelings after having taken the deposition of Marcus. They discussed pretrial strategy and the need to file an official demand. Omar wanted to ask for a million, but Brandon told him that would not be constructive. It was better to make an offer that would be acceptable if accepted—but one that would be in the ballpark to exceed if trial was successful. Brandon had a feeling that Knight would not be making any tempting offers no matter what in any event, and he would be right.

Over the course of the next several weeks, Brandon's investigators finished digging up the arrest and police calls to the college for the months prior to this incident and finished taking statements of the witnesses that could be found. Brandon completed his pretrial disclosures and prepared the case for pretrial conference. He filed an official demand in the case with Omar's reluctant permission in the amount of $150,000. This was done in official form in a proposal for settlement wherein the event the jury returned a verdict more than 25 percent larger than this amount, the plaintiff would be entitled to add his fees and costs to the verdict instead of paying them from the verdict amount. The defense was allowed the same strategy in the form of an offer of judgment, and Mr. Knight responded with an offer of one hundred dollars, which meant he was confident of obtaining a defense verdict. The battle lines were drawn, and a settlement was obviously out of the question. The pressure on Brandon was ratcheted up a few notches because a defense verdict would mean that Omar would walk away owing money to the defense for its attorney's fees and costs. That, on top of all his unpaid medical bills, would be a nightmare.

A few days later, at the pretrial conference, the judge looked over each party's submissions and saw that everything was in order. He inquired as to the possibility of settlement. Hearing silence from the lawyers, he inquired as to how many days the trial would take, and Brandon and Knight agreed upon one week. Discovery cutoff dates were set, jury challenges were agreed upon, and timing for all motions in limine and other pretrial motions to be heard was set. With that, a trial date was assigned, and Brandon and Knight cordially bid each other good day and went their separate ways. Now it was up to six Walmart shoppers who had driver's licenses but were without the good sense to get out of jury duty.

Brandon was becoming increasingly stressed about this trial. Liability was going to be a stretch, and it was all going to come down to how sincere and believable Omar was on the stand—and whether or not Brandon could get in some licks against the college, enough to make the jury want to punish them for letting him get bonked on the head by a mob on campus. Then, if by the grace of God, he got by that hurdle, he then had to convince them that the injury sustained by Omar when he jumped from a third-floor window was also the college's fault. Then, stretching beyond unbelievable, he had to get them to give him a sum of money that was not just a reflection of his medical bills and the pain of a broken ankle; they had to give him something for the loss of a career as a Major League pitcher! Well, at least he had the argument that he had lost his ability to enjoy pain-free walking and running for the rest of his life; for the rest, he would have to pull a rabbit out of the hat.

Back at the office, Brandon answered some phone calls and shuffled papers. One of them was a new criminal case. A frantic mother called about her little boy; twenty-year-old Paco had a thing for young girls, always consensual, she claimed. Unfortunately, he was fooling around with a fifteen-year-old wild child, and her parents took issue and had him arrested. Unfortunately for Paco, it was a second offense, and he was still on probation from the first one.

Brandon always said, "You can't coach stupid when the little brain is driving the train." This kid was looking at ten years, and the mom was not happy about it. More work to be done.

Brandon decided that he needed to blow off a bit of steam, and he recalled Genie had invited him to join her for a yoga class. *What the heck? How hard can that be for an ex-jock?* He gave her a call and made plans to meet her at six o'clock that evening at her yoga studio. It was a small nondescript joint in a little plaza that held the usual Realtor, chiropractor, and nail salon. In Florida, there are several time-honored truths. First, everyone is required to have a real estate license; second, there are more chiropractors in Daytona than there are taxis because there is a school for them here, and third; if you are a Vietnamese refugee, you must own a nail salon in Daytona Beach. Brandon wasn't sure why this was; he just knew it was.

So, when he pulled his truck into the shopping plaza and saw the sign for "Bikram," he knew he was there. She had told him to come dressed in a Speedo and sandals—with or without a shirt—and to bring a large towel. Fat chance on the Speedo! Upon arrival in his surf baggies, he found a few very fit-looking women standing around and chatting.

The girl working the front desk took his money pleasantly, rented him a mat and a towel, and sold him a bottle of water. He wasn't sure why he needed one, but when in Rome.

Genie popped in, gave him a hug, and started gushing about how glad she was that he had come. She looked good enough to eat: trim in her pink short shorts, tube top, and blonde hair tied up in a ribbon. "You are so gonna love this. I'm not kidding. It's, like, the best workout ever!"

"Right," said Brandon, "If I get a workout, I'll be happy."

"Oh, darlin, you *so* will!" she said.

A couple of the other ladies giggled.

Whatever, he thought. He felt silly standing there in his old gym shorts and an FSU T-shirt. He was the only guy in the place, which he did not necessarily view as a bad thing.

Genie led him into the room, and the first thing he noticed was that it was dark and hotter than Hades. He wanted to ask her what was up with the heat, but she immediately shushed him and said, "No talking." When she invited him, she mentioned something about hot yoga, but it failed to register in his brain until now.

She led him to the right side of the room, which had no furnishings, just three lines on the carpet and mirrors on the front wall and a little square podium in the middle. She unrolled his mat, put his towel on top of it, and did the same for herself. She lay on her back on her mat and told him with her eyes to do the same.

He was already sweating, and he grabbed his water bottle.

She slapped his hand and whispered, "No drinking until after the first warm-ups!"

He decided to follow the rules and pretended to meditate like everyone else, but in reality, his mind was racing through plans for escape. His mind was formulating the perfect plan when the lights came on like Wrigley Field and a voice boomed, "Good afternoon, everyone." Brandon recovered from the sudden blindness in time to see everyone standing up, putting their toes on the lines, and standing up straight. Brandon couldn't see through the sweat in his eyes, and breathing was not coming easily, but he managed to stand somewhat at attention like everyone else while the desk clerk/instructor explained how to perform the first breathing exercise.

It was hard to hear instructions with sweat filling his ears. After two poses, Brandon was ready to call 911 and report either a fire or a flood; he wasn't sure which, perhaps both. Throughout the workout, Genie was mercifully supportive, although there was only so much she could do to assist him in his misery.

The instructor kept telling them to breathe normally, which meant calmly and through the nose.

Fuck this, he thought. He was panting and drooling and leaking from every pore, and his shoulders were much too broad to allow his arms to cross at the elbow. Instead, he just grabbed his upper arms and held on. He would have laughed, but he couldn't breathe. The best he could manage was bending a bit at the waist and leaning in the general direction of his foot, which he managed to lift about a foot off the ground. He stole a glance at Genie, and she was standing on one leg with the other straight out in front, foot in hand, and head balanced on her knee, perfectly still. It wasn't fair. Two sets of that nearly dropped him. In all, the class lasted just under ninety minutes.

At the end, there was a breathing exercise that left Brandon so dizzy that he nearly checked out. mercilessly, after that it was over. They were told to spend between two and five minutes relaxing in the room after class in the flat-on-your-back position, but Brandon feared he might actually melt for real, and he crawled out after only a minute. He made it outside to the cool concrete in front of the studio. Girls exiting class had to step over him to egress the building.

Genie finally came out and dragged him up to his feet. "Well, how'd ya like it?"

He looked at her and contemplated a response that would neither emasculate him nor leave him unable to ever again access her goodies. "It was interesting," he said, and he meant it.

Later that afternoon, Brandon went back to his office feeling like Gumby with all the moisture sucked from his body. He couldn't get enough to drink. But after drinking several bottles of water, he started feeling really good. *Maybe there's something to this yoga stuff.* He had a couple of appointments that he couldn't cancel just because he felt like lying on the couch and becoming jelly.

Wes Brickman, an old family friend, was in for a divorce consultation. Brandon didn't specialize in divorces, but he would do them if it meant just divvying up the stuff and not fighting over the kids. How many times had people come to him with "uncontested divorces," which usually meant they both wanted it—and they were going to fight tooth and nail over every asset, dog, and toaster. Those he had no use for. Brandon had watched his parents go through it when he was nine, and he wouldn't wish the process on any kid.

"So, what can I do you for?" Brandon asked.

Wes was a forlorn middle-aged dude with a large belly, unkempt clothes, and a defeated look. His dirty brown hairline was receding at the same pace his beltline was gaining, and he had a sad look in his watery eyes. "Brandon, ol' buddy, me and Eileen are splittin' the baby."

"Oh, man," Brandon said. "I'm so sorry to hear that. I thought you guys were doing fine."

"Well, so did I, but I guess we were kidding ourselves—and she finally called me on it."

"Is there someone else?" Brandon asked with raised eyebrows. He wouldn't doubt it if Wes said Eileen had someone since she was still quite a looker, but he'd crap if the cheater turned out to be Wes. His shopping days were over: been there, done that, got the T-shirt.

"I don't think so," Wes said. "It's just like we ran our course. We've been together twenty years, the kids are all gone, and now we want to be friends and spend what time we've got left chasing new horizons while we're still young enough to do so."

"That's good work if you can afford it," said Brandon. He had always wondered how it would be to be married to the same woman forever. *How do you keep it interesting? How do you keep it fresh?* He didn't know— and obviously neither did Wes—but things were looking good for Genie so far.

"What brought all this on?" asked Brandon.

"Well, if you really want to know, I can explain it because I have given this situation lots of thought. You see, I've been noticing for quite some time our passion level has been going downhill. It's been a gradual but steady decline. It's something we guys notice. As best I can tell, most women are romantics and want life to mimic a chick flick with everyone always in love and smashing their faces with passionate kisses.

"When that kissing and hugging slows down, they seem to lose interest in the sex part. My theory is that it's inevitable, because with guys, they do all that passionate stuff when they're trying to get laid, but once they are getting it regular, they slack off on that other stuff. I don't know which came first, the chicken or the egg, but in this case, when one slows down, the other does the same. Eventually the train's stopped—and everybody's getting off!"

"So, what you're telling me, Wes, is that your train is at the station, and the engineer's trying to decide which track to take from here?"

"That's about the size of it."

"Have you tried counseling?" Brandon asked.

"No, I don't need some headshrinker telling me why my marriage failed, or even worse, giving that woman a chance to tell me how she feels cheated!"

"Well, is everything functioning? Are you sure it's not something medical, like low testosterone or estrogen?"

"No, my plumbing works just fine," Wes replied. "It just isn't getting enough work to keep it interested."

"I guess there may be something to that Mars and Venus stuff," Brandon said. He gave Wes a dissolution questionnaire to fill out while he surfed the web, all the while wondering if he and Genie would ever get tired of making love with one another. He certainly hoped not.

CHAPTER 25

TRIAL DAY ONE

Several months later, the case went to trial. In the interim, Omar and Diandra had gotten married in a small ceremony in the hospital chapel, during Omar's rehab. With his doctors and nurses as witnesses, they had committed their lives to one another. She had been a rock for him throughout the rehabilitation process, and now she was with Omar as they met Brandon at the courthouse on City Island.

Brandon exited his truck with his lucky leather trial bag, which looked more like a small suitcase, and it was bulging with files and law books. He gave Diandra a hug and said, "My dear, you look lovely as always."

Diandra was wearing a professional-looking tan pantsuit, a white shirt, and a pearl necklace. She smiled and hugged him back.

Brandon turned to Omar, and the two men exchanged a quick manly hug. Brandon stood back, held Omar by the shoulders, and appraised his outfit. Omar was sporting a nice navy blue two-piece suit with an open-collared dress shirt, and no tie. He looked very cool and athletic—until he tried to walk. His limp was still a pronounced wobble, probably always would be, and Omar didn't give it much thought anymore. Brandon whistled and said, "You look perfect, dude: sharp but not better than me. We don't want the jury to get confused about which one of us is the lawyer here!"

Omar laughed and said, "You look pretty good yourself. If I didn't know any better, I'd think you were a professional."

"Come on, you two," Brandon said. "Let's get in there and get the first pick of trial tables." As they approached the courthouse entrance, they spotted Bob Knight pulling boxes, law books, and files from the trunk of a large black Mercedes. His minions scurried around and gathered up his stuff like ants surrounding their queen. Brandon recognized Kevin Doyle as one of them, but the other two didn't look familiar from a distance.

His partner, Jim, was waiting by the front door of the courthouse, holding it open like a Wall Street butler. "Come in, gents. Welcome to my world."

Brandon nodded thanks, and he and Omar entered the lobby and prepared for the security ordeal.

Jim was going to assist with jury selection and anything else Brandon needed in order to get the case heard. Brandon would question prospective jurors, but if he gave proper attention to the person he was questioning, he couldn't watch the reactions of the other jurors, and those reactions were sometimes more telling than the answers themselves. Jim would keep an eye on them while Omar sat respectfully, quietly taking notes if anything important occurred to him and scanning the jury for telling looks or the stink eye from someone who just didn't like his vibe.

After clearing the metal detectors, Brandon, Omar, and Jim took the elevator to the third floor, which was where the circuit court courtrooms were housed. They entered courtroom 10, the westernmost courtroom on the third floor, through double doors. It was a recently renovated courtroom, with church pew-style seating made from blond oak in the rear for the audience seating, two four-by-eight oak counsel tables, and a black bench for the judge, which was flanked by a witness corral on one side and a clerk's bench in the front. The judge's bench was made of black Formica and had the seal of the state of Florida on the front.

The room was nicely appointed with earthy colors like burnt orange seat cloth, ochre carpeting, and dark brown soundproofing on the walls. Next to the jury box was the door to the jury deliberation room, and behind the bench was a concealed escape hatch for the judge to enter and exit from his chambers.

Lisa was setting up her stenography machine at the clerk's table, and John the bailiff was standing next to her, flirting as usual. Lisa was a stunning blonde court reporter who Brandon had known for years. Her legs went on for months, and she had a world-class chest.

He headed for the table on the right that was closest to the jury box and began laying out his files. Brandon liked to keep things in order and had each witness folder in the order he planned to call them. Each folder contained a copy of the witness's deposition, where it had been taken, or if not, a recorded statement from his investigator, or at the very least, notes from a conversation between Brandon and the witness. His theory was that the only witnesses you needed to depose with a court reporter and the other lawyer present were those you couldn't speak to through other means to find out what they were going to say, those who might disappear before trial, or those who were likely to change their story between the time of the statement or deposition and the trial. An old trial lawyer adage was to "never ask a question whose answer you don't already know." Brandon generally stuck by that, but he thought that "men plan, God laughs" was a more appropriate adage for trials.

As he was unloading his gear, Knight and Kevin dragged in enough stuff to fill a library. Knight scowled at Brandon when he saw that the choice table was already taken, and he dragged his stuff to the table on the left nearer the judge. Both sides would still have a clear view of everything that went on, so choice of table was not that big a deal to him.

Bob looked over at Brandon and said, "Sure you don't want to pocket ten grand to drop this turd and save everyone the trouble?"

Omar looked like he was going to reply, but Brandon gave him a nod, smiled, and said, "I think we'll take our chances."

"Fat chance is what it is," Knight muttered.

A few weeks before they held a mediation or settlement conference, and Brandon had sought to settle the case for what he felt was a very reasonable $150,000, but Knight's best offer was $10,000, which would barely cover the costs incurred—and would not even touch Omar's outstanding medical bills, future medical bills, loss of income, and prospective future losses of the ability to earn, albeit somewhat speculative truth be known.

Kevin was helping his boss get set up when the bailiff announced, "All rise. The circuit court in and for Volusia County, Florida, is now in session, the Honorable Fred Stamper presiding, please be seated." Brandon had tried a case before Judge Stamper and found him to be even-tempered and fair. He was in his fifties, and he looked as anyone would imagine a judge should look: big shoulders, white hair and beard, and a booming voice. He was a former "silk stocking" civil trial lawyer from a big firm who understood how trials worked, and he ran his courtroom like a general. Everyone sat down, and the judge took his seat as well.

"Good morning, everyone. Today, we are hearing the case of *Omar Steele v. Martin Luther College*. Mr. Michaels, is the plaintiff ready to proceed?"

Brandon stood and said, "We are, Your Honor." He sat back down.

"Defense, Mr. Knight, are you ready as well?"

"Yes, Your Honor."

"Then, Mr. Bailiff, when you are ready, you may fill the first fourteen seats of the jury box."

The rules provide for a state court trial in the civil division to seat six jurors and one alternate. (Twelve are required for criminal cases in which the death penalty is in play). Long-duration cases sometimes used multiple alternates, but this case was not of that ilk and would take less than a week.

Each side would be allowed to question the prospective jurors individually and strike from the panel anyone who had cause to be unable to render a fair verdict because some prejudice or preconceived notion infected their mind, they knew the lawyers or the parties personally, had personal knowledge about the case or the parties, or had some really good reason why it would be a hardship to attend. The lawyers would each have three strikes or peremptory challenges for any reason whatsoever—as long as it wasn't some impermissible bias such as attempting to exclude all members of the plaintiff's race.

In many cases, there would be no strikes for cause, and if each side struck three of the fourteen, then there would be eight left—and the jury could be empaneled on the first round of jurors. Folks who had jury duty for the week had to sit in a boring jury room until called, and sometimes they would have to be a prospective juror on several cases that first day before being released if no one picked them to serve. Once chosen, they were bound to see the case through to the end—even if the trial took months. They were paid a whopping fifteen bucks per day. For retired folks, it was like attending live TV, like *Judge Judy*, lots of drama added to their otherwise mundane existence, but for folks with families and jobs, it was not so great.

Judge Stamper liked to get the general questions out of the way for each juror: name, where do you live, work, what is your education, are you married, do you have kids, a job, have your ever been arrested, have you ever served on a jury in the past, and any reason why you can't hear this case. He then handed it over to the lawyers to get more in detail.

Brandon, as the plaintiff's lawyer, would go first at this and every other stage of the case. He made his way to the podium after the judge went through the prelims. This panel was a normal Florida jury panel: lots of older folks, mostly white, and mostly born up North. This was definitely not going to be a jury of Omar's peers. Brandon worked his way down each row of prospective jurors; his style was similar to standing in a bar and getting to know everyone. He didn't have a particular person in mind for the jury; he just wanted to avoid seating anyone who was defense-oriented or had reason to side with the college on this case, like someone who worked in the insurance industry and would be skeptical of any claim, or someone owning a business subject to this type of negligent security suit who would relate with the defense. Also, anyone with family members associated with the police or security services were to be avoided since negligent security was the theory of liability. Also, anyone who didn't like black folks was an obvious no-no, but Brandon knew that no one would admit to that.

Prejudice was very subtle and hard to identify, but it still existed. The liberal media had poisoned the well to some extent by publishing fantastic stories of greedy people cheating the system by tricking juries into large verdicts for BS claims, like the famous lady who spilled her own hot coffee in her crotch and reportedly got millions from McDonalds. What the rags didn't report was that the woman's verdict actually got reversed on appeal, and she ultimately got the goose egg that she deserved. He mostly just tried to make nice with the jurors, build up a rapport so they would trust him and like him and his client, and ultimately do them right by their verdict. He tried to root out bias with questions they could relate to: "Mr. Brown, I like my BBQ dry rubbed and salty, as opposed to wet and sweet, so if you asked me to judge some ribs, and one was a Memphis-style dry rub and the other was covered in sweet tomato-based sauce, well, that Memphis-rubbed rib would have a leg up before it even got to my mouth, and try as I might to be fair and objective, that wet rib would already have a strike against it. Bottom line, all things being equal, I'd probably vote for the dry one even if the other one was just as tender and cooked to perfection. That is what I want to know here. In a personal injury case such as this, where we are seeking money damages, some folks may already have a slight bias or feeling against these kinds of cases. So, if you were to assign your feelings a number value, let's say from one to five, with one being I have no problem whatsoever with this kind of case and five being I can't stand this type of thing, what value would you assign to a personal injury case like this?"

Mr. Brown would hopefully then answer honestly with a number, and if his number was higher than one or two, he would be admitting bias against the case, and Brandon would strike him for cause. The difficulty came when prospective jurors who actually wanted to be on the jury hid their prejudices in order to stay in the case, and those were the hardest to ferret out.

Knight, on the other hand, would slip them each a check if he thought he could get away with it in order to win. After Brandon finished questioning, Knight jumped right into his questions: "Mr. Brown, what do you think of people who ask others for money? What is your opinion about people who get into fights and blame others for their problems?"

Brandon objected to improper questions several times, and the judge sustained him. He usually didn't like to object too much during the other lawyer's presentation, but sometimes it was called for when the other guy was being a dick—and the jury needed to be made aware of it.

Jury selection took well over two hours, but they finally had an acceptable six jurors and one alternate to sit and hear the case: two men and five women, all white, all middle-class, and all wishing they had been clever enough to think of something that would have gotten them out of jury duty. Omar and Jim had been helpful in eliminating a couple of questionable characters, and Omar was generally happy with the group they had left.

Once the jury was empaneled, the judge announced it was time for the lunch break. He admonished the jurors not to discuss the case over lunch, instructed the attorneys and witnesses not to discuss the case in the hall if jurors were present, and told everyone to return for opening statements at one thirty.

Brandon, Omar, and Jim went back to the office for sandwiches and drinks in the conference room.

Omar said, "I have to say, I like the jury. No one seems to be giving me negative vibes, and the ladies were smiling at me on more than one occasion."

"I agree," said Brandon. "They seemed attentive and not at all anti-plaintiff, but you never know. They can smile into your face while driving a knife into your back, and you will never know what hit you." Brandon gave the office girls the play-by-play on the jury selection, and Omar chowed down on some Subway. Brandon never ate much during jury trials; the nerves and adrenaline seemed to fuel him plenty.

After lunch, the jury was again empaneled, and the judge gave the opening instructions regarding burden of proof and giving both sides a fair opportunity to present the case before deciding, yada yada, and then handed it over to the lawyers to give their opening statements.

Mr. Knight promptly stood and said, "Your Honor, I would like to invoke the rule." He was referring to the rule that required all persons who might testify be excluded from the courtroom until they have testified so that their testimony would not be affected by the evidence as it was presented. This required Diandra, who would be a witness, to wait outside the courtroom until her turn. Brandon had expected this, and she was prepared with a book to read while she sat in the hall.

A favorite tactic of some lawyers during opening statements was to humbly tell the jury that their opening remarks were not evidence but merely a road map of what they were going to prove during the trial.

Brandon, on the other hand, wanted the jurors to believe what he said as if it were gospel, and he never made such self-effacing remarks. After going through the basics of introduction, he said, "Ladies and Gentleman, I am going to show you why the college was negligent, why on the night before graduation, a night that everyone would be keyed up and partying, where families and friends would swell the local population, and where alcohol mixed with celebration and excitement, and sometimes, drugs, had the potential to cause problems, and they knew it or by God they should have. As a result, your common sense will tell you that graduation night was a night in which security should have been heightened— doubled or tripled—and instead it had been almost nonexistent, and that as a direct result of this lack of security, this negligent attention to foreseeable events on campus, Omar's life was permanently altered when he became the victim of a gang attack that should never have been allowed to happen. And, finally, I am going to ask you to make them pay for that negligence. Thank you for your time and your attention to this case. Omar and I appreciate it very much." And he sat down.

He had kept it simple and short, just enough to give them a taste, while hopefully leaving them wanting more sordid details.

Knight stood for his opening, and he delivered a defense favorite: an attack on the plaintiff's character and an attempt to shift blame to anyone other than his client. "We will show you that Mr. Steele caused his own injuries. No one pushed him out of that window. He jumped of his own free will, and there was nothing added security could have done to prevent it. He had been drinking, and he and his buddies started a fight they were too drunk to continue, so they were running away, and he left his bleeding buddy and ran and jumped out a window. A cowardly act to be sure. So, ladies and gentlemen, the evidence will show that this was not the college's fault, nothing we could have done to prevent it. And even if there was from a fight—he left his buddy and ran—and he jumped out of a window. There is no liability on our part for these injuries. And even if there was, the evidence will show that Mr. Steele was a troublemaker, had very little chance of ever playing baseball in the pros, and was the cause of all of his problems. He was his own worst enemy, someone who went looking for trouble and found it." He also railed on about how cases like those drove up the cost of doing business everywhere—it was not permissible to speak of insurance—and promised the jury that he would prove to them that this case had zero merit.

Brandon wanted to object several times, and he had to restrain Omar from jumping out of his seat and punching Knight on more than one occasion.

"And furthermore, Omar Steele has fully recovered from his injuries, and now he is here for some easy money from you good people. We urge you not to give it to him." And with that, he took his seat. Brandon thought, *Obviously, he hasn't seen Omar walk lately.* He made a mental note to make sure the jury got to see his limp and his scars.

After openings, Brand put Dr. Gaines on the stand. The surgeon who had treated Omar at Halifax Hospital on the night of the incident put Omar's x-rays on a viewing box. The doctor stood in front of the jury and pointed out where the ankle was twisted and angled in ways the maker never intended—with the dislocated foot actually pointing in the reverse direction to normal. The jury was shown pictures of the foot turned around sideways as it appeared in the ER before the surgical repair. Most of them had to look away, and the ones who didn't made faces that revealed they knew the injury came with great pain.

Dr. Gaines explained how he had to open up the ankle and insert screws into bone, forever fusing them together, so that Omar would ultimately be able to walk—but never run again. He also showed the after x-rays in which the screws appeared as bright white objects embedded the gray bone structure.

Brandon had Omar join the doctor briefly so that he could point out what was done on Omar's ankle as Omar held up the leg for the jurors to see.

Knight screamed, "I object, Your Honor. This is a stunt to inflame the jury with no probative value whatsoever!"

"Overruled."

"But, Your Honor!"

"Sit down, Mr. Knight. I am going to allow it."

Knight had steam coming from his ears as he sat.

Dr. Gaines pointed to the ugly scars, which looked like permanent worm trails on Omar's lower leg, and most importantly, he demonstrated the limited range of motion in the fused ankle, which would permanently prevent Omar from playing any kind of sports involving running. This obviously meant that his football and baseball playing days were over. For a world-class athlete considering the very real possibility of a professional career and a huge payday, this news was devastating. Two of the female jurors looked at Omar with eyes that seemed to say, "I am so sorry." The men tried to remain stoic, but even they were squirming uncomfortably at times.

Through Dr. Gaines, Brandon also introduced all the medical bills: the hospital and surgery bills as well as the extensive physical therapy bills. Dr. Gaines spent two hours explaining his care and treatment of Omar, showing grisly operating room photos—again, over Mr. Knight's vigorous objections—and describing the formation of scar tissue, the limited range of motion after repaired bones and ligaments heal with scar tissue, and the physical limitations, pain, and rehabilitation still to come. It was a picture of anguish for a young athlete with an otherwise bright future.

Aside from a midmorning break of fifteen minutes, his testimony consumed the rest of the morning. When they broke for lunch, everyone seemed relieved, especially Omar, who had clearly not enjoyed reliving that part of the case. Thankfully, Mr. Knight's cross-examination of the doctor was short. His focus was all on liability and not on damages. In fact, it was his hope that the jury would never even get to consider damages in this case. The doctor didn't know much about that other than what Brandon had told him, and most of it would be inadmissible hearsay. There was no denying it was a nasty injury, and in Knight's mind, the less focus on it, the better. Brandon was relieved they were able to finish the doctor's testimony before the lunch break, because at six hundred dollars an hour, he had to pay for his time from door to door. Having to recall him after lunch would have made for a very expensive day, but he hoped it was well worth it.

After the lunch break, Brandon called Steve Allen, the physical therapist, who went through an impressive list of qualifications before being accepted over Knight's objections, as an expert in his field. Brandon said, "Mr. Allen, tell the jury what role you played in Omar's recovery."

As instructed, Allen turned toward the jury and said, "I spent four months teaching Omar how to walk again. In the beginning, it was painful for him to stand up, and walking unassisted was impossible. His muscle had atrophied from weeks in a hospital bed, and I had to hold him while he cried after taking his first steps. You have to understand, this young man was a world-class athlete who once ran a forty-yard dash in 4.3 seconds; who ran for over a thousand yards every year playing football; who stole dozens of bases playing baseball at the college level, and who ran track and field; to walk ten feet without assistance or tears of pain. His recovery took months before he could walk with only a minor limp, but it will never end, and as he ages, the stiffness will get worse. Before he is old and gray, he will again have to use a cane to get around."

While Allen was testifying, there was not a dry eye in the jury box as Brandon walked him through those weeks and months in painstaking detail. It was like hearing the chronology of a war veteran learning how to walk after a leg amputation, and everyone in the room could feel Omar's pain—even the judge.

"These injuries are permanent, and this ankle will never be far from his mind. It will literally define his life."

Knight said, "Oh please—"

Judge Stamper said, "Overruled."

Knight sat back down.

During Mr. Allen's testimony, Mr. Knight would stand and say, "I object, Your Honor. these questions and answers are irrelevant, repetitive, and clearly being offered only to unfairly inflame the jury's passion."

Most of them were overruled by the judge and were clearly designed to break up the flow and make the testimony difficult to follow. Brandon hoped they were as irritating to the jury as they were to him.

In the end, after an afternoon of testimony, Knight barely cross-examined Mr. Allen. He wanted to continue giving the jury the impression that it didn't matter what the medical situation was because the accident was not his client's fault, and if the jury did not assign liability to the college, all of the damages in the world would never become an issue.

By the time Mr. Allen had finished giving his testimony, the afternoon session was over. The judge called it a day, admonished the jurors not to speak about the case to each other or to anyone else, and reminded everyone what time he expected them in their seats in the morning.

Omar and Diandra went home to try to relax and get him ready for his time on the stand. It would be a stressful evening—another one in a long line of many.

Brandon went back to the office to organize the file for the morning, return some phone calls, and unwind a bit. He had a decision to make on the order of proof, now that he had the jury thinking about damages. Brandon was thinking about putting Omar on the stand first in the morning, knowing that this would most likely eat up the whole day going over both liability and damages. Then he would fill in day three with liability and "scene of the crime" witnesses, concluding with some "before and after" witnesses and finally Diandra to shore up the damages.

The alternative would be to fill in the liability picture with witnesses and leave the jury waiting to hear from Omar, the "horse's mouth," last. There were many psychological theories, but Brandon liked the one about recency over primacy, that juries remember best what they hear last, and he was leaning toward the latter strategy.

Back at the house, Brandon poured himself a large glass of dry red zinfandel, grabbed his spin-casting rod, and headed out to the end of the dock with Steve to fish and think. The sun was setting, and the scattered high cirrus clouds formed a tapestry of orange, yellow, and red colors in the sky. It was a beautiful evening to be in Florida, and he tossed his bait far out into the gently flowing river and sat back in his chair, petting his dog and thinking that this life certainly did not suck—unless your name was Omar.

CHAPTER 26

TRIAL DAY TWO

Brandon, Omar, and Jim settled into their seats moments before Judge Stamper took the bench for the second day of the trial. Diandra had stayed in Orlando; her day on the stand would be day three, and she couldn't miss another day of work.

"Are the parties ready to proceed?'

Brandon and Knight stood and said, "We are."

"Bailiff, bring in the jury," he said.

Randy, a portly sheriff's deputy who had obviously not passed any physical fitness tests or buffet tables recently, opened the door to the jury room, and the seven lucky jurors filed in with their notepads.

Brandon and Omar watched their return, smiling politely and trying to detect any hint of where they were leaning from their body language, which was purely speculation at best.

Judge Stamper looked at Brandon and said, "You may call your first witness."

Brandon had decided the previous evening to go with his plan of calling Omar last, so this morning, his first witness was Omar's friend, former teammate, and current Major League star. Brandon stood and announced, "The plaintiff calls Marcus Jones."

When Marcus made his way into the courtroom, both male jurors recognized him immediately—as did every other male in the courtroom. The females certainly appreciated his physical presence. Marcus was obviously athletic, a fact not well concealed by the custom-tailored blue suit he was wearing. He glided more than walked, and he exuded confidence and comfort in his own skin.

The starstruck bailiff showed Marcus to the witness chair next to the judge, and the clerk made him raise his hand and swear to tell the truth.

After promising to tell the truth, the whole truth, and nothing but the truth, Brandon had him state his name and occupation, which was center fielder for the Montreal Expos.

"How do you know the plaintiff, Omar Steele?" Brandon asked.

"Omar and I grew up together in Tampa," Marcus said. "We played sports together. Depending on the season, we played football, baseball, basketball, and ran track. If it wasn't raining, and sometimes when it was, we were ballin'."

"Did you play organized sports?" Brandon asked.

"Yes, sir, every kind, Little League, junior high, high school, college, and for me, now, pro baseball."

For the next hour Marcus related his experiences of playing ball with Omar, a good friend and running mate, who he considered to be of equal athletic ability to his own, and in some respects greater. "Omar had a better arm than me, but I was no slouch, which is why he was an excellent quarterback. I played wide receiver just as well, his favorite, I would say. We were both were very fast, but I am a bit faster." He winked at Omar, who smiled back. "And we both had very good hand-eye coordination and plain old God-given athletic ability and physical talent. But everyone loves the quarterback."

Brandon could tell that Marcus was a bit envious of Omar, even though he was older and had now made it to the big time. He came across like a kid talking about his hero, and he became visibly emotional when speaking about Marcus's post-incident limitations.

"So, Marcus, have you spent time with Omar since this incident?"

"Yes, sir. Every time I am back in Tampa."

"Have you noticed any changes in him?" Brandon asked.

"I couldn't begin to describe them. He can't run, he can't play sports, he's in constant pain, and while he tries not to complain, I can see it on his face. I know it depresses him, man. It wears him down, but it is what it is, we make do." Marcus wiped a tear, looked at Omar, and nodded.

After exhausting the emotional well, Brandon shifted gears and started to question Marcus about professional athlete salaries.

Mr. Knight promptly exploded from his chair. "Objection, Your Honor. This is bald speculation. There is no way anyone can predict what salary this plaintiff may have earned in sports—or if he ever would have made it to the pros at all for that matter—and any evidence of professional athlete incomes would be completely speculative, prejudicial, and irrelevant to these proceedings. We strenuously object!"

Judge Stamper looked at Brandon and said, "Counsel, I have to agree with Mr. Knight. Do you have a response?"

Brandon replied, "Yes, Your Honor. We have pled loss of the ability to enjoy life in this case, and every time Omar goes home to Tampa for Christmas or on vacation and hangs out with his friends like Marcus and others who are now playing in the big leagues, some baseball, some football, close friends from high school and the neighborhood, who are now living in big houses and driving sports cars, he is going to feel the loss of what might have been, experience from a distance the exact lifestyle he might have been able to afford, had this not happened. It is no secret, and everyone, including this jury, knows that top athletes make millions of dollars per year. We are not offering this testimony in an effort to prove his loss of wages in the future but to show one very important aspect of his emotional damages, namely, his loss of a lifestyle, and how this will change his, and make him different from his peers."

Judge Stamper pondered for a few seconds and said, "On that limited basis, I'll allow it. You may answer, Mr. Jones."

Knight, who was still on his feet, sputtered, "But, Judge, this is ridiculous. This jury will now speculate on lost income with no basis in fact!"

"Sit down, Mr. Knight. When the time comes, we will instruct the jury accordingly, and you are free to clarify it for them during your summation."

Knight turned three shades of red, took his seat, and mumbled something about the judge's primate ancestry to his associate who no doubt assured him that he was right and the judge was very wrong on this issue.

Marcus went on to describe his multimillion-dollar annual salary as well as that of other players in both baseball and football who had grown up in the same neighborhood as he and Omar. Another close friend had become an All-Pro football player, and he cruised the strip in Tampa in his Bentley and bought houses for seemingly all his relatives. This was not uncommon in a country that rewards sports stars and actors on a much higher level than it does the president of the United States. Brandon had to be very careful with this evidence since it was a golden goose that could crap on his case if he allowed Marcus to come off as greedy. So, he moved on and closed his direct examination of Marcus after the numbers came in. No doubt Knight would take his shot on cross.

Knight got up and started hammering Marcus with statistics. "Did you know that there are 117 Division I college football teams, with an average of around eighty players per team? That is more than 9,300 players?"

Marcus said, "I am aware."

"Did you also know that there are only around 250 of those players drafted each year?"

"Yes," said Marcus.

"So, if my math is correct, that is a little under 3 percent—and more than half of those don't last more than two years in the minor leagues, and of the other half, only 10 percent ever play in the Major Leagues?"

"If you say so," Marcus answered.

Brandon could have objected that Knight was testifying instead of asking a question, but he let him dig his own grave.

"Furthermore, there are thirty Major League teams, each of which has twenty-five players. That means there are only 750 players in all of Major League Baseball."

"Correct," Marcus answered.

"Did you know that the average salary in the minor leagues is $1,500 per month, plus meals? And that is only for the six months the season lasts, which totals around $9,000 per year?"

"Yes, but the average annual salary in the pros if you count the huge superstars is more than three million—with the vast majority making nearly one million per year."

Knight shouted, "And the chances of making it to the pros is just above zilch!" He grunted disgustedly and sat down.

His associate patted him on the back and looked over at Brandon smugly.

Brandon stood back up for redirect. "Tell me, Marcus. In your opinion, as someone who has intimate knowledge of the athletic abilities of Omar Steele, and as someone who has reached the pinnacle of his sport, what are the chances, in your opinion, that without this injury or some other unforeseen tragedy robbing his health, that Omar would be in your shoes both professionally and financially as we sit here today?"

Knight was out of his seat objecting before Brandon finished the question. "Objection! That is utter speculation and beyond the scope of direct, Your Honor." He was spitting on his desk as he shrieked his objection.

The judge looked at him and said, "Sit down, Mr. Knight. Overruled—you opened the door with your statistics."

"But, Your Honor—"

"I have ruled. Now sit—or I will hold you in contempt. You may answer, Mr. Jones."

"There is no question in my mind that Omar would be doing as well as me—if not better."

"Thank you, Marcus. That's all I have, Your Honor." He turned to Knight and said, "Your witness."

Marcus had tears streaming down his cheeks.

Knight declined to re-cross-examine the witness, and the judge announced that it would be a good time to break for lunch.

Brandon, Jim, and Omar went to lunch at a pizza joint to work on the presentation for the rest of the day. Brandon wished that Marcus could have joined them, but he had a flight to catch.

Brandon said, "This afternoon, we will bring in the people who were present on the night of the incident: your friends who were witness to the fight at the house, Ronnie Short who got stabbed, Cooter and Speed who held off the mob while you crawled into the dorm, Erma Baldwin who let you in, Carol Brown whose room you jumped from, and John Gamble, the cop on the scene who protected you on the ground until the ambulance and the cavalry arrived. Everyone has been subpoenaed and has checked in. Jim, you will stay in the hall this afternoon to keep them coordinated. It is a tall order, but we have everyone lined up to testify. I want all of these witnesses to flow, one after the other, or we will put the jury to sleep—and I don't want that. This will use up the entire afternoon, and tomorrow will be all you, Diandra and we'll finish with your mom."

Omar said, "I know the boys will be ready, and tomorrow, we'll bring it home."

The afternoon went as expected, and Ronnie Short was the star. You could have heard a pin drop in the courtroom as he described the fight in the alley and Omar dragging him across campus in search of help. How they found an empty security office and then encountered the girls' dorm where Omar could not get anyone to open the door as the gang returned to finish the job. How Cooter and Speed showed up at just the right time to join the fight after Omar went down after being clubbed in the head, how somehow the dorm door finally opened, and how they were dragged inside, about his losing blood and finally, consciousness.

The jury heard from Speed how the police finally arrived with lights and sirens blaring, and that he and most of the other combatants were in the process of getting handcuffed when he heard a scream and saw someone falling from the sky and landing in the bushes next to the building. He had no idea at the time that it was Omar.

Carol Brown tied it all together.

Brandon said, "Tell us what happened on that night when a stranger came into your room, Ms. Brown."

"I was getting ready to go out. I had my music up pretty loud, so I didn't hear any commotion downstairs." She pointed to Omar. "All of a sudden, that dude came bustin' in my room. He had wild eyes and was bleeding from his head, and he sort of looked right through me like I wasn't even there. He was mumbling stuff, and I screamed, 'Who are you—and what are you doing in my room?' I was sitting on my bed in my underwear, brushing my hair, so I covered myself with a towel. It was like he didn't even hear me. He ran over to my window, yanked off the shade, opened it up, and just jumped out. I screamed again and looked out, and that's when I saw all the police outside. It was too dark to see where he landed. I guess he landed in the bushes next to the dorm. I got dressed and ran downstairs into chaos. There was cops and people everywhere. I saw them load him into an ambulance, gave a statement to the police officer, and that was it. We finally all went back inside and resumed our night. A crazy night for sure."

Mr. Knight stood and said, "Ms. Brown, was anyone chasing the plaintiff when he entered your room that you could see?"

"No, sir."

"In fact, did any other boys come up to the third floor that night before Mr. Steele jumped from your window?"

"No, sir."

"And, ma'am, did you or anyone else threaten Mr. Steele or in any way make him jump from that window?"

"No, sir," she said.

"Nothing further." Mr. Knight took his seat.

With that, Judge Stamper called it a day.

Brandon was emotionally drained after the day's festivities, and after spending a couple of hours back at the office, catching up on emails and returning calls, he went home to crash early.

CHAPTER 27

TRIAL DAY THREE

On day three of the trial, the ambulance and hospital personnel took up most of the morning describing the scene, the emergency room, and the carnage that was Omar's ankle.

Brandon was able to get all of these witnesses on the stand to tell their compelling stories in the morning session, mostly because Mr. Knight waived cross-examination of most of them. These were mostly damages witnesses; it was clear to Brandon and Jim that Knight was continuing his theme of wanting the jury to believe he was not concerned with damages because he did not feel there was any liability. Without liability, jury deliberations would never get to damages.

Brandon, Jim, and Omar spent the lunch break going over Omar's direct exam and coaching him on what to expect from Knight on cross-examination. Next would come Diandra, and then they would close the day with Omar's mother. She was regal, well spoken lady who would tell it like it is, and hopefully, the jury would eat her testimony up.

At the end of the day, Brandon and Knight would submit to the court their prospective jury instructions, and then, on the morning of the final day, they would hash them out, do closing arguments, and hopefully, bring in a verdict for the plaintiff that afternoon.

The afternoon session began as it always did. Judge Stamper came in and ordered everyone to take their seats, and then he looked to Brandon at the plaintiff's table to call the next witness.

Brandon said, "I call the plaintiff, Omar Steele, to the stand, Your Honor."

Omar got up, walked stiffly and slowly to the witness stand, raised his hand, and told the clerk he would "tell the truth, the whole truth, and nothing but the truth, so help me God."

"Good afternoon, Omar," said Brandon.

"Afternoon."

The jury had been waiting to hear Omar's side of the story, and they were all leaning forward and paying rapt attention.

"Tell us your name address and occupation, Omar," Brandon said.

Omar stated his name and particulars, speaking and looking at the jurors and not at Brandon as he had been instructed. One of the female jurors was a middle-aged white lady who clearly found Omar attractive, and she was glued to his testimony like a woman watching her "stories" as they often referred to soap operas. Omar was clear-eyed and spoke clearly and confidently. All seven of the jurors were clearly very interested, and they all had their pens and notepads handy—even the two men. Brandon took him through his history, childhood, schooling, and athletic accomplishments.

Mr. Knight tried to limit this testimony from time to time by objecting to relevance, but Judge Stamper wanted to hear it all. The complaints were routinely denied.

Brandon spent a good deal of time going over Omar's collegiate accomplishments, his being voted All-American in both baseball and football, being MEAC player of the year the year before the accident, and some detail on the recruiting he had experienced from pro scouts in both sports. Omar had wanted to be a professional ballplayer since he knew what one was, and all he ever watched on TV was sports.

Omar said, "I was one of those kids who left his house in the summer right after breakfast or a bowl of cereal, and spent the day playing pick-up games at the local ball fields, oftentimes with boys much older than myself. I was fast and had really good hand-eye coordination, which made me an excellent hitter and a nimble runner. I hate to brag, but I also had a terrific arm and could throw a baseball over ninety-five miles per hour with accuracy and movement. I could throw a perfect spiral over seventy yards in the air and hit a receiver in stride."

Even if the five female jurors were not sports enthusiasts, Brandon thought they had to appreciate the fact that they were in the presence of a rare athlete. He just hoped Omar wasn't coming off as a bragger by tooting his own horn.

After this buildup of his self-esteem, Brandon took Omar to the day of the incident—the day that changed his life forever.

Omar said, "I drove down from Tallahassee, rounded up my boys from Tampa who were hangin' out at Speed's place, and hit the graduation party scene." Omar emphasized that he had very little to drink, as was his norm since he was not one to allow himself to lose control. "No more than one beer." The party that turned into a short skirmish was not the sort of thing that he worried too much about, just some drunk dudes letting off steam, and after he and Ronnie left there looking for their girls, they didn't give it another thought, until they were confronted by the gang in the alley.

Omar said, "Ronnie getting stabbed took me totally by surprise. It was the last thing I saw coming that night, and after it happened, and the gang took off, I was never so scared as I was dragging my best friend across campus. Ronnie was bleeding out in front of my eyes and holding his guts in with his bare hands. I knew I had to get Ronnie some help, and nothing was going to stop me."

The trek across campus to the security office was a blur to Omar, and finding it empty was a crushing blow. Ronnie half-carried him across the street to the nearest dorm and began to pound on the door. He could not believe his eyes when he saw a truckful of dudes pull up and get out with bats and pipes. He pounded on a door that would not be opened from the inside due to campus policy.

Their big break came when the head of security took the stand. He was not cooperative, but when pressed, he admitted that two security guards were assigned to man the little office that night, and one was supposed to be intermittently patrolling the campus in a golf cart. One carried a handheld radio to keep in touch with the other guard who was to remain in the security office at all times. Unfortunately for Ronnie and Omar, the roving guard had encountered trouble in the form of a pajama party in one of the girls' dorms and had radioed his mate to come join him on the double. When the shit hit the proverbial fan, those two yo-yos were standing on the golf cart a quarter of a mile away, peeking into another girl's dormitory window. Knight tried to prevent the testimony, and when that failed he asked the Judge to strike it as irrelevant and overly prejudicial. The judge denied both motions.

Omar had very little recollection after he was hit on the head, and he had no recollection of being dragged into the dorm, coming to and stumbling up the stairs, or barging into Carol Brown's room—and he certainly didn't recall jumping from her window. He had flashes of memory from the ambulance and the emergency room until he was sedated, and the next thing he knew, he was waking up in his hospital room with his leg in a cast—and pain was his new reality.

Getting through the testimony was grueling, and the judge ordered a fifteen-minute break so everyone could catch their breath.

During the break, Omar and Brandon conferred briefly and then repaired to the hall to walk—or limp as the case may be—off the pressure. Mr. Knight spent the time reassuring the insurance adjuster sitting in the back of the audience that all was going according to plan, no worries. The jury sat in the jury box and talked about what a jerk Knight was. Since they weren't supposed to talk about the case, they usually spent the breaks talking about the lawyers or the witnesses in general terms, but it was really impossible for them not to discuss the case at all under the circumstances.

After the break, Brandon spent the afternoon going over the aftermath, the multiple surgeries, the physical therapy, the scar tissue, the limitations, the pain, the pills, and the regret. The hardest pill to swallow was that his athletic career was over. Sure, he could amputate the foot and compete in the Paralympics or something, but this was not just his job prospects, which were huge, but also his career and a lifelong dream of becoming a pro athlete. It was every red-blooded American boy's dream, and it was gone. They talked about depression, about how Omar had lost interest in girls and the day-to-day stuff that normally motivated him to get up in the morning.

Brandon noticed that Knight looked like he couldn't wait to get his turn to make Omar look like a whiner.

When Knight got his chance on cross, he did all but suggest that Omar get in line with the rest of his "people" who collected welfare benefits and just got on SSI disability.

Omar had not chosen that route, and as he fought back against Knight's snide and bigoted remarks, he described how he had turned his attitude around and made it through the excruciating physical therapy. He was walking with a limp, but he was walking, and he could even jog a bit. If nothing else good came of the incident, Omar hoped he could coach and prepare young people for the reality of life without sports. For those who were good enough, he could help keep them focused and make every effort count toward their ultimate goals.

In the end, Brandon felt like Omar did a great job on the stand, and he felt like they had a really good chance to get a positive verdict— certainly more than the poke-in-the-eye ten grand being offered by the defense at mediation.

Brandon closed with Omar's mother on the stand, and he took her through the painful process of watching her son live in pain, of his profound disappointment, and her heartbreak of having to watch it all while he went through physical therapy and slowly recovered.

Brandon rested the plaintiff's case, and the judge closed the proceedings for the day. Brandon retired to the office to prepare for the defense and had another early night on the river with Steve.

The fourth day began with both sides arguing motions for directed verdicts to the judge outside the hearing of the jury, and as expected, the judge denied both. Judges were very reluctant to take the decision away from juries and preferred to correct errors after the fact.

When the jury was brought in, the defense began its case by calling a rehab expert to discuss exactly how the injury was a good thing for Brandon because 90 percent of all athletes don't make the pros and most athletes who do make the pros only last two or three years. Those who make it longer often suffer season-ending injuries or long-term debilitating problems such as early-onset dementia or crippling arthritis.

Brandon couldn't believe it, but by the time he was done, it had started to sound like the whole thing was Omar's lucky day. Brandon spent the better part of an hour trying to get the guy to admit that there were actually good things to come of sports, but he wasn't having it. To hear him talk, anyone who spent their spare time watching sports on TV or attending the events was wasting their time. Brandon, who loved to watch football and golf, wasn't buying it, and he hoped the jury was not either.

Knight called a couple of the kids who were at the party, and they portrayed the fight as instigated by Omar and entirely his fault. It was clear from the way they squirmed uncomfortably on the stand and testified through a lot of hums and haws that they were not comfortable with the false version they were selling. Brandon barely questioned them on cross to emphasis the fact that he didn't believe a word they were saying.

Knight closed the defense with a school official who described all the efforts the school had undertaken to make the campus safe that weekend. He claimed to know all the troublemakers at the college—and none of those involved in the stabbing were active students. He emphasized that there was nothing the school could have done to prevent the incident, especially since Omar and Ronnie were not students or subject to his discipline. With that, the defense rested.

The judge felt like there was plenty of time to hold closing arguments and jury instructions and deliver the case to the jury for deliberation were presented after everyone agreed on a set of jury instructions. Brandon argued passionately for Omar, emphasized the pain, the rehab, and the loss of a lifestyle. He also spent considerable time talking about liability, about how the collage utterly failed to secure the campus on the busiest night of the year, and he pointed out the defense's attitude was "So What" we didn't do our job, but so what?, he hurt himself!" Several jurors looked visibly angry by the time he finished. Knight's closing was as expected, cocky and belittling, and after an hour or so, the judge released them for a late lunch, and the lawyers and he crafted a set of jury instructions that were acceptable to all involved. It was a very difficult process—Knight quibbled about each and every one—but after an hour, they were ready to be presented.

Closing arguments went much the same way as the openings had, and after an hour or so, the judge released the alternate, and the six jurors went to the jury room to deliberate.

Brandon always felt a great weight release from his shoulders at that point. He had done all that he could do, and it was up to those six folks to decide the fate of the case and Omar's future. Brandon and Knight shook hands and exchanged perfunctory platitudes about what a good job both had done, neither of them meaning it, and the parties went back to their offices or hotel rooms to wait for the verdict.

The general theory in civil cases was a quick verdict was bad for the plaintiff because you were getting zilch, and they only had to settle on who would act as the foreperson of the jury. The foreperson would deliver the verdict in court. Two or three hours of deliberation was good for the plaintiff since it showed they were carefully considering the amounts requested and awarding an amount commensurate with the damages requested.

Brandon had not asked for a specific amount, but he ran through some examples of a yearly payment based upon Omar's life expectancy, most of which ran into seven figures. Knight had told them to send Omar home empty-handed. If the deliberation went past three hours, the theory was it was bad for the plaintiff because the jurors could not agree on a unanimous verdict, and a hung jury became a possibility. If that happened, they would be back to square one since the judge would declare a mistrial, and they would have to retry the case. Nobody wanted that.

Brandon checked emails, and Omar paced about the office and drove the staff crazy with unanswerable questions concerning the predictability of the outcome. Brandon told Omar to chill out several times, but he wasn't having it.

"This is my life. This is my damn life!"

After about two hours, right around dinnertime, Brandon got the call that the jury had a verdict. They piled into the car and hauled ass back to the courthouse. When they arrived, Knight and his team were already seated at the defense table, but the judge was nowhere to be found.

Brandon nodded to the bailiff by the door to the jury room, and he nodded back. Brandon mouthed, "Verdict or question," and the bailiff silently replied, "Verdict."

The jury could come back with a question they need answered from something confusing in the evidence or something not included in the evidence, and the lawyers had to scramble to figure out what was admissible and what was not, whether the question was relevant, and if answering would invade the providence of the jury. It was always a delicate situation to balance.

The judge finally waltzed in, and when everyone was seated, he told the bailiff to bring the jury back into the courtroom. The six jurors filed in very stoically and took their seats.

Judge Stamper said, "Ladies and Gentlemen of the jury, have you reached a unanimous verdict?"

"We have, Your Honor," said the woman in the front row who had seemed to be particularly enamored with Omar during the trial.

"Please pass the verdict form to the bailiff."

The bailiff handed it to the judge, who looked it over, and then he handed it to his clerk to publish.

She stood up and read, "In the matter of Omar Steele versus Martin Luther College, Case Number 1345, today's date, yada, yada. Was there negligence on the part of Martin Luther College, which was the legal cause of injury or damage to the plaintiff? Answer: Yes. Was there negligence on the part of the plaintiff, which was the legal cause of loss or damage experienced by him? Answer: No."

Had they attributed some of the fault to Omar, the judge would calculate a reduction in the amount awarded, but they did not.

"What is the total amount of damages sustained by the plaintiff for medical expenses? Answer: $35,000. For pain and suffering and loss of the ability to enjoy life in the past? $1 million. for pain and suffering and loss of the ability to enjoy life in the future? Answer: $2 million. So, say we all, this yada, yada date."

No one heard the rest.

Omar, Jim, and Brandon were too busy embracing and trying not to break decorum by shouting too loud.

Mr. Knight muttered, "This is bullshit."

The judge whacked his gavel and said, "Order in this courtroom."

Everyone settled down so that they could poll the jurors individually to be sure each agreed with the verdict, and then he thanked them for their service and released them.

Omar had tears flowing down his cheeks as the jury filed by him on their way out. Most of them looked him in the eye and silently wished him luck.

When the jury was gone, the judge said, "Any objections to the instructions or the verdict?"

Knight stood and said, "I object to this whole circus and move for a judgment for the defense notwithstanding the verdict."

Judge Stamper said, "Denied. Anything else?"

Knight said, "At this time, we will reserve all objections and will be filing several motions, including for remittitur and new trial."

"I expect you will," said the judge. "Then, with that, we are adjourned." He slammed the gavel one more time, got up, and retreated to his chambers.

Brandon, Jim, and Omar gathered up their stuff and headed out.

Brandon said, "Drinks are on me. You want to join us, Mr. Knight, Kevin?"

Knight said, "Fuck you," slammed his trial bag on the floor, and stomped out of the courtroom—with his minions trailing behind him.

Omar was jubilant and immediately began calling and texting everyone.

Brandon called the office and told Patty to have everyone meet at the pub for a posttrial party. They left the courthouse like a pack of football fans whose team just won the Super Bowl, and the after party was epic.

Meanwhile, the traveler was in route in the travel pod, with arrival on earth scheduled in just a few short hours.

PART II

THE AFTERMATH

Brandon staggered into his house the morning after the after-party. He had passed out in his truck, rather than drive home wasted, and six hours later, he was probably still wasted, but he had made it home. He was annoyed with himself for leaving Steve alone all night, but she knew how to push the bottom of the bathroom door open and let herself in and out. He was not overly concerned about any little poop messes, but she was probably hungry—unless she found some dead critter to gnaw on or roll in.

"Steve!" he yelled as he stumbled in the door. Hearing no responsive bark, he grew more concerned. He dropped his trial bag on the kitchen table and walked back toward the pool.

Seated at his computer, a gorgeous girl who looked vaguely familiar was working on his computer. The TV was playing a golf tournament, and there was music coming from the computer. This woman was very muscular—with brown hair and a killer body—and he knew he had seen her before. She was wearing a strange clingy jumpsuit made of a shimmering substance. "Who the hell are—"

She looked at him, and his whole body froze. "I am sure you are wondering who I am and what am I doing in your house, and I will certainly tell you, but I don't have time just now. Why don't you mosey on into your bedroom and take little nap—and we'll speak in a bit?"

He took the suggestion as a command, walked into his bedroom, joined a slumbering Steve on the bed, and promptly went to sleep.

The traveler went back to work on his computer, her fingers whizzing across the keys as she mined the internet for information critical to her task at hand. Several dozen hours later, she allowed Brandon and Steve to awaken. She stood over the bed and said, "Awake."

Brandon thought he was having a dream. Standing over him was none other than that Holly chick from the golf channel—one of the hottest women on TV. He wanted to speak to her, but he could not form words.

Steve was also awake, sitting calmly and silently.

The woman said, "Okay, I'm finished on the computer for now. You can come back into the other room and have a seat, and we'll talk." She walked into the other room, and he followed her. Steve did as well. He had never seen his dog so quiet with someone new in the house; she was usually all excited and introducing herself. Something was very strange about this whole thing.

The woman sat down and indicated that Brandon should do the same. Steve sat beside him.

He glanced at his watch, and according to the date, it had been four days since he was last awake. He tried to speak but found that he could not.

She said, "First of all, my appearance is that of a person I mimicked from your television when you walked in. This look is not my real look, but you probably could not handle that so this will do for now."

He was very confused but agreed with that statement wholeheartedly.

"I will let you speak in due time, but I don't want you interrupting me with questions while I explain, okay?"

Like he had a choice, he managed to nod.

She began, "I am a traveler from a place far from here, from this planet. I believe the proper term using your language would be ... alien. I have come to your planet to collect certain things and to make some changes."

He was fairly freaking out. A million questions were trying to bubble up to the surface, but her control over him was absolute.

She said, "My presence here in your house was purely random, but my landing in this part of your world was not. I come from a planet many light years from here, where life is much more advanced than here, but just as fragile. I have downloaded the entire frame of knowledge from your planet through your internet, and it is obvious to me that the course your humankind has plotted for itself will lead to disastrous results in the not too distant future.

"You see, we have been here before, in fact, I, personally, have been here before. More than two hundred of your years ago, I came here for some plant and animal specimens and some seawater. I found that your planet had just over a billion of you inhabiting it, but life here was still quite primitive. That sounds like a lot of people, but you must know that my planet is five times the size of yours, and our population is less than one hundred thousand souls."

Brandon was busting with questions, and it must have shown in his pleading eyes.

She said, "You may speak."

"You are shitting me, woman. That is the craziest shit I have ever heard—"

"You may communicate slowly and without expletives, and I will understand you better."

"Can I call you Holly?"

"If that makes you happy but let me assure you I am telling you the truth. We learned how to perfectly clone the human genome more than three thousand years ago. After that, we began to reduce the population by nonrenewal, so to speak, as we no longer needed huge numbers."

Nonrenewal? We're not talking about subscriptions to Playboy *here. We are talking about people!*

"How do I put this so you will understand? So, after we mastered human cloning, we also mastered what you call 'backing up' the brain's contents or 'downloading' for lack of a better word, all of its memories into new bodies. It is far more complicated a process than that, but the simplified version is that every twenty or thirty of your years, we clone ourselves and download all of our knowledge and life experiences into the new clone. In effect, we renew ourselves. I have two to four clones in the clone farm of various ages, waiting for my use, as we speak. This body I am currently inhabiting is only twenty-four of your years old, but my memories date back more than 1,500 years."

Brandon nodded at her dumbly, and as crazy as it sounded, he believed her.

"You may speak."

He said, "What do you do with the clones as they grow up?"

She said, "The young bodies are kept in isolation where they do basic exercises and strength training—but no learning, socializing, or nurturing. Basically, all they do is eat, sleep, and exercise. Their minds are nearly fresh blanks when we need them. Then we anesthetize them, wipe their memories, download the collective consciousness and knowledge of the worn body, discard it after keeping some select parts and DNA samples, and wake up the new one as me all over again. It feels no different to me than waking up refreshed in the morning."

He said, "But you are not really you—you just think you are? Right?"

"Technically, physically, yes, but what difference does it make? When I awake fully programmed, I remember everything I have learned over the course of dozens of lifetimes, and all of my memories are intact."

He said, "What happens if you get hit by a bus and get killed before you can download?"

"Good question. In order to prevent that, we do a periodic memory dump just in case, kind of like when you back up your computer. This information is kept in the master computer for emergencies just like what you suggested—although we lack buses as well." She smiled.

"And you can make yourself look like anyone you want?"

"Yes, kind of like what your TV actress from *I Dream of Jeannie* could do. Along with downloading every piece of information from your internet, I have also downloaded everything ever written or shown on TV that was accessible to the internet. There is little to no knowledge on this planet that I do not now possess, except perhaps some oral histories from the ancients, if anything. Everything else, I possess."

"Okay," Brandon said. "Let's say I believe you ... why can't I move or speak unless you want me to?"

"Because I can control you and your dog with my mind. For that matter, I can control all of humankind with my mind—all eight billion of you."

"That is ridiculous," Brandon said. "I may have been born at night, but it wasn't last night!"

"You'll see soon enough," she said. "Now, you must be starving. Let's get something to eat."

All of a sudden, Brandon was ravenous. Hell, he hadn't eaten in over four days. When got out of bed, his limbs were extremely stiff, as if he'd been in a fight.

He followed "Holly" into the kitchen.

"Show me what you eat," she said. Of course, she already knew since she had downloaded the entire internet, reading as she went, but she was ready to stop working for a while and play with her new human friend before she disposed of him.

Since he hadn't been to the grocery in days, there wasn't much to eat in the fridge that wasn't spoiled or unappetizing, but he managed to cobble together a salad and a turkey sandwich that hadn't quite turned bad. He fixed Steve a bowl of kibble, sat down at the table across from the alien goddess, and began to eat. What she ate looked like an energy bar—only far less appetizing.

She caught him staring at her breasts while he was chewing, and she said, "If these are going to be a distraction, I can become Samuel L. Jackson or Fat Albert."

"No, sorry, Holly … can I call you Holly? I couldn't help it, but you are gorgeous. I'll get used to it … please don't change for me."

She said, "We'll see."

"So, assuming you are not bullshitting me, what are you doing here exactly?"

"I'll get to that a bit later. First, I have some questions for you."

"Fire away," he said.

She said, "In the past two hundred years, people on your tiny little planet have made great strides in computer technology, electronics, and science. You have advanced in leaps and bounds, yet you have allowed yourselves to pollute your planet with nearly eight billion souls—in spite of having several wars in which millions were killed. What is worse, every day, dozens of species of animals are erased from the planet. How could a so-called intelligent race allow that to happen?"

"Wow, that is a heavy statement," he said. "To my knowledge, only China has tried to limit population growth, and I don't think it worked out too well. I don't think any government wants to limit the growth of its people. More people means more power and more money. Everything always has to be bigger to be better, especially when it comes to currency."

"You are a nasty, stupid species," she said. "It's time we fix that situation—and soon."

Brandon didn't like the sound of that.

"This planet has an incredible and diverse biostructure, plants, and animals not seen anywhere else in our known galaxy, but you are polluting it with humans, and I am here to fix it."

"What do you mean?"

"You'll see," she said ominously. "You'll see." She stood up and said, "So, now that you have been fed, explain some things for me. When I was here, in around your year 1800, your country, America, was dirt-poor and one of the weakest countries on the planet. How did that turn around?"

"I thought you said you downloaded all of our history?"

"I did, but I didn't read it all yet. That will take me days!"

"Right," he said. "Well, it really is all about power, money, and war. We nearly wiped ourselves out in the 1860s when we fought the Civil War among ourselves, but then along came World War I and World War II, and we turned America into an industrial powerhouse, and the former top dogs ended up on the bottom."

"Amazing," she said. "Why doesn't America rule the whole planet? It would be much more efficient."

"We don't want to rule the planet. We want all people to have their own say in running their own governments."

"That is incredibly naïve. The majority of humans don't have sense enough to do that, and they need to be led."

"Well, that is the American model. It's called democracy, and it seems to be working pretty well."

"Bullshit," she said. "It's leading to a population hemorrhage that will soon result in this planet's demise." She turned on the computer and typed in Hong Kong, New York City, and Tokyo. The images were teeming with throngs of people. "This has to stop!" She put down the computer. "Listen, you people live what seventy, eighty years, sometimes more? That is a mere blip in time compared to the age of this planet, of your sun, of the universe, which is more than thirteen billion years. For an ecosystem like this to survive, it needs to be carefully managed, not have seven or eight billion humans ravaging it. You need one central government, which never changes, and everyone must get along and have the best interest of the planet and all its creatures at heart—and population must be strictly limited.

"You can't accomplish any of those things with seven or eight billion humans all trying to exert their freedom to do what they want while reproducing like insects. They aren't smart enough to do the right things. They are largely greedy, stupid, and selfish, and they cannot be allowed to do whatever they want to this place."

Brandon said, "I have to agree with you there. In my view, most people are selfish idiots, but I work in the legal system, where all the criminals live."

She said, "We have no criminals. Anyone who does anything that is contrary to our system is simply ended—erased. You think that is harsh, but we wouldn't have it any other way."

"I get it but tell me about where you come from and where you have been."

She ignored him and said, "Think about this for a moment. There are millions and millions of stars in what you have named our Milky Way galaxy, most with dozens of planets with dozens of moons around them. You do not yet have the technology to reach any other stars, let alone another planet, in one of your lifetimes. If I told you where I am from, it would mean nothing to you. The closest star that you have named is Alpha Centauri, which is 4.22 light years away. That is around twenty-four trillion of your miles. Currently, according to your internet, humans have not yet managed 10 percent of light speed. At that rate, it would take you nearly a lifetime just to get to the nearest star—and there is nothing there!

"A light year is just under six trillion miles, and our galaxy is over 100,000 of those light years across. Ours is just one small galaxy. There are billions of galaxies in the universe which is at least a hundred billion light years in size, and we have no idea how many inhabited planets exist in the universe. Hell, my kind may be relatively primitive compared to some, but we have not found any of them yet, except here."

"We have found a way to, as you have imagined in your science fiction, to fold space, so that we can travel in excess of the speed of light by jumping huge distances folding space and using what you call wormholes within the galaxy, but we have not yet managed to travel to other galaxies. I haven't the time to explain it all to you, human, but we have only scratched the surface of this galaxy in our travels, and this is so far the only other habited planet we have found—and we are not about to let you humans ruin it."

Brandon was starting to believe this thing was for real, and he was not excited about her plans.

"My planet is five times the size of your earth, It is very far from here, but it is not as rich in resources, especially the abundance of water. What brought me here, more than anything, is that you are getting close to a planetary water crisis, and even though your experts have recognized this pending crisis, nothing is being done about it but talk."

"So, you plan on non-renewing some folks here to bring the population in check in order to preserve resources, is that it?"

"No. I have a more aggressive plan that that, but for now, we need to rest. We'll speak more later." She closed her eyes and sat back in the chair.

Brandon and Steve took an unsaid cue and returned to bed. He had no idea it was even happening.

She had no idea why she hadn't erased him and his dog the minute she arrived. Probably because she got to know the Aussie first, and the dog convinced her to let her master live.

Brandon awoke a few days later with a head full of questions. Holly was back at the computer when he returned to the living room. As Steve ran outside to do her business, he sat down on the couch and watched her tapping away on his computer. "So, what happens now?"

"That remains to be seen," she said. "I have some decisions to make, and while my leaders have given me a great deal of discretion in making them, I still have to decide what is best for my people—and what is best for this planet. Certainly, having someone manage the various ecosystems is not a bad thing, but we have not planned for any of our people to come here and live full-time in order to do so. We are working on other more important ventures at the time. So, I am going to try to calculate the best resolution for the planet before I depart. Most importantly, a significant population reduction is a priority."

Brandon had been thinking about the issue, and beyond self-preservation, he did not want to see billions of human beings eradicated. "What if you just make it so we naturally non-renew? Make it so that only a small percentage of us can reproduce, and then the population will reduce itself to the desired level in less than a hundred years, which as you said, is a mere blip in time."

She smiled. "You are using my words against me, a wise move."

He said, "Well, it's true, right? There is no need to kill huge numbers of people. As they die naturally, they will be properly disposed of and if only—say less than 1 percent—are capable of reproduction, the population will naturally reduce while those left behind manage the diminishing population."

She considered the argument and then replied, "A valid argument, but it lacks the ability to work. First, I don't have a hundred years to sit around and monitor it. Second, humans seem to be obsessed with the act of reproduction, and if all of a sudden it stops happening, they will riot in the streets looking for a scapegoat to blame for their failures. Further, when those rare children are born, your greedy upper class will probably commandeer the children for government use and cause civil wars—or worse—and destroy the planet in the process. You humans are simply too greedy and selfish to manage this situation yourselves.

"Humans have demonstrated the ability to reduce this planet to dust with their weapons, and your own government nearly did so at the end of World War II in Japan, and again during the Cuban Missile

209

Crisis in the sixties. Imagine the wars and chaos that would result if only a very small number of children were born in the near future. If the population is not reduced, and very soon, there will be equally ugly wars over fresh water and food. The planet cannot support the number of people who are coming if nothing is done. It is estimated by some that earth will be populated with fifty billion people in only thirty years. Your grandchildren will be born into a world at war."

Brandon said, "I don't believe that."

She said, "It comes from your own records, the population of the earth was around 500 million in 1750, by 1802 it reached one billion, by 1935, it reached two billion, then your World War II happened, and although somewhere between eighty and a hundred million were killed in that war, your population has more than tripled to now nearly seven billion only seventy-five or so years later. Your world wars barely slowed it down. I have another related question for you. What is the fascination with reproduction and sex on this world? Also, it seems that once the children are born, the males become far less interested in the process, and the marriage unit often breaks up after the birth of children. Divorce, I think you call it. Why do they choose monogamy only to reject it at a later date on a large scale?"

Brandon thought, *Boy, this chick is clueless.* He said, "Are your people monogamous?"

She said, "We don't have couples at all."

He was shocked into silence.

She explained, "All reproduction is done in the lab through cloning, so we have no need for mating or coupling. We leave such activity to the animals, such as yourself."

"Wait a minute. Do you mean to tell me that there is no sex on your planet, no marriage, no nothing."

"Exactly. There is no need. We are all the same, and all reproduction is done in the lab. We can change our appearance at will, so there is no prejudice. Look at how many people through the ages have been killed because they are different on your world. You have Catholics killing heretics and protestants, Germans killing Jews and gypsies, Muslims killing everyone non-Muslim as infidels, and white supremacists killing gays and blacks. What does any of this accomplish? Unfortunately for the planet, the killing is on such a small scale that it doesn't really affect population growth, but it is counterproductive to having a harmonious planet."

Brandon said, "I have to agree with that, but what about this? You have no sex, no mating, and no courting, and everyone looks alike?"

"By choice. Actually, by necessity."

"Wow," he said. "I think I like it here better. What about kissing?"

"Nope," she said.

"What about partying? Do you have intoxicants, alcohol, weed, or dope?"

"No need," she said. "Those things are counterproductive to optimum health, and we can stimulate our own pleasure centers with our minds for optimum rest and relaxation."

"I don't think I want to come home with you—not that it was an option."

She laughed. "Tell me about religion. It seems that every civilization recorded since you people created writing has worshipped some sort of god or divine entity, but no two seem to be the same. Each one thinks they have it right, and many kill people from other religions who don't believe likewise, yet they all come and go."

Brandon said, "Yes, that is tough to explain. Basically, most of us are born into a family that believes one way, and that is the way we stay, for the most part. Strangely enough, you can also switch if you find one you like better, which begs the question, who is right? Also, I think it mostly helps people live without fear of death, and the threat of punishment keeps the peace to some extent, which is a good thing. Each religion installs a moral compass or set of controls to its people so that there is law and order. Also, believing in an afterlife makes it less stressful going through life, knowing that your life will inevitably end."

"That makes some sense, I guess, but if you clone and download, then, in effect, you never have to die. And as far as religion goes, we are pretty secure in the knowledge that while there may be a divine force in the universe, it isn't a white-haired old man sitting on a cloud focused on any one people, and it's certainly not focused on any one person. And yet, down through time, almost every species of human being has worshiped something or someone. My people are certain that the universe was formed in a chaotic explosion more than thirteen billion years ago, that there is a guiding physical force or inertia pushing everything that moves. We study it, but we don't deify it—and we don't need its fear because we have no crime. Then again, we are probably several hundred years ahead of you technologically speaking."

"We call that chaos theory," Brandon said, "but I think you are missing out on one of the most important features of being human: love."

"Bah! Unnecessary! Now, go play with your dog. I have work to do." She shooed him away.

Brandon went outside and sat on the dock. There were no boats in the river and no aircraft that he could see, which was very unusual for Daytona Beach. This whole thing was just getting curiouser and curiouser. He wished he had his phone, but she took it, and he hadn't seen it since. He certainly wanted to keep her talking and not doing anything drastic, but he also would love to get in her shorts, assuming she had the proper equipment, especially if this was his last day on earth.

He played catch with Steve until she refused to return the tennis ball, which was her sign that she was done playing. He was freaked out by the lack of noise, any kind of noise, so he went back inside to see if he could pry some more information out of this alien goddess.

Over the course of the next several days, they discussed many things—history, politics, ethics, sex, you name it—and he was really beginning to develop feelings for this strange being, alien or not. Strangely, he was getting the feeling that those feelings were becoming mutual.

About a week after her arrival, they were on his bed. She was working on his laptop, and he was watching her—astonished at the speed with which she worked.

She said, "Brandon, we already discussed your theory for reducing earth's population gradually, but let's assume that is not an option. How would you do it if you wanted to leave a few hundred thousand people around—even a few million—but not necessarily all over the world?"

"You mean like, what if we eliminated everyone in certain areas and less than everyone in others?"

"Yes. How would you decide?"

"Well, I guess the optimum way would be to find a diverse population somewhere that could be self-sustaining without the rest of the world and eliminate the rest."

"How would you keep them at home? What would prevent them from traveling to the places where people weren't and re-inhabiting them?"

"Well, I guess you would have to use your mind control to keep them in place—or else take away all forms of transportation but putting that genie back in the bottle would never work. They would just build new ones. Why couldn't you just tell them what you were doing and forbid them from leaving by using your mind control or something?"

"Well, I could do that if I stayed, but after I left, my control would wear off. On the other hand, I could just stay here and rule."

He looked at her. "Is that an option?"

"Possibly," she answered.

Brandon looked into her eyes and felt a pull. "Can I kiss you?"

She closed her eyes, and he planted his lips on hers. At first, she didn't respond or move, and then he slowly began tracing her lips with the tip of his tongue, and she began to mimic his actions. Soon, they were full-on making out. She was doing it right, but not with passion, and then she pulled back. She looked him in the eyes and said, "That was not altogether unpleasant." She got up and left the room.

Brandon stayed on the bed. *This is the strangest situation I have ever been in. I had better play it right—or I might end up eliminated.* He could not help but feel he was the only person left on earth, especially since she wouldn't let him access the internet, the TV, or his phone. He did not know that she was in the process of ordering all vehicles back to their homes—planes, trains, ships, subs, cars, and trucks—where they would be made to exhaust all onboard fuel and be put away.

She had the whole human world preparing to put all vehicles in dry storage so as not to pollute the earth with crashing, smoking vehicles when the population reduction happened. She had not yet decided on the extent of that, but she needed the vehicles put to bed, both military and civilian, and then the oil and natural gas drilling secured, and lastly, the nuclear, coal, and electric power plants secured. This she could accomplish with mind control since she obviously couldn't be everywhere. The preservation of the planet was her primary goal.

As of now, she had total control of every human mind on the planet. People were carrying out her instructions without question, basically becoming docile servants of her mind control. They were otherwise simply hanging out in their homes, waiting for further instructions. She had not yet decided on the final solution. She had the power to direct each and every person to commit suicide—or she could simply return them to their basic elements, mostly water and dust, where they stood.

She could save a select few, only the smartest and most useful, or save only certain areas. For those decisions, she was going to solicit help from Brandon. He was one of them after all, and they, through him, could provide valuable input. She was practical, but she was not a monster, but her definition of rights was vastly different from ours. She went outside and contacted the mother ship. It had maneuvered closer now that the humans were under her control—and there were no possible threats to the mission.

Her superior accepted her report, complimented her on her progress, and told her that he was near if she needed support. She was going to have to make a return trip at some point for fuel for herself since she hadn't risked eating the earth food Brandon was eating. She returned to the house and asked Brandon to join her at the computer.

She brought up a large-scale map of the earth and asked him to tell her in general terms about the different races and populations inhabiting the earth. "Take me through the continents as you call them, starting with the one we are standing on, North America."

He booted up his computer, accessed Wikipedia, and said, "America is North and South America, Canada, the US, and Mexico, with some smaller countries forming a bridge called Central America. The US is considered the only superpower, but the Chinese and Russians would probably disagree since they both possess enough nuclear weapons to destroy the earth several times over."

"It just blows me away that anyone would develop technology solely for the purpose of destroying the earth on which they live?"

"Human beings are not very good at weighing out the long-term consequences of their actions," Brandon said. "Altogether, there are a little more than two hundred sovereign countries, most of which belong to the United Nations. Of those, America, China, Russia, Great Britain, France, India, Pakistan, Israel, and North Korea possibly all have nuclear weapons, but the use of nuclear power is widespread."

She gave that some thought. "And I assume the largest countries are included in this list?"

He nodded.

She thought, *These, we eliminate first.*

He said, "After the Americas, heading east, you have Africa, Europe, Asia, Antarctica, and Australia."

She said, "Which is smallest?"

"Australia, for sure."

"What is the population of Australia?"

"More than twenty-five million."

She pondered this info. *Way too many.* "Are there any island nations that could be totally self-sustaining?"

Brandon said, "Certainly—maybe in the South Pacific, like Fiji or New Zealand. Fiji has just under a million, and New Zealand has just under five million."

"Let's check them out!" She grabbed his hand, and the next thing he knew, they were crammed into her single-person transport and flying high above Fiji's turquoise waters.

It was very claustrophobic, but he did not mind the closeness to her tight body. If she noticed his growing excitement, she failed to mention it. He pointed out geography as they passed over land far below.

She commented briefly and took it all in through a micro-viewer that allowed her to see much more detail than Brandon. She seemed especially intrigued by the two islands of New Zealand, with its diverse ecosystems and terrains. It seemed to spark her interest more than any other place.

When they returned to his house, the trip was a blur to Brandon. At some points, they were moving so fast the ground below blurred, and the whole trip seemed to only cover minutes despite the fact that they had traveled thousands of miles. Back in Daytona, she got back on the internet and trolled for information.

Brandon asked, "So, what did you think of our planet?"

She said, "I have always loved this planet, especially its plants and animals. It's the utter infestation of humans that I have a problem with."

"So, what exactly does that mean?"

"I am still working on the bottom line, but I need to consult with my superiors. I am going to return to my ship for a bit. You and Steve stay put—and I will be back."

"Can I go too?" he asked.

She looked at him for a moment, actually considering it, and said, "No, too cramped for that long a trip." She packed up her notes, went out to the backyard, launched her ship without a sound, and was gone.

Brandon stood on the deck as Steve whined longingly as the ship disappeared. "Hey, are you getting attached to her too?"

Steve barked and ran back into the house.

Brandon suddenly had a terrific urge to take a nap.

Holly arrived on the mother ship and immediately checked in with the commander.

"How is it going?" he asked.

She replied, "I need supplies, and I want to enlist the aid of one of the humans to supervise my actions. I want to bring back a two-person transporter."

"What are you thinking regarding the reduction of the population?" he asked.

She said, "I am currently securing all transportation and fuel stocks using mind control for the entire human population. Once that is done, we will decide how many humans we wish to retain, empty the zoos, free the animals, and let most of the earth return to a natural state of plants and animals without the human element. Nature will eventually erase most, if not all, evidence of humanity in a few hundred years."

He said, "Their kind is not without value entirely, so we don't want to eliminate them all. It's a delicate balance."

"Yes," she said. "I am thinking of retaining a self-sustaining island or two and taking away their power to travel outside of their land. I have to admit that they are a fascinating but largely greed-driven mob that has much work to do if they reach our enlightened state, but it is like looking into our own history. Many of the problems our ancestors had to overcome, they face as well. Perhaps we can help bring them up to speed and make them allies once we bring their numbers down to manageable levels, I'm thinking a worldwide human only flu virus pandemic with a 100% kill rate should do it, outside the island we chose to preserve of course."

"I agree," he said. "Let me know what you decide. We'll run it by the council and implement the final solution from here."

She nodded and left the bridge to gather her supplies for the return trip.

When all the decisions had been made and final solutions were implemented, Holly returned to earth in the larger ship. She landed in Brandon's backyard and went into house. He and Steve were asleep on the bed. "Have a nice nap?" she asked.

Brandon was groggy, and he said, "Wow, how long were you gone? It seems like minutes."

"Something like that," she said. "You need to pack up enough clothing and stuff for an extended vacation. We are going on one shortly."

"Where to?" he asked.

"You'll see soon enough," she said with a smile. He packed his things along with a box of Steve's toys and food. They loaded up the vehicle together, and without so much as a goodbye to his lifelong home, they took off into the sky.

She put them both to sleep for the ride, and after a short couple of hours, they touched down in a new place. She carried the sleeping Brandon and dog into the house, unloaded the transport, and covered it with a shimmering cloak that hid its existence to human eyes. Then she went to bed.

When Brandon awoke, he was on a king-sized bed, the most comfortable ever, and it faced a huge picture window. They were obviously very high up the side of a mountain, and he could see a series of turquoise lakes with many islands and signs of civilization below. He had never been there before, but it was the most beautiful place he'd ever seen.

Holly was next to him—her lithe body covered in blankets—and she was watching him. "What do you think?"

"Are we still on earth?" he asked.

"Yes," she replied. "This is our new home." She leaned over and kissed him long and deep. When she pulled back, she looked into his eyes and said, "I have been given permission to control and monitor this planet for a while. We will do it together, and I'll give this love idea of yours a shot."

He smiled and kissed her again. "You will be my queen—but where are we?"

She looked out the window at the gorgeous vista and replied, "Queensland, New Zealand, of course—the last bastion of humanity."

Steve jumped on the bed and wagged her nub of a tail. They both hugged her and fell back onto the bed together.